Executive Sick Days

Maria E. Schneider

Bear Mountain Books

A Bear Mountain Books Production
www.BearMountainBooks.com

Executive Sick Days
Maria E. Schneider
Copyright March 2011, December 2022 © Maria E. Schneider

Printing History:
POD printing June 2011
E-format March 2011
Second POD printing July 2012

ISBN-13: 978-0615498126 (Bear Mountain Books)
ISBN-10: 0615498124

Acknowledgments

Thanks go to the real Holly who, I know, read this with great trepidation. You just never know what you'll be guilty of when a fiction writer gets going. To Cinderspark for once again diving in with enthusiasm and swatting errors with her wand; to Diane for spending time in my fictional hospital; to Irene for her eagle-eyes and bright-red pen; and to LeAnn because I cannot choose between toward and towards. To Joan because you not only my support my dream, you support everyone around you. And to Elisabeth for being the best fan ever. Leo, once again, you came in late in the day, improving things with your blue pen. Thank you. All of you made this a better book. I would be lost without you.

A special thanks to Mom because she was the inspiration behind much of this story, and the best nurse I ever knew or worked with. She really did think about taking a rattlesnake into work in a coffee can although for different reasons. I think we can safely stop wondering where my sense of humor came from. And to Randy, my husband, because he puts up with that sense of humor and more than matches it with his own.

To find out what I'm currently up to, visit me at: www.BearMountainBooks.com.

Executive Sick Days

Chapter 1

Decisions, decisions. It was flattering to have everyone want me, but it was also a little frustrating. My head was currently swelled with the privilege of choosing between working for two computer companies: Strandfrost or Acetel. Strandfrost tried to fire me, but then relented. They feared a lawsuit because they mistakenly believed I was pregnant. To avoid the non-existent lawsuit, they offered me my job back at my old salary. I could live almost lavishly right until they realized that my sister-in-law was pregnant, not me.

Acetel, on the other hand, had never fired me, but my boss, Jacques, was back in residence after having recently survived his heart attack. I wasn't sure I wanted to be around for his next one. More to the point, I didn't want to be responsible for his next one.

The pay was better at Strandfrost, but I'd definitely be on rockier ground. Unfortunately, I was not certain Acetel paid enough to cover my lifestyle. It wasn't that my lifestyle was extravagant, but it did include me, a single woman, making payments on a small two-bedroom patio home.

I wouldn't have been working at Acetel at all had it not been for the nemesis in my life: Steve Huntington, undercover investigator of corporate issues. He'd had the brilliant idea that I could work at Acetel and discover who was pilfering money from the company coffers. That had been great, but once the case was solved, Huntington stopped supplementing Acetel's not-so-generous salary. I could make my house and car payment on Acetel's salary, but only if I didn't eat.

Of course, Strandfrost was a riskier job overall because if I was fired again, there would be no income at all, and that would really put a rumble in my stomach.

Instead of weighing the pros and cons of my problem, I used my Saturday to peruse Hawaiian brochures. Both Strandfrost and Acetel would be closed for the week of Christmas and since my parents had just visited for Thanksgiving, I had fulfilled my daughterly holiday obligations. Hawaii seemed like an awesome way to celebrate Christmas. Denton, Colorado was heaven for skiers, but not for beach-going, and I was really looking forward to trying out the latter.

The phone rang, rudely interrupting my daydreams. Since it wasn't likely to be a travel agent with free tickets to Hawaii, I was inclined to ignore it.

Curiosity was going to kill me someday.

The voice on the other end was that of my sister-in-law, Brenda O'Hala. I spontaneously started praying that she wasn't cooking anything.

"Hi Sedona! Remember when, uh, Huntington got shot and ended up in my living room?" Brenda whispered, a habit she had picked up after she became pregnant. In this case, however, she was probably keeping her voice low because she was discussing one of my more unsuitable acquaintances.

"It would be rather hard to forget." I accidentally tugged too hard on my ponytail holder. Flyaway brown hair suddenly obscured my vision, but didn't inhibit my hearing.

"Well, yeah, for me I'm sure, but you're involved in a lot of that sort of thing."

Patently untrue. I was never involved in underhanded, thieving, dangerous or ridiculous capers, at least not on a regular basis. In fact, I never had been at all until I met Steve Huntington. He had a way of bringing out the worst in me. His brother Mark brought something out in me too, but my feelings for him were even more alarming. Mark was…dangerous. Dangerously handsome, sexy and I was finding, dangerously irresistible. That didn't mean I shouldn't stay away.

"Do you remember when Mark mentioned the investigation at Crestwood Hospital?" Brenda asked.

It was understandable that Brenda remembered the comment. As a part-time nurse at Crestwood, she was there all day, every Thursday and Friday. "Yes, why?"

"I've been doing some digging," she continued. "And I think I know what they are investigating."

Now that got me up out of my chair. The brochures scattered across the table as I changed grips on the phone. "*What?*" Brenda involved in anything remotely resembling "investigating" could get me thrown in jail by my overprotective and just-so-happened-to-be-a-lawyer-brother, Sean. "Brenda, are you crazy?" Perhaps pregnancy had used up all her available brain cells or maybe they had transferred to the baby, leaving her senseless. "Do I have to remind you that the last case resulted in Huntington getting shot, and he wouldn't let us take him to the hospital? You're pregnant! You can't go around looking into things!"

There was silence for several seconds before she responded, her voice meek. "I just checked on a very *few* things. I've seen Huntington--Steve--there now and again lately so I know he is still working on a case. And I have access to records--"

"Have you mentioned this activity to Sean?" Just how long did I have to get on a plane to Hawaii before my brother came after me?

"Of course not! He'd have a fit!"

More like a diabolical plan to have me committed to a mental institution where his wife couldn't contact me. "Brenda," I squeaked out, "I really don't think you looking at records is a good idea."

"I know. I'm not supposed to access them, and if the supervisor finds out she'll fire me. We're only supposed to look at what is pertinent to patient care on our own patients. And I saw Radar the other day, so I figured he was probably investigating anyway, so what does Huntington need me for?"

My heart, already beating fast, went into overdrive. "You saw Radar at the hospital?" I had assumed Radar had gone back to San Jose. He had quit Acetel, and I was furious with him for leaving without a word of good-bye. Not that we were close friends, but I felt basic courtesy counted for something. "When did you see him?"

"Just yesterday. I'm positive he works at Crestwood now in the IT department."

My big head, inflated over two possible job offers and the successful solving of the crimes at Acetel, shriveled. Huntington had hired Radar to help with the case at the hospital. And I hadn't heard from Huntington since the Acetel incident had ended over two weeks ago. My heart slowed. I slumped back onto the tabletop, scattering what was left of the brochures onto the floor.

It was true that Radar was more capable than me. He could hack his way into God's own database. His expertise was the primary reason we had been able to solve the case at Acetel. He probably didn't argue about how to investigate things either. But...I was unreasonably hurt.

Huntington was often recruited to solve corporate cases because executives and board members preferred someone who spoke their language. It also let companies investigate without calling in nosy authorities such as police, FBI or heaven forbid, the IRS. Unfortunately for Huntington, since he was busy schmoozing with the upper echelons, he had to hire someone else to mingle with regular employees and sniff out suspicious characters. That had been my job, and I *had* helped him solve the cases.

But it appeared I had been replaced. Summarily pushed aside by...

better talent. I sighed. My two job prospects were already less than ideal. This news made them look even more like booby prizes.

"So I was wondering," Brenda broke into my depression, "do you think I should tell Huntington or Radar what I've found?"

A tingle of hope or...stupidity...started up my spine. "Well," I said slowly, sitting back upright, "that really depends upon what you've found, doesn't it?"

Chapter 2

Meeting with Brenda was awkward lately even when she wasn't trying to play secret agent. She had it in her head that she was disguising her pregnancy. To do this, she walked around dressed as Mrs. Santa or an oversized elf. She was headed into her fifth month, and her build was slight. The only person who could possibly be fooled was a five-year old distracted by the fact that Christmas was only a few weeks away.

There was little in life more embarrassing than sitting with a grown woman dressed in a Christmas costume except for sitting with one in a badly rendered Christmas costume. Brenda's latest Mrs. Santa outfit consisted of a large red cape, a red felt square on her head, black boots and a tent-like, checkered red and white dress. The woman looked as though a naked Little Red Riding Hood had grabbed grandma's tablecloth and ran.

Luckily, Happy Family Chinese didn't question my appearance or that of the people who accompanied me. They just welcomed me. One of these days a real weirdo was going to be sitting at a table and the proprietor, Mrs. Chang, was going to lead me to the guy thinking he had to be one of my friends.

Brenda wasn't all bad habits. I loved the fact that she didn't stand on ceremony. She had already ordered and was just finishing her egg rolls when I arrived.

It was a hard choice between starting with soup or egg rolls, but seeing Brenda's empty plate clinched it. "I'll have an order of egg rolls and beef with broccoli," I told Mrs. Chang as I sat. "And a water."

I greeted my sister-in-law by getting right down to business. "If we have this discussion, you're going to remember to tell Sean that I advised you away from this completely, right?"

Her brunette curls, tucked under the square of red felt, nodded emphatically. "Sure. That's if he finds out at all. I'm not planning on mentioning it."

"Good. Me neither."

"I've really only noticed a couple of little things," she said. "It could be honest mistakes. It would help if you told me what Huntington thinks is going on."

Be still my beating, dismayed heart. Even Brenda thought I was on the inside. "I'm not really sure." My chopsticks were of sudden importance. I picked them up and positioned them carefully as though I already had food. Shoot, even after Huntington officially hired me on cases, he tended to leave out pertinent information. "He implied one of the doctors was adding inflated charges to patients' final bills. It sounded like it occurred after the patient had already checked out of the hospital." Mark had actually said that, not Huntington, and Brenda was present when he mentioned it. She knew as much as I did.

"Mrs. Olsen," she whispered.

I leaned in. "Mrs. Olsen?"

"She's a mean old lady, and she's in the hospital all the time; practically lives there. Frankly, I think Huntington is mistaken about it being the doctor who adds bogus charges. Of course, the doctor could be checking her in for no justifiable reason, but Mrs. Olsen is more likely to be responsible for the extra charges. She's such a whiner. She demands all kinds of things. The funny thing is that she's always watching her bill as if she were paying every cent from her personal retirement account, but she has good insurance."

"How do you know about her insurance?"

"Easy." She paused to dish out the food that Mrs. Chang set in front of us. Neither of us was going to concentrate on anything else with it sitting there. After she had a few giant bites, she elaborated. "If a patient doesn't have good coverage or doesn't have any at all, the admitting office is in a rush to get the patient checked out. Patients without insurance almost always come up from the ER. They don't generally get checked in by one of the staff doctors, because if people don't have insurance, they wait until it's an emergency."

"So how does this make her guilty of...umh, what is she guilty of?"

"Because even though she is always refusing little things like Tylenol or toothbrushes, there are a lot of those types of charges on her bill, and those charges are ones that Medicare or insurance isn't likely to question. It looked small at first, things like the Tylenol, ice chips--we charge for the cups, you know. Then there was a lot of lotion and toothpaste charges. She has dentures so that should never show up on there at all, but of course these things happen."

I chewed on this. "So how much can that add up to?" Even with hospital prices, it would be a lot of risk just to pocket a hundred dollars here and there.

"Not a lot. Except I also noticed that there were three admissions that I couldn't remember."

Now that was more like it, but I had to be cautious here. Brenda was a woman who hadn't noticed she was pregnant until she was twelve or thirteen weeks along. Brenda also only worked part time, two days a week. The hospital had at least three floors. "Would you have necessarily seen her?"

"I checked my schedule. For two of the admissions, I was definitely working. So I'm wondering if she somehow has the insurance company pay her and then later she disputes the bill with the hospital, but pockets the money." She leaned over the table and whispered, "I could be wrong, but I really don't like Mrs. Olsen so I'm not likely to forget when she's there. She rings the call bell about forty times a day. When I make the rounds with meds she wants to double-check everything. She won't allow us to give her a sponge bath either. Every morning she wants a regular bath, and I know she asks her doctor for whirlpool privileges."

"Whirlpool privileges? I didn't know you could request whirlpool privileges in the hospital."

"Sure, for physical therapy. The whirlpool is to improve circulation, and the old lady swears she has bed sores on her back and shoulders twenty minutes after she is checked in."

"Oh."

"So, do you think we ought to tell Huntington?"

I sat back. I wasn't all that pleased with Huntington and had I stumbled across this information without Brenda, I would have hoarded it. I would have insisted he pay me for it, maybe by the word in a lengthy, typed report. But my main concern at the moment was to figure out how to convince Brenda to leave the problem alone. I couldn't do that unless I promised to tell Huntington.

"Okay," I gave in, knowing my chance of profiting was nil. Protecting Brenda had to take priority. "I'll call him."

"Good." She shoved an unmarked brown paper bag at me. "Just pretend it's a doggie bag from the restaurant, and no one will know I'm passing you information."

It was futile to point out that we didn't have a rice kernel left between us or that the restaurant used plastic bags with the Happy Family Chinese logo on them. I accepted the bag.

Brenda broke eye contact and focused intently on her now empty plate. Her felt doily hat started to slide sideways, but she didn't reach up to stop it. "I think there are a couple of other patients in on it, but I can't look at their records. I only obtained Mrs. Olsen's bill because she wanted a copy before she checked out. I sort of volunteered to request the bill on her behalf, and then requested a tad more back information than Mrs. Olsen asked for."

She took a very obvious covert look around the restaurant before leaning across the table and whispering loudly, "Copies of her billing information are in the bag, along with the names of the other two patients."

"Ohboy." I had to do something fast before she got herself into trouble. Maybe I could turn Radar onto our suspicions. Then I wouldn't have to call Huntington at all.

Besides, I owed Radar for helping me the last time, and he'd look good if he found clues. He didn't have to tell Huntington how he obtained them.

Chapter 3

Mark and Steve Huntington were a lot alike in appearance: drop-dead handsome. They both had dark hair, but Mark had dreamy chocolate brown eyes, while Steve had piercing blue ones. With colored contacts and dim lighting, I knew all too well one could temporarily replace the other.

As far as personalities, no two brothers could be further apart. Huntington, that was to say, Steve, was suave, cool and comfortably rubbed elbows with board directors. Mark was not likely to ever bother attending a board meeting, nor would he blend well there. His jeans fit well on a body that looked like it spent more time outdoors than drinking coffee at a boring office meeting.

Both of them worked on inside company investigations, and they were both adept at their respective jobs, although the exact nature of those jobs was often a mystery.

Huntington had a rude tendency to assume he was welcome anywhere, anytime, even if a home wasn't actually occupied by its owner--or maybe especially if it was unoccupied. In the past this even involved him picking my locks and waiting inside until I showed up.

Unlike Huntington, Mark didn't sneak inside or make any arrogant assumptions about my hours of availability. Like a normal human being, he waited at the curb until I happened home from the grocery store. He then pulled his motorcycle into the driveway behind me.

There was something that shouted, "Bad Boy" about a motorcycle, especially one with a sword and lightning bolt custom-painted down the side. I was pretty sure that Mark had a tattoo on his left arm that matched the sword on the motorcycle, but it could have been part of his disguise for an earlier case. Since it was wintertime, he had on a black leather jacket, and I couldn't see his arm.

"Hey beautiful," he greeted me, setting his helmet on the bike and joining me in the garage.

That kind of greeting will buy forgiveness of just about anything, including not calling me for two weeks and leaving me out of the latest case.

I tried rolling my eyes, but my face was stamped with a big foolish grin.

Who can know if he planned it or it just worked out that since I was standing there blocking the way into the house like a star-struck idiot, he decided to take advantage of the situation? Either way, he wrapped his leather-clad arms around me and bent to touch my lips. I was still trying to say hi, and he took the motion as encouragement and pretty soon it was definitely along those lines.

"Wow. You sure know how to greet a guy." He pulled back and smiled. "You look good."

I think he had already said that, but I was not one to complain about redundancy of that kind. "Hi," I said breathlessly, unable to keep my eyes from giving him a quick top-to-bottom inspection. At just over six feet he towered over my wish-I-were five seven. "You too," popped out of my mouth with more enthusiasm than I probably should have allowed.

He raised an encouraging eyebrow, but feeling shy, I scooted toward the inside door before he could gain further advantage. On the way in, I started to think about Crestwood Hospital. "I hear you're working a new case at the hospital." I stopped in the hallway. "And that Huntington hired Radar." I tried not to sound jealous, because, after all, I had job offers, just not very secure ones.

Mark didn't seem put off. He gently tucked my hair behind my shoulder and then left his hand resting there. "You wouldn't be upset about that now, would you?" He moved in again, and I had a bad feeling that in a minute, I wasn't going to care where anybody worked.

"A little," I breathed as his brown eyes got closer to my gray ones.

He started a slow seduction, kissing me gently and then asking questions as if he was interested in the answers. "But why? I thought you didn't like working for my brother." Another light kiss, just a gentle one, no tongues. It was like seeing a picture of your favorite food, but knowing you couldn't have it.

Focus, Sedona, focus…my mind drifted. I licked my lips and so did he. *Oh, my.* Then he pulled back.

Bad boys weren't good for me. I had a sneaky feeling I was being manipulated. I forced myself to step out of reach. "I have some information on the case. I promised Brenda I would get it to Huntington, even though I'm not working on it." I crossed my arms in front of me, hoping to stop the tingling in my hands, toes and lips. The motion made me realize how fast I was breathing, and it drew Mark's eyes downward.

His eyes flashed back to mine. "It isn't a good idea for me to date people I work with," he said softly.

"What?"

He looked me over, almost longingly, before stepping backwards. "Sedona, the last case you worked on, you almost got yourself blown up."

I wasn't sure where he was going with this, but it wasn't as though I had gone looking for a dangerous situation. How was I to know I'd have to deal with a lunatic and a propane tank? "Mark…"

He stopped me with one hand up. "Steve is talking about hiring you again, but I think Radar can handle anything we need. It would make things a whole lot easier if you didn't take the job." He grinned. "I have absolutely no designs on Radar. He doesn't distract me, nor do I spend a lot of time… worrying about him."

It didn't sound as though "worry" was quite the word he wanted. He might have been thinking, "fantasizing," and that word was a lot better than "worry." Worry was something my brother Sean did when he thought I was going to screw something up. "Oh. Well."

"Well?" He gave me plenty of room.

Mark sounded like he was trying to tell me that we could either date or work together, but not both. I didn't like that idea. It made perfect sense, but that didn't mean I liked it. I had other jobs or at least job offers, even if they turned out to be temporary. It was dates I was short. Not only had it been a long time since I'd had a date, I could state with certainty that I had never, ever had a date with someone like Mark. He was looking at me now as if I was the only person in the whole world that he wanted to date.

When I didn't say anything, his grin turned wickedly suggestive, but he didn't push. That was irritating. At least if he seduced me, I could blame the whole mess on him.

"I actually came by to invite you to dinner tomorrow." He very helpfully upped the ante.

My eyes narrowed. Had he really been going to invite me out or had he just now decided that such a suggestion might persuade me? "That's--"

The front doorbell rang. I glanced at it, but decided it couldn't possibly be important enough to postpone this discussion. I wasn't expecting anyone so it was probably a solicitor. Or worse, my brother.

After a scant second, there was a scraping noise from the front door. Mark frowned, moving to stand in front of me. "Expecting company?"

"No." We watched in fascination as the door swung open.

Huntington stepped through and grinned at us. "Hope I'm not interrupting anything," he said cheerfully. "I saw your bike. I'm glad you changed your mind about including Sedona. We need someone on the inside."

"I didn't," Mark said.

Huntington ignored the comment, but looked briefly confused.

With the sunlight coming in behind him, the two could be twins. His self-assured grin didn't melt my knees and generally speaking, neither did his suggestions, including the one he decided to voice now. "What do you think about volunteering at the hospital, Sedona? I figure you need a few good deeds written in the book somewhere." He pointed up toward heaven.

I looked back at Mark. He wasn't looking at me. There was a muscle in his jaw that clenched and unclenched. He stared at the carpet, waiting for my answer.

"Let me get this straight," I said. "First you wanted me to work at

Strandfrost, and you helped me get promoted to a nice, fat paycheck. Then you wanted me to take a pay cut and work at Acetel. Now, you want me to work and not get paid at all?" Don't get me wrong, I had the utmost admiration for volunteers. My only problem was the house and car payment. Even if I got rid of the Civic and drove the Mercedes that Huntington had given me at the end of the first case, I still needed a paying job.

"I'm sure we could work something out," he said nonchalantly.

Now Mark did look at me. Actually, he stared over my head so he could see my reaction without making eye contact.

This was turning ugly. "Okay, guys." I pinched the bridge of my nose. "Here is what I know." I stuck to business and gave them the information Brenda had detailed. I omitted her name in the telling.

Huntington looked disgruntled when he realized I already had some information. "You think Mrs. Olsen is siphoning off money because she is grumpy?"

"No, I'm telling you she might be up to something shady because she's the type of person who would notice extra billing, especially if she wasn't in the hospital when the billing took place. Why couldn't some of the patients be part of the scheme? They agree to over-billing, take a cut and give the doctor a cut."

Huntington tilted his head and then nodded in agreement. "We can get Radar to start watching that account."

"That won't tell you who is adding the charges to her account."

"Who is Mrs. Olsen's doctor?"

The doctor would be the most likely person to claim Mrs. Olsen was hospitalized when she wasn't. "I don't know who her doctor is. It really doesn't matter because she could be admitted by more than one doctor. Maybe Radar can figure out who is admitting her when she doesn't actually show up."

"Doesn't sound like there is much for you to do," Mark said, looking right at me now. His eyes asked for a lot.

My choices appeared to be a drop-dead gorgeous guy and one of two lousy jobs, or a possibly dangerous job with a decent paycheck and a non-existent love life. Huntington had already hired Radar; if I dawdled over my decision, he might discover he really didn't need me. When Strandfrost fired me again, I'd have no job and no leverage to negotiate a decent salary.

"What do you mean there's not much to do?" Huntington disagreed sharply with Mark. "We need a lot more information, and it's going to be difficult to obtain. She'll have to work damn hard to blend in this time. Volunteers are supposed to be nice, caring individuals. Sedona, this is going to be a tough assignment for you."

I cut my eyes to him. "You have such a charming way of convincing me."

Before I could blast him further, Mark sighed. "I have to go." He stepped close to me, put his hand on the back of my neck and leaned in. There was no pressure in the kiss. He massaged my neck once before turning to leave. "See you."

He strode out the front door before I had a chance to respond. I guessed this meant no dinner date. Unconsciously my hand went to the back of my neck, and I stood there until Huntington's voice broke into my thoughts.

"What the hell was that about?"

I frowned and turned my attention to Huntington. "Ask him," I said crossly. "He's your brother."

Besides, I really didn't know myself.

Chapter 4

Volunteering was not, in my opinion, one of those things that brought instant gratification. Maybe some people were immediately satisfied because they knew they were helping someone in need. As for me, my first day of volunteering involved training--and regret. The bedpans were a large part of the regret, but my heart knew most of it was really Mark. He didn't want me working on another case. That was a fifty-fifty split for me, but only because I didn't like to be told what to do. He meant well. He wasn't trying to control my life before we even went on a first date. Right?

Either the situation with Mark or one bedpan in particular actually brought tears to my eyes. It was going to be a tough assignment, but not for the reasons Huntington had outlined.

In addition to changing bedpans, I learned how to deliver breakfast trays and wheel people to various parts of the hospital. The trainer, Ellen Garcia, informed us very carefully of the list of "do nots." It was hard to believe that any volunteer would get a sudden urge to start an IV or put a breathing tube up someone's nose, but Ellen repeatedly warned us against such actions.

The last part of our training on Tuesday included decorating the nurses' stations on all the floors with Christmas wreaths and a tour of the rest of the hospital. I was introduced to the head nurse, Brenda's supervisor and soon to be mine, Sally Rendal. Long black hair framed a stunningly flawless face, but like a stately blue jay, when she opened her mouth, the noise that erupted was in direct contrast to her beauty. "Nice to have a new face to lead." She cawed like a cross between a dying crow and the smoker in room three-oh-five.

Since I had specified on my application that I wanted to work with elderly patients, my assignment was on the third floor, reporting to her for scheduling. "Nice to meet you," I murmured, shaking her outstretched hand.

No delicate flower, this woman obviously spent some time at the gym. Not only was her grip painfully strong, there wasn't an ounce of fat anywhere on her frame.

Sally introduced me to Crissa Sheldon, one of the technicians. Crissa completed a couple of mouse-clicks at the nurses' station's computer before turning and giving me a nod. "Welcome." One mischievous green eye winked. She gave a casual wave and headed off down the hall.

Sally executed a military turn to bring her attention back to me. "If you need anything or have an emergency situation, the nurses' station is a good place to come." She did not point out the employee break room tucked behind the desk. Apparently it wasn't important for me to know where the refrigerator, snack machine and chairs were located. Stabbing a finger toward the patient call lights, she cawed, "These are the call lights that you will be answering."

Two of the lights flashed madly. Sally noted the blinking with a frown that could have frozen Medusa. "It will be good to have more help. We obviously need it." Without another word, she marched off, no doubt to look for the remiss employees.

Just then, both call lights stopped blinking.

Hmm. She looked hell-bent on scolding someone, but by the time she found a nurse or technician, there wouldn't be a reason to complain. I bet that wouldn't stop her.

Ellen, the trainer, seemed to miss the tension. She continued to beam as she inspected the Christmas greenery and the red bow she had just installed across the front of the desk. Like a mother hen, she ushered all of us trainees on to the next task, not the least bit perturbed to have had someone half her age take over, ignore her completely and then stomp off. "Let's go find the floor nurses," she chirped energetically. "There are two working each floor on any given day, on any shift. Most of you will work day shifts, so you will work closely with the people you meet today."

We followed dutifully and met several nurses and another technician before trooping to the linen cabinets to collect our cute little striped aprons. Good thing there weren't any guy volunteers because our "uniforms" were pink and white.

I tied the apron on while Ellen informed us, "You can wear jeans if you like, or if you have the money, the loose uniforms that the technicians wear are wonderful. You can choose your own hours, and if you want to expand your experience, just apply to volunteer in a different section of the hospital."

My eyes widened before a smile broke across my face. Apparently when it came to volunteers, management was not only nice, but flexible. Maybe they actually wanted volunteers to keep showing up. In my experience, this was in direct contrast to a paying computer job where management was often bent on running employees off by saddling them with ridiculous schedules designed to cause extreme stress and a nearly constant sense of failure.

My theory about volunteers versus paid workers was confirmed when I called Brenda after I got off work. "Is everyone always so nice at the hospital? I get to choose my own hours," I explained happily.

She paused before shouting into the phone. "Nice? Who's nice? Hours? You mean Sally hasn't tried to schedule you for overtime and explained that you won't get paid for it because the budget hasn't been approved yet?"

I got my first real lesson in nice by twelve o'clock Wednesday morning. Someone stole my lunch. It was taken in broad daylight, right out of the refrigerator in the employee break area--the little room that was tucked protectively behind the nurses' station. I couldn't believe it, but after a thorough search of the entire fridge, including the freezer, there was still no sign of it. It had vanished.

I marched down the hall to the empty visitor's waiting room and called Brenda. "Someone stole my lunch!"

"Oh, did you leave it in the nurses' station's fridge?"

"This has happened before?" I had expected her to have some other explanation. Who could be that desperate? What if I spit in my food?

"It's hard to believe, I know," she confided in one of her quiet whispers. "But some of the nurses aren't very good cooks."

Brenda was by far the worst cook I had ever encountered, but I stifled the urge to comment. For a scant moment, I was even suspicious of Brenda, but she wasn't working until Thursday. It was doubtful she would have driven to work just to steal my lunch. Then again, she was pregnant. "I'm hungry," I whined.

"You'd better run out and get something. You don't want to eat in the cafeteria," she warned.

I knew that. No one in any line of work wanted to eat in a cafeteria. "Okay, you're right. I'll sign out."

"Don't worry about your lunch container. The thief always puts those back."

Well, wasn't that nice of the thief. "I only brought a sandwich in a plastic bag." At least I hadn't wasted a gourmet lunch on a low-down crook.

I hung up and went in search of food. Since I was signing out anyway, it was probably a good time to locate Radar. The computers were kept in the basement; we had seen them on our tour of the hospital.

I made my way down to the bowels of the building, a clogged underground floor containing furnace and air conditioning equipment, closets and of course the ice room. The morgue, or the ice room, was just an empty room by the back entrance. We had peeked inside long enough to see the walk-in refrigerator used for patients awaiting their final trip out.

The basement was kind of spooky now that I was down here alone. Since the servers weren't near the ice room at the end of the hallway, I picked the first door available, but it was a broom closet. On television drama shows and soaps, opening the janitor closet meant you were going inside to make-out with some irresistible doctor. This closet was full of buckets, mops, and a cleaning cart. It didn't smell like a place that would bring out romance either.

I couldn't even picture anyone I had met going into the closet. The doctors were all over fifty and intently focused on patient charts. The head nurse, Sally, had to be a relative of Attila the Hun. It was no wonder Brenda didn't want the woman to know about her pregnancy; Attila might cancel it. The one male nurse on the floor, Paul Labrowski, looked like a fish. He had a round mashed face with bulging eyes and as a quirk of fate, walked around with his mouth hanging partly open.

No, this closet wasn't going to get a lot of romantic use.

I closed door number one and had to choose between a door across the hall labeled "Records" and an unlabeled door a few feet past the closet. Since I was pretty sure the "Records" room contained old patient files and x-rays, I picked the unmarked one.

A few dangling wires and two computer monitors indicated I had chosen correctly. It didn't take long before I located Radar's legs. He was underneath a desk at the back. His jeans, sporting a couple of holes, were the only visible part of him.

"Hey buddy. I thought you left town without bothering to say goodbye." My voice pierced the steady hum of technology. There was a clank as Radar dropped something. After a pause, he scooted out.

"What did you say?" He was still thin as a scarecrow, and his long hair must have been near the computer fan. It was full of static and blown every which way.

"Wow, you ought to be careful. You're going to get your hair stuck in a computer fan one of these days."

"Yeah, thanks." He pulled the mess away from his face. I noticed that he had shaved his dark-blond goatee. It was a vast improvement.

He stood up and after a short inspection of my own person, he added, "Nice apron. Pink. Heh-heh-heh."

Okay, pink was not my color and with my personality it was like putting an apron on a convict working in a prison kitchen. I chose to ignore his humor because I had two brothers and knew there were some fights you couldn't win. "Did you move to Denton or what?"

"Yeah, at least for now." He grinned. "Huntington had this job for me. Guess you're working for him again too?"

Radar seemed to like working for Huntington and didn't mind the possible danger. "Did Huntington tell you about the three patients we're supposed to be watching?"

Radar nodded and seated himself at a console. "I found the records in question. And I can tag patients that are currently admitted to see if their records get tampered with once they are discharged. In the case of Mrs. Olsen," he typed quickly, "and these other two," he pointed to the computer monitor, "there's an interesting pattern, but not exactly proof of illegal activity."

"What pattern?"

"The charges are remarkably similar."

I looked over his shoulder at the Excel spreadsheet he had created. He switched back to the bill and then to the records. I read down the bill. "Check in, fluids, x-rays...wow and a few thousand dollars later, checkout."

"Yeah, the bills have a bunch of different diagnosis codes, but the tests that were ordered look remarkably similar. I couldn't make heads or tails of the medical record." He looked over at me. "Be careful with this history stuff. It belongs to a specific someone, and we wouldn't want it to fall into the wrong hands. It is a breach of their privacy to have access to these records."

He, who could hack into any computer system faster than I could walk through a doorway, was warning *me*? It wasn't as if I would be standing here staring at them without his help. "The wrong hands?"

"Yeah," he agreed, missing my pointed glare.

I surveyed the spreadsheet again, but didn't see how it was going to help. "How can anyone tell if these services are fake?"

Radar grinned up at me. "That's the point, right? I'm guessing you take a patient who has a slight heart condition and check him in a few extra times for "heart events." Run some tests, some x-rays and check them out. Then for some old lady like Olsen, well, she didn't drink enough, got herself dehydrated and needed a few days of recuperation. This other guy, who knows why he was checked in initially? He got fluids, looks like a couple of inconclusive tests, x-rays and then out."

"And nothing on the bill is enough to get anyone's attention."

"Except the patient. If the patients know they weren't in, they'll notice."

I agreed. But Mrs. Olsen wasn't young and just because she complained loudly, didn't mean she actually sat and read her bill. Of course if she had found some way to profit from it, she certainly wasn't going to say anything. "I'm not sure how we're supposed to figure this out, but if you see records that indicate these three are admitted again, now that I'm here, I can find out if they are physically here or not."

"Mrs. O is supposedly in right now," he said.

I nodded. "Yes, she's on my floor."

"We can watch the discharge date and the itemized charges," he said.

My stomach rumbled its displeasure. I glanced at my watch and decided to get a move on because I wasn't supposed to stay clocked out forever. As a volunteer, I could take all the time I wanted for lunch, but the other volunteers were very interested in collecting a certain amount of hours for college credit. In order to fit in, I couldn't be too lax. "Do you know of any good places to eat around here?"

"There's a sandwich place right next door. It gets a lot of the hospital business. There's a pizza place across the street next to The Pavilion physician complex and a place down from there that has great gyros."

I grimaced. "Impossible. There is no such thing as a great gyro."

"I guess you'll want to go with sandwiches or pizza then."

"You could say that."

"I can live with that."

He grabbed his coat and followed me out.

The sandwich shop was already crowded so we settled for the pizza parlor. I ordered a pasta salad and Radar got a calzone that looked like an eighteen-inch pizza folded in half. If it had been anyone other than Radar, I would have assumed most of it would go to waste, but he dug in like it had legs and was trying to escape.

"So what do we know so far?" I asked.

Radar raised an eyebrow and chewed. "Does Huntington ever tell you what is going on when he hires you or is it always like this?"

Last time Radar had helped me with a case, he had come to me for answers, answers he mistakenly thought I had since Huntington had hired me. "Maybe we'd better compare notes," I hedged.

He shrugged. "Okay. Basically Huntington wants me to scour the records for suspicious transactions tied to any particular doctor."

"How in the heck are you going to figure that out? That can't be easy."

"No, it's not. I have to compile all kinds of statistics about which doctors order what medications or treatments more often than others--the expensive stuff like MRIs or CAT scans. It's hard to do because those things generate a separate bill, and I have to match the bills with the doctor's orders. Then there's the fact that for accidents, the emergency room doctor is likely to order more of those procedures than another doctor anyway. It doesn't make pointing a finger easy."

"So what about patients like Mrs. O being overcharged?"

"My fancy statistics won't show anything at all if that is the case." He was well over halfway through his calzone.

"You aren't actually going to eat all of that, are you?" Not even my brother Sean could devour food like Radar and if he did, he wouldn't stay skinny.

He shook his head. "No. I've been cutting back. I'm going to save a sliver for later so that I don't have to cook tonight. This place is great," he said happily. "I can get a large pizza and still have leftovers."

The large pizza was a twenty-four inch dynamo designed for parties of six. "Uh-huh." My salad was large enough that I would be taking part of it home. "I'll ask Brenda again about the billing. We need to figure out at what point these things are entered into the computer so we have a better idea of who is doing the entering."

"Good call. Hey, I saw Mark around the hospital the other day. What is he up to?"

My heart stuttered a bit, but I made sure my voice didn't. "No idea. He...doesn't usually work by day from what I've seen."

"Heh, heh, heh."

I didn't like his knowing little laugh. "What is that supposed to mean?"

He just smiled and took another giant bite of his calzone.

Chapter 5

After lunch I was assigned to help Dr. Brian Staple. It didn't take long to figure out why none of the technicians had volunteered to go on rounds with him. Dr. Staple looked like a mature version of a handsome surfer, right down to sunburned cheeks and dark hair that lightened before splitting into frazzled ends.

The resemblance ended with his looks though; he snapped orders like a drill sergeant with constipation. Maybe it was just me, but it seemed that all his patients had blockages too. Not a one of them smiled, and Dr. Staple spent an inordinate amount of time asking questions about bowel movements. Maybe all surgeons were like that, or maybe it was some sort of disease that people caught whenever they were around the doctor.

Even Paul, the nurse on rounds with us, looked haggard. He already resembled a fish, and walking around with his lips pursed didn't improve his image any. A constipated fish was not a pretty sight.

I stayed out of the way. The most attention I received was when Dr. Staple looked up, stroked the perfect cleft in his chin and barked, "Isn't it your job to give sponge baths?"

His icy blue gaze was on me, but I knew the routine. Never look a vampire directly in the eyes, and you won't lose any blood. I bravely stood my ground, avoided his killing stare and mumbled an unintelligible answer.

Eventually he gave up frowning down at me and proceeded to his next patient. He was marginally nicer to the frail lady in the bed than he was to the hired help, but his very lack of conversation was unsettling. Everyone knows that vampires hold very still right before extracting blood. I could easily picture this man adding charges to bills to siphon money out of patients.

Before we were halfway through rounds, I managed to trail far enough behind to slip into the visitor room instead of following. "Yeesh." There had to be an easier way to spy on people. This wasn't going to prove anything. Dr. Staple gave orders and lots of them. He could easily slip in orders for things that weren't needed and who would know? Paul certainly wouldn't question anything, because it wasn't his job to do so. If he tried to ask an innocuous question, Dr. Staple would probably cut him to pieces.

I needed more information about how doctors' orders translated into money. I knew the perfect person to educate me. It was close enough to the end of my shift for me to visit her too.

My pasta salad, when I went to retrieve it on my way out, had vanished from the fridge. "Unbelievable." Not only was homemade lunch not sacred, leftovers, *things I had already had a fork in*, were not off limits. The nurses' station was supposed to be for nurses and other employees only. Who would walk back here and take my leftover lunch?

Who would *want* to?

Perplexed and disgruntled, I stopped wasting time. Since my shift ended at three, Sean would still be at work, and I wanted to talk to Brenda about the billing before he even thought about going home.

I made it to her house in record time, but it was for naught. Brenda wasn't much help. "I don't know how someone would be able to make a lot of money from extra hospital charges," she mused from her relaxed position on the couch. Her feet were starting to swell frequently so she kept them elevated. Maybe keeping them up might offset the effect of the salty snacks she was chomping on.

Around a handful of cashews she said, "All the various charges get entered from different computers. For example, if I get items from central supply, like gauze or toothbrush kits, there's a sticker on it and that gets put on the patient card. At the end of each day, central supply picks up the cards and scans them in. As for medications, the pharmacy enters the medications before they even come up to the floor. Admitting starts the charges for the bed on the day the patient checks in."

"Couldn't you enter a bunch of charges for toothpaste whether or not it was used?"

She shook her head and then nodded. "I guess I could scan in the toothpaste code six or seven times, but I don't know how much each item costs because I only see the code for toothpaste, not the price." She looked worried. "I enter all kinds of things that result in a charge somewhere. Technicians use supplies all the time too. Do you think it's one of the nurses? Or a technician in on it with the patients?"

I shook my head. "I don't think so. But I don't know who is doing it. And I can't see a nurse or a technician making much money by racking up Tylenol and gauze charges. How would they get the money from the insurance company anyway?"

Brenda looked slightly relieved. "You're right. Mrs. Olsen would have to get the money and then turn some of it over to the nurse or technician. I don't think she would be willing to share profits with anyone."

"What about a doctor?" The doctor charges were the highest, and if charges were fabricated for a patient visit that never happened, it could really be a large amount of money.

"The doctors don't enter the information or the supply stickers. They don't even enter their own orders. Clerks transcribe all the doctor orders, and one of us nurses has to sign it to make sure it all makes sense and is correct.

You'll never see a doctor actually sitting at the computer entering sticker information. They will enter medical notes, but that's about it."

"But after a patient is admitted, doesn't the doctor have to know about it?"

She nodded. "Sure. When a patient is admitted, the doctor has to examine the patient. But for actual admitting process, someone else does all the entry work on the computer. The doctor just shows up and orders tests."

"So if a doctor were the perpetrator, he might have an accomplice to enter patient data and charges." I switched to a specific example. "If Mrs. Olsen wasn't in the hospital on those days you noticed, someone from admitting would have to be involved, right?"

"I guess. Someone has to input that the patient was there and someone else has to generate a request for a test and normal supplies, otherwise the bill would be flagged. Admitting admits the patient, but they don't enter test requests or supplies."

Interesting. If Radar could find one computer where false information was being entered, perhaps we could pin down a single person breaking into the system for the sole purpose of entering false records. Otherwise, there had to be two or three culprits and that meant even more money would be needed to keep everyone happy. "Thanks. Oh, and don't tell Sean I was here. Remember, you aren't working on this."

"Of course. You didn't happen to bring any cookies, did you?"

"Brenda, Sean would know I was here!"

"Nonsense. I bake cookies sometimes."

There was no winning that argument. I wasn't going to tell her that Sean could easily distinguish my cookies from hers.

At home, I called Huntington at his condo. To my relief Mark answered. I knew it was him from the hello because my toes tingled. "Hi Mark."

"What are you so happy about?" he asked.

"You answered instead of Steve," I said reflexively.

There was a pause followed by a quiet chuckle. "Okay. What can I do for you?"

Now why did that sound like he wasn't talking about the case? I grinned, hoping his attitude meant that he wasn't still annoyed about me helping with the case. "I was talking to Brenda about how hospital charges are generated and trying to piece together who could profit from over-billing." I proceeded to explain how if a doctor were guilty, the doctor was either hacking into the system or he had someone helping him enter charges.

Mark never got frustrated with my meandering way of providing information. He just waited patiently while I backtracked and explained all my theories.

When I was finished he said, "That's interesting. You know the hospital was owned privately until a few years ago. Makes you wonder if this was going on all along or if it started after it went public."

"Hmm. Do you think that someone is trying to make the hospital appear more profitable by adding charges? "

"I doubt any one person would bother. I was thinking that it might be easier for a few individuals to profit now that the hospital is public. New auditors were hired, and the public doesn't have the records for the hospital prior to it going public. It would be the optimal time to insert changes because no one would notice if profits or patient stays went up."

"Ah, and as long as profits are high, no one is going to look too closely at past statistics."

"The board has already turned the audits over to Huntington. He's also been going over the other finances. Have you told Radar your suspicions yet?"

"He's the one who found similarities in the three patient bills, but we haven't discussed how patient charges are entered. Radar is monitoring the three patients that Brenda mentioned. If they get admitted again, I will find out if they are physically in the hospital."

"I'll make sure Steve is updated. You keep Radar informed."

Seemed like more than a fair split to me. "Excellent," I agreed with a smile.

As I put the phone down, my euphoria evaporated. It occurred to me that despite the friendly conversation, Mark hadn't brought up going out to dinner again.

I sighed. Apparently, I couldn't have my cake and eat it too.

Chapter 6

Who knew that even in the medical field, they had pep rallies? I thought such meetings existed only in computer companies and were designed for the sole purpose of providing executives with a captive audience. Apparently Dr. Johnson, the Chief of Staff at the hospital, shared a bond with computer executives. He had almost the same mantra, only instead of "propelling the company to number one in profits," he wanted to reach number one "in patient care and eliminate inefficiency and waste." The hospital marketing gurus probably couldn't find a way to discuss profits tastefully.

The old, "number one in customer satisfaction" didn't change at all, which I thought odd since customer satisfaction in health care might mean different things to Dr. Johnson versus the patient. Was his intention to keep all patients healed and happy or was he after profitable, chronic returning patients? Theoretically, the most dissatisfied customer was a dead one, but that customer wasn't likely to affect satisfaction surveys. On the other hand, no one was going to reap additional proceeds from the dead guy either.

In the computer industry, executives set unreasonable goals, but promised bonuses if by some quirk of fate the goals were achieved. The bonus program at the hospital was different, but just as impossible.

Dr. Johnson offered, "You lose, you win." He chuckled as though he had told a fabulous joke. "No, seriously folks, thanks to a great suggestion by one of our newest head nurses, Sally Rendal, we are instituting a weight loss program. If health professionals lose weight, it sets a good example for patients and," he stopped to wiggle his very large, menacing white eyebrows, "Crestwood will pay you for every pound you lose!"

What if a person gained weight? Could someone end up owing the hospital a bundle? I scanned the room, but no one raised a hand to ask if a "fat" fee would be charged.

Dr. Johnson droned on to his next topic. "A week from Friday is team player day. Mark your calendars!"

I would have marked mine and planned to be out, but I had promised Brenda I would volunteer on the days she worked, so I was on the hook.

Because the rally meetings were done in shifts to ensure the floors were always staffed, Dr. Johnson couldn't talk as endlessly as some executives. As soon as we were released, I headed for the stairs, thinking it would look bad to hop on the elevators after the "be healthy" lecture. There were only three of us pretending we cared.

I ran into Brenda as she headed downstairs to attend the rally. She looked rushed, but she stopped to ask, "Did you bring your lunch? It's really hard on days when we have these meetings. I forgot to tell you that you end up using your lunch hour for the meeting. And what with the," she looked around quickly and then whispered, "that *person,* you can't leave your lunch in the fridge!"

"The lunch lifter?"

She nodded. "I usually bring something that doesn't have to be refrigerated and lock my lunch in my locker. Have you eaten already?"

I eyed my sister-in-law. Was she hungry and scouting for food? She *was* pregnant, and she had eaten enough of my cooking to covet the occasional dish. Currently dressed as a round green elf, she looked as though she might be capable of just about any crime. If she put her green nylons over her face, she could rob a bank. "What are you going to do when Christmas is over and you can't dress like that?" I asked.

A smile burst onto her face. "Oh, do you want to go shopping with me? I've decided to come as Cupid and then as a leprechaun in honor of St. Patrick! And then the Easter Bunny!"

Far be it for me to tell her I had heard her doctor, Dr. Evans, and Ellen, the volunteer trainer, discussing a baby shower for her. "Whatever."

"Just keep it a secret," she warned, shaking my arm.

"Okay, okay." I walked back downstairs with her and dashed out for a sandwich rather than attempt two lunch breaks.

Because of the rally, there were still some lunch trays to be distributed to patients when I arrived back upstairs, but I didn't mind. Even the craziest patient, Mr. Silva, enjoyed lunch. He didn't need help eating it either, because he was in good shape physically. He just had a little trouble with reality.

Today he was a member of Congress. He'd be with us until his medication was properly readjusted, but like a lot of people with...imaginative outlooks on life, he wasn't very reliable at taking his medication. His records indicated he was in and out like clockwork.

"Here's lunch, Mr. Silva. How are you today?" I placed the tray on one of the little wheeled stands, slid the open side across the top of the bed and lowered it to the proper height so he could eat.

"Just fine," he responded heartily. "I'm working through lunch. Lots of legislation to consider."

"Can you lower my taxes? Would you like to get up and go to the window?"

"Got to work. Don't have time for lunch!"

No window today. The patient who shared the room with Mr. Silva grumbled, "Crazy old man." The two of them had been talking yesterday at lunch, but the other patient must have finally figured out that Mr. Silva was inventing various careers. For a while they had been having a pleasant time swapping war stories. Too bad Mr. Silva's weren't real.

The dreaded Mrs. Olsen was scheduled for x-rays at two, so after lunch was over, I packed her into a wheelchair and rolled her to the elevator. The x-ray department was on the first floor near the ER. The whirlpool that Mrs. Olsen so dearly loved was also on the first floor. Apparently that was where she thought she was headed, because she got very irritated when I rolled her into the x-ray room.

"Today is my whirlpool day! I'm not getting x-rays, you stupid bimbo. I want my whirlpool!"

Mrs. Olsen had a tendency to call people names. This was the hardest part of my job because under no circumstances would I tolerate such abuse in any other job. At least in the computer world, I'd get to call names right back. "Sorry Mrs. O. You'll have to reschedule your whirlpool. It was on Thursday last time you were in the hospital, but the doctor has to put in a new request for this stay." Mrs. O relied on her Cadillac insurance plan, which apparently didn't balk at paying for the whirlpool regardless of her malady.

The x-ray technician didn't look thrilled to see us; she must have already met Mrs. O. "Hi," I said, trying my best to sound cheerful. "I'm Sedona O'Hala, a volunteer. Do I wait here, or should I come back?"

"It shouldn't take long. I'm Holly Long. Can you help me get her on the table?" Holly was a tiny little thing and Mrs. O was not. In addition, Holly looked as though she had already dealt with about ten Mrs. O's today. Long blond hair framed a delicate face that was decorated with a smattering of freckles. Her light complexion made the dark circles of fatigue under her hazel eyes rather prominent.

"No problem." It was either volunteer down here or go back upstairs and do whatever needed doing up there.

I should have clarified that there were no problems for *me*. Mrs. O, of course, had more than a few complaints as we gingerly moved her to the x-ray table and positioned her properly. Granted, the table was cold, but she wasn't likely to get better service by whining about it. Her calling Holly an "incompetent imbecile" was completely out of line, but Holly politely ignored her.

"Why don't you save those pleasantries for someone really incompetent?" I suggested.

That turned Mrs. O's attention to me, but at least the distraction allowed Holly to load the x-ray cassettes in peace. Unfortunately, Mrs. O wasn't holding still.

"This is going to take longer if you don't hold your breath like Holly is asking," I chided.

"I need the hot tub. I want to see my doctor! This is torture!"

"The doctor ordered these x-rays, ma'am," Holly pointed out. "I need you to turn on your side."

We finally got through the x-rays, but then Holly pleaded, "Can you wait with her? She was moving a lot and some of these might not turn out."

"You're going to develop them now?" Apparently Holly was a one-woman show, loading, taking and developing.

"Yup." She pointed to the little door where she had put the cassettes. "The dark room is behind that wall. I'll have these ready in a few minutes. It doesn't take long."

Mrs. O wasn't so accommodating. "I want off this table! Instantly!"

I would have much rather gone into the darkroom and learned how to develop x-rays than sit with Mrs. O. "There, there, you old...dear. Lemme get your blanket." I tried to sound like Brenda rather than myself, but my patience was tested when Mrs. O compared me to a sheep, a cow and a mangy dog.

Holly finally came back out holding one of the x-rays high. "We'd better do this image again." She showed me the chest x-ray. It was blurry on the edges. "I really appreciate you waiting. Sometimes the nurses or techs can't wait and then depending on the patient, I can't develop them because the patient requires supervision. I end up taking the patient upstairs, coming back to develop and if the shots don't turn out, I have to go get the patient and do it all over again."

"Here or there, doesn't matter to me," I said.

We took the shot, and this time Mrs. O must have been tired of the table because she held still.

"This will probably be good," Holly said.

"I'll wait."

"No, you won't! I want out!" Mrs. O tried to get off the table. The surface was not only cold it was slippery, and Mrs. O was in danger of sliding herself right off the table and onto the hard floor. Still, I wasn't about to let the old hag get away with her bad behavior because it would be me dragging her back down if more were needed.

"You just settle down," I snapped. I had to practically lie on top of her to hold her still. "If you don't, I'm going to tell the doctor that it's too dangerous to transport you around the hospital, and I'll request he cancel your whirlpool."

That earned me the glare from hell, but she stopped wiggling in order to more effectively yell at me. "You snippety little bitch! I don't have to put up with this. This is malpractice! I'll sue!"

"Yeah, yeah, yeah," I muttered, wishing Holly would hurry up. "You're in for pneumonia, aren't you?"

Only Mrs. O seemed worried it was pneumonia, hence the x-rays. Apparently her doctor didn't want to take any chances. The woman had probably threatened to sue him just as she was threatening me now.

Holly hurried back out and nodded.

We practically threw Mrs. O in the wheelchair. "Thanks for the help," Holly whispered. "Anytime you want to volunteer down here, come on down. I can always use a hand."

"Really?" The work seemed marginally more interesting than what I did upstairs. Maybe she would teach me to develop the x-rays.

"Absolutely."

"Sounds good to me. I'll stop back down in a bit!"

Her eyes lit up. "That would be really, really great."

Mrs. Olsen bellyached all the way upstairs. "I want the whirlpool! It's damn cold in this hospital."

The physical therapist could probably hear her and might resign before Mrs. O could get permission to go to whirlpool. Geez, no wonder Brenda remembered when Mrs. O was in.

I got the old lady back to her room and suggested a walk so that she could warm up. I only did it to be irritating. I knew Mrs. O wouldn't actually walk.

The afternoon was wearing down to my normal end of shift, but since I had promised Holly I'd stop back down, I told Crissa, the technician, that I was going to go help out in x-ray in case anyone was looking for me.

"Okay," she said. "But Sally will not be pleased if she finds out." She swished her shoulder-length blond hair and wagged her finger in an imitation of Sally.

"Well, then just tell Attila I took a patient down there for x-rays."

"Attila?"

"Sally," I corrected.

Crissa grinned. "If she finds out you're moonlighting, she'll start paging you every five minutes."

"Thanks for the warning." Rescheduling officially was probably a good idea, but I was supposed to be up here spying so I didn't want to make a habit of farming myself out. "It's almost quitting time anyway."

Things hadn't slowed down any by the time I got back downstairs. Holly was working with a patient and had one in the wings. About all I could do was take patients back upstairs when they were done. She didn't have time to train me in anything else.

After delivering a few patients back and forth, Holly said, "The work down here can be a lot more fun, honest! If you come again I can teach you to develop the x-rays and then you'll be more than just a taxi service."

On what I hoped was my last run, I asked, "Can I take the x-rays next time?"

She laughed. "I could let you push the button after I set the machine up." She pointed to a chart on the wall. "There's a science to the positioning and the exposure. But if you volunteered down here permanently you could learn a lot."

Regrettably, I couldn't avail myself of her offer. I had a real job to do. "I'll stop by when I can," I promised.

It was really too bad the criminals didn't work in areas that would be more interesting for me. How inconsiderate of them.

I went back upstairs and delivered the last patient to her room. Before I could grab my coat and leave, Brenda waved me over. "I didn't know you were still here. Come with Dr. Burns and me on rounds. It'll be fun."

I doubted it, but how could I turn her down? She was a pathetic pregnant woman, for crying out loud. At least the doctor wasn't Staple. Dr. Burns was about as far from Staple as a person could get. Instead of a blondish, handsome vampire-type, he was short, plump and quite ordinary looking. Although he wore the ubiquitous white lab coat like other doctors, his looked as though he had wadded it up and sat on it in the car for a few days.

As we were introduced, he studied me carefully, possibly scanning for diseases. He let go of the stethoscope around his neck long enough to shake my hand, but then, as suddenly as I was his focus, he shifted. He turned and marched into the first patient's room.

Brenda and I followed. If an actual exam were to be done, I wouldn't stay, but for normal rounds, unless something came up, I was allowed to "learn and assist."

Mrs. Swartz was a dainty little lady and since she was allowed to have all the food she wanted, her son brought in snacks all the time. She had a tray over her lap with a couple of leftover finger sandwiches, carrots, and cherry tomatoes. I quickly wheeled the little stand out of the way so that the doctor could talk to her.

"How are you feeling today?" Dr. Burns asked. He was completely focused on her chart, but as I moved the tray, he reached out and plucked off the remainder of a sandwich.

I stared in astonishment as he began eating it. He never lost a beat; his questions and review of her blood pressure and other stats went off like clockwork. When he finished eating the piece of sandwich, he dusted his fingers off on his white jacket. He patted Mrs. Swartz gently, said some encouraging words, and we proceeded to the next room.

I followed in consternation. Eating food from a patient's tray could not be normal. Besides being rude, it couldn't possibly follow any good hygiene rules.

I looked at Brenda, but she just smiled serenely and lifted her eyebrows once. There was no way I could tell if she was trying to tell me that Dr. Burns was a likely candidate for stealing my lunch…or even adding charges to patient bills. Did stealing a leftover sandwich from a patient goodie bag constitute a pattern? Had she invited me on the rounds to see the evidence of deviant behavior? Given that she was dressed as a giant green elf, would she even recognize deviant behavior???

I was obviously tired and losing my mind. Instead of leaving at three as planned, it was almost five o'clock. As a volunteer, my hours should be nice and easy. Only one of the other volunteers scheduled as many hours as I did. If I was going to have any time for other investigative activities, like cornering Huntington for information, my schedule needed to be rearranged.

With that in mind, when I saw Attila at the nurses' station, I mentioned that I wanted to change my hours. "I've had a change in my personal schedule, and I need Wednesdays off." It occurred to me that I could ask for a couple of days, but it was better if I didn't get carried away. The case *was* at the hospital. There was only so much outside footwork necessary.

Of course, as soon as I told Attila, she frowned. With precise, staccato movements, she sat down at the computer and pulled up the schedule. "How about we replace Wednesdays with some afternoons? You're only scheduled for days right now, and we need late afternoon shifts as well as mornings."

"Well, actually," I kept my voice at its sweetest, which for me was a cross between strained and a high-pitched yell, "I'm already leaving well after three. I don't want to tie up my afternoons permanently."

"Hmm. How about a weekend day? We're always short on weekends."

My eyes crossed. "No thanks. I date a lot so I'm rarely free on Saturdays." A complete lie, but I thought it was a good one.

She glared at me. "Wednesdays," she muttered in her best harpy voice. "You're going to leave us short."

She was being greedy. I was a volunteer for crying out loud. Rather than point this out, I shrugged it off. With an extra day off in the middle of the week, this job now easily beat all the others that I had ever worked.

Chapter 7

Work at the hospital wasn't hard, although changing bedpans really was as bad as you might imagine. I tried to be helpful, though my main purpose was to hang around and spy on people. Since there were doctor rounds both in the morning and afternoon, it was easy to "watch and learn" at least twice a day. I verified pretty quickly how charges were logged and who did the logging.

Crissa, the technician I had already met, was a font of information via her complaints about lazy nurses. "What does Paul think, one of us is going to follow him around, get the stickers out of the trashcan and enter them for him?" Her blond hair was fluffed model-perfect with a wash-and-wear look that probably took hours with a blow dryer. For someone who was just over five feet tall and sported little-girl freckles, her bright green eyes threw some pretty mean sparks.

"Do you have to enter his numbers if he throws the bar codes away?" I asked. The technicians were assistants to the nurses, but that seemed over the line.

"Not in this lifetime! He might like us to, but he isn't stupid enough to suggest it. He's just lazy. I caught him napping--*napping*," she spit out, "in one of the patient beds one time. Do you know that he then commented that the sheets should probably be changed before we checked anyone in?"

After "assisting" him twice, it became obvious that Crissa wasn't exaggerating. Paul quite often unwrapped gauze or band-aids and threw the outer covering away without looking at the sticker, much less logging it. He certainly wasn't adding extra charges to the hospital bills, unless he went in at the end of the day and willy-nilly added charges to make up for his laziness.

Unfortunately, the most likely culprits were the doctors, but I couldn't tell bona fide orders from bogus ones. The only person who might detect such was another doctor. Luckily, I had one in mind who might be of help: Dr. Evans, Brenda's obstetrician. She just happened to work closely with four of the other doctors, sharing a building with them in the fancy physicians' office across the street. She would be a great inside source.

When she came on the floor to check on a couple of hysterectomies, I approached her. "Hi, Dr. Evans." I couldn't decide between asking her to lunch or making myself an appointment. An appointment would be more private, but what if she insisted on an exam? I kept up on my exams and even had birth control pills, but once in her office, I'd be at her mercy.

"Sedona! Brenda mentioned she recruited you. How do you like volunteering so far?" She was an elegant lady, taller than me by a few inches. Her numerous tiny cornrow braids were piled up on her head giving her even more height and elegance.

"So far so good."

"What made you decide to look into health care?" she asked.

"Uh, well. Computers are so…nonhuman." And part of the reason I had chosen them as my real career. I continued the lie, hoping to guide her toward which doctors or procedures might generate the most cash. "I'm looking into different specialties, trying to decide which areas fit my personality, but still allow me to make a decent living."

"Good to start right in the thick of things," she approved before opening one of the drawers at the nurses' station desk. "Have you seen the stack of doctors' business cards? I need to refer one of my patients to Dr. Burns. I know we all have cards in here somewhere."

"Dr. Burns?" If she did referrals for someone like Dr. Burns, maybe consulting with her wasn't such a good idea. The man had eaten food right off of a patient's tray, and he was my number one suspect for the lunch thief. Sure, it wasn't proof of overcharging, but he was still weird.

Dr. Evans turned and grinned at me, completely unconcerned. "Yes, if you're in need of a good internist, Dr. Burns is the one. He's the best."

"Oh." Then since I sounded disbelieving, I added, "He has an office at The Pavilion with you, doesn't he?" Maybe Dr. Evans referred patients to him because he was part of the group of doctors at The Pavilion. That sort of business exchange was common in the computer business. Some executives would throw business to their golf buddies without caring whether the guys were any good or not.

Brenda, who had come up behind us, laughed at me. "You can't let a few bad habits get in the way of a referral. He's really good!"

Dr. Evans agreed as she turned to go down the hall to do rounds. Before Brenda followed I asked, "Are you guys serious?"

She nodded. "Honestly, working with him beats half the other doctors. Think about it. Can you imagine letting Dr. Staple take a knife to you?" She shivered.

"Uh, no." But while Dr. Staple doled out smiles as if they were the cause of all disease and strife in the world, he probably didn't steal patient's food. "Doesn't Dr. Staple work at The Pavilion too?"

"Yes. He's a surgeon, but has his private offices over there like Dr. Evans. He's actually extremely talented, but he doesn't have bedside manners, not a one. He gets results and that's all that matters to him."

"Are there any other internists here?"

Brenda nodded. "Of course, but don't you worry. Dr. Burns is the best. I really like him. If I--" she stopped suddenly. With a snap, she closed her mouth and mumbled, "All the doctors here are really good."

I turned around. Dr. Staple must have been lurking in the break room because he was now standing in the doorway with a fierce frown on his face. I hoped he hadn't overheard Brenda's remark about him.

"Mrs. Pierce's bed needs changing," he said.

Since it wasn't Brenda's job to change sheets, he was obviously addressing me, although he didn't even lift his little cleft chin from his chart. "I'll get right on that," I responded, heading for the linen closet.

Mrs. Pierce didn't seem to like her doctor much. Whatever exam had been performed had either frightened her into losing control over all her bodily functions, or more likely, she had been aiming at Dr. Staple.

Computer work paid better and rarely smelled bad. Even when electronics were on fire and smelled like singed hair, it beat sewage. "Ohboy." This was going to take some doing.

Paul came in the room just then and stopped on a dime. His little fish face worked as though his gills had suddenly realized that he required water to breathe. He must have decided to go in search of some because he disappeared faster than a tadpole.

"Hey," I called out after him.

"He's never a big help, is he?" Mrs. Pierce murmured. She patted my arm.

I wasn't certain whether to be dismayed or relieved when a knock sounded. It wasn't Paul. Holly, from x-ray, poked her head around the doorway. Her long blond hair was pulled back into a tight ponytail. "Eh-yew. Smells like there was a code brown in here." She wrinkled her nose.

"You got that right." Brenda had explained that "code brown" was nurse talk for "emptied bowels." It wasn't an official code. Those were saved for the intercom, because it wasn't considered good form to blare out, "Patient stopped breathing in room 302, bring emergency equipment." Instead, a "code blue" was announced. I had a sheet with all the codes and their meanings in my volunteer packet.

Holly swished her head back and forth before pushing a wheelchair into the room. "Mrs. Pierce is due in my shop for some x-rays." She sucked in a breath like she was going to laugh, but she coughed instead, waving a hand in front of her face. "At the moment I'm wishing I had called in and a sub were here, but since there's only one x-ray tech in at a time, I guess it's me." While she was talking her hazel eyes searched slyly for a graceful exit. She shuffled her feet. "Doesn't look like Mrs. Pierce is quite ready."

"I'm working on it," I grumbled. "Paul was here, but he didn't exactly offer to help."

Grudgingly, she took the hint. After putting the chart down on the wheelchair she grabbed clean linens. "Some of the nurses will help out, some won't. Technically it's a technician's job--not an x-ray technician," she clarified, "a nurse's technician, you know, the aides."

"Yeah, I know. Or a volunteer's job."

"In Paul's case, he probably wouldn't help his own mother. If you ever need to move someone and need help, don't ask him."

"You'd think he could put some of that male muscle to work," I said.

Holly snorted. "Yeah right. Have you met John or Charles? John is an ambulance driver and Charles works in the ER. Mm-hmm, now there are some muscles."

"No, I guess I've missed them."

"Oh, I miss them too." She shivered delicately. "Next time you have to come in, Mizz Pierce, call the ambulance. I-am tell-ing you! That Charles can give me a ride any old time!"

Mrs. Pierce smiled vacantly, a little dopey. I wasn't sure how anyone could have romantic thoughts about men during a code brown cleanup. I had never washed my hands so much or changed my apron so often as I had since I started this job.

Once we finished, it was only polite to offer to go down with Holly to bring Mrs. Pierce back up. After all, she had helped with the mess.

We were just rolling out of the elevator onto the first floor when Crissa called out for us to hold the doors. She was pushing a patient bed all by herself. "Can you help me?" she asked. "This guy needs to go upstairs for emergency surgery."

Holly waved me onward. "Go on!"

I hurried to help Crissa get the patient into the elevator. The guy didn't look very healthy, moaning and breathing erratically. He had an IV in his arm and without my help, it would have been almost impossible for Crissa to control the bed and the IV pole.

The surgical rooms were at back of the third floor, behind an extra set of doors for additional privacy. Crissa didn't waste any time. When we got through the double doors into the surgery area, someone with green scrubs took over and rolled the guy into a procedure room.

"Thanks," Crissa said. "The ER is crazy today. We normally have more help, but I was left holding the bag this time."

"No problem." I turned around and almost slammed into one of the doctors. He stopped short to keep from plowing me over. He steadied me with one hand while asking, "In one?"

"Yes, sir, doctor," Crissa replied, saluting playfully and giving him a saucy wink.

He looked down at me then and caught me staring. "Sorry," I said. He was the kind of doctor mothers dream about; professional, good-looking and emanating doctor with every step.

He moved to one of the sinks, but didn't break eye contact. "You must be new."

I was about to follow Crissa out, but common courtesy demanded I answer his question. "I'm Sedona, one of the volunteers." I would have offered my hand, but his were under the running water. Just as with the other doctors, I got a thorough inspection, but this one seemed more personal and a lot more complimentary. I didn't feel at all diseased.

"Dr. Fox. Alex Fox." He said his name like, "Bond. James Bond." The man even looked like James Bond, except his eyes were green rather than blue. He had a hint of gray at his temples. "Wash up. Grab some scrubs. You can watch."

My eyes about popped out of my head. "Really?"

"Sure. It's a routine appendicitis. We encourage students to observe as often as possible."

Technically, I wasn't a student, but I didn't argue when one of the nurses took pity on me and tossed some scrubs in my direction. "I'm Stacey, welcome aboard." Her hair was already covered, and after introducing herself, she donned her face mask and followed Dr. Fox.

"Thanks, I'll be right there!" I hurriedly pulled on the protective uniform. We had learned in training to wash up properly. Ellen had put goop all over our hands and then checked them under ultraviolet light to see how much we had actually washed off.

I barely washed my hands long enough, even though rushing wasn't necessary because my presence wasn't critical to anyone. The doctor wouldn't care if I wandered in late, but I didn't want to miss anything, or worse, *distract* him in the middle of something important.

This was the most exciting thing to happen since I'd started. Too bad it had nothing to do with the case. Feeling very privileged, I went through the door and stood out of the way toward the patient's head. I made sure I was well away from Dr. Fox so that I couldn't bump anything, especially his arm. The video screen was on the other side of the patient so everything was within easy view. An anesthesiologist was already putting the mask over the patient's face. There was one little spot with the guy's abdomen exposed.

Dr. Fox didn't waste any time. He didn't even have to say, "scalpel," because the tray was right there with all kinds of instruments. Stacey stood next to him, efficient and professional. Dr. Fox blocked most of my view of her, but he was better to look at anyway.

I admit, I couldn't watch when he made the initial cut. Sure, it was all for a good cause. I still closed my eyes. When I peeked, Dr. Fox had finished inserting a tube underneath the patient's bellybutton. He said something about "inflate," and then he made a second incision and then a third. I forgot to close my eyes.

There were a lot of long instruments and giant tubes. Dr. Fox moved a long tube around, and pictures of a whitish wormy looking thing surrounded by red capillaries appeared on the video monitor. Dr. Fox seemed to be going after this wormy, disgusting body piece. I hoped the images were meaningful to Dr. Fox because they were indistinguishable to me. All of the flesh looked, "infected" and "swollen" not to mention disgusting and oozing.

"Not ruptured," Dr. Fox commented.

It was hard to watch the monitor and Dr. Fox's hands at the same time. The patient looked like a weird voodoo doll with all the instruments poking out of his abdomen.

Dr. Fox made a small cut underneath the worm. He then used something else to clamp one end of the white mass. A few more movements and another clamp, and suddenly there it was, a grotesque bundle of flesh. *Plop*, he dropped it into a specimen bag that the nurse held out.

"Good thing the guy didn't ignore the pain," Dr. Fox said.

Wow.

I stayed out of the way while he bandaged the patient up. He snapped his gloves off just like on television and strode out of the room. It took me several minutes to follow because I was too amazed to get my feet working.

There it was, the workings of life and death. Just like that, the doctor went in and removed the problem. This guy would wake up and heal and move on with his life. I felt heroic and all I had done was *watch*. My own appendix wanted to be taken out at that moment.

In a daze, I wandered back out. I hadn't even gotten a spec of dust on me, never mind blood or gore. This surgery watching was a lot more captivating and a good deal more sanitary than bedpan changing. Truthfully, with all the computers involved, it should have been nothing more than another lab exercise to me, but it wasn't. There was a *patient* with real blood and everything!

Dr. Fox had already removed his mask and scrubs. "What did you think of the surgery?"

"Totally impressive," I said in awe.

He smiled. "How long have you been here?"

"A...couple of days...a week now," I stuttered. "I'm trying to decide on whether or not to choose a medical career. How long have you worked here?" It was a stupid question, but mentally I pretended I was furthering the investigation by asking questions, rather than being nervously flattered by his attention.

He flashed perfect white teeth. "About fifteen years, give or take. I did my residency in Houston, but I've been doing surgery here ever since."

"Oh."

"I'm on my way to check on room 305--removed a tumor yesterday. You headed back that way?"

Without his prodding I might have stood there all day thinking about the amazing surgery. "Sure. I'm supposed to be helping."

He grinned at me, his emerald eyes flashing.

I followed along and wondered if he would mind if I asked a few thousand questions. Before I could form an intelligent thought, a voice from down the hall hailed him.

"Oh, Doc-tor Fo-ox! Yoohoo!" There was no way that cawing voice could coo. Attila's attempt was worse than a howling cat.

Like a race car driver, she zoomed in. Her muscular arm grabbed mine and nearly squeezed it off. Since she was the head nurse and rarely helped with the grunt work, I doubted she got those muscles from lifting patients. She must spend all of her free time working out at the gym.

"Sedona, you need to check the supply cabinet and restock it," she grated out before turning her dark-haired vixen wattage on Dr. Fox. To my disgust, he didn't seem to mind. Like Bond, he seemed willing to give any female his amused attention.

Attila wasn't all that well endowed, but what she did have, she pushed out in a parody of either a strutting peacock or some weird chest exercise that I didn't know about. His eyes, as intended, strayed to the target.

"Thanks again," I said to the doctor.

He acknowledged my appreciation with a wave. "Anytime. We usually set up a time for students to come in and watch. Check with your administrator. I'm sure she will know when we have the sessions planned."

By the time Attila and Dr. Fox went into room 305, he had a hand on her shoulder, but I couldn't tell if that was to keep her from becoming velcroed to his lab coat or if he was encouraging her. At last, the closet romances that television dramas always seemed to portray.

"Hmph," I muttered.

"That woman is determined to marry herself a rich, handsome doctor and retire before she's thirty. She's not the only one either."

I jumped and turned to find Holly behind me pushing an empty wheelchair. "He doesn't look all that unwilling,"I said.

Holly shrugged. "That man gets whatever he wants. Then again, most of the doctors do. Sally is too blind to see that." She paused and raised the pitch of her voice, "Alex, oh Alex," she fluffed at her hair even though hers was blond to Attila's long dark hair, "isn't a one-woman kind of man."

"He's not married?"

"Nah, messy divorce years and years ago. He's a surgeon--the head surgeon--and like most of them, he's married to his work. He manages to date, and I happen to know that he and Sally," she wiggled two of her fingers together and then hurried on, "but I think he's currently dating at least *one* of the girls downstairs. Since his daughter works here too, he keeps a lid on things, because you know, people would talk."

Like we were doing. She went on to confide, "From what I've heard, he isn't dying to settle back in with one woman. You should probably be careful. He has a reputation, if you know what I mean." She leaned forward and stared at the door where he had disappeared. "He sure is nice to look at though."

I had to agree on both counts. In fact, he was probably one of the few doctors who wasn't completely weird. Really, most of them were as geeky as engineers; they just lacked the nerd reputation.

Thinking of weird must have been a beacon. Dr. Burns came out of one of the patient rooms, eating a cookie. I winced. Mrs. Starksy liked to keep her meal trays and dawdle, especially if she had pudding. She also nabbed the cookies or brownies and saved them for later.

I went into her room and sure enough, there she was with her very empty lunch tray. "Hey, Mrs. Starksy."

"Anna, dear. Just call me Anna."

"You ready for me to take your tray?"

She nodded.

What else could she do? There wasn't anything on the tray but a lonely empty plastic bag that the cookie had been wrapped in.

I shook my head. Maybe there was a pattern, and Dr. Burns only took food from patients who didn't have incurable or contagious diseases. Much as I liked food, there was no way I was that greedy. I hated to think badly of the doctor, but who else could be guilty of stealing my lunch?

The real question, of course, was whether or not he was guilty of stealing something even more valuable.

Chapter 8

Instead of wandering around aimlessly looking for non-existent clues or doing my volunteer work, I went looking for Radar. Surely by now he had more information.

I entered his lair and called out a greeting. He jumped about three feet in the air. The wheeled chair he had been sitting on spun halfway across the concrete floor before stopping. "You trying to parachute off that chair or what?" He wasn't a particularly nervous person, but maybe the creepy basement was getting to him.

"Couldn't you knock?"

"Would you have heard?" There were far too many clanks and echoes across the concrete floor for anyone to distinguish a polite knock on the door.

Radar retrieved his chair.

I checked my watch because I didn't want to be gone too long. "Find anything yet?"

"I looked up the admitting doctors and went through more of the codes, but I'm not sure any of the information is going to help. The charges are almost exactly the same for two of the patients, but the third one is kind of off."

"Who admitted them?" If it had been the same doctor, Radar would have been more excited.

"Dr. Evans admitted Mrs. O for the dates that Brenda mentioned. The Brown patient was admitted by Burns and the third guy by Fox." He shrugged. "I went back into Mrs. O's records. She has been admitted by Burns several times in the past and also by Dr. Staple."

"Typical hypochondriac," I said.

"Dr. Evans has also admitted Brown. I charted all this, but since it isn't the same doctor, it doesn't prove a thing. Maybe that is why someone picked these patients to overcharge. They have more than one doctor so how is anyone going to be able to keep track?" He pulled out a three ring binder. Instead of flipping through what appeared to be blank pages, he dug out papers from a very carefully concealed slit in the plastic. "I know you like hard copy so I printed these. Be careful with them. Don't leave them lying around where someone could see them."

So far as I could tell, Radar and I were the only ones who had ventured down to the basement in several years. Even if he posted it on the wall, no one would be likely to discover the sheets of information.

He laid out the copies. "Brown and Mercer had colonoscopies. Mrs. O had a hysterectomy on the dates you originally gave me, *but,*" he held up his eureka finger, "I found another stay where she had a colonoscopy so I included that. She's also been in for ulcers and had a couple of tumors removed--not all at the same time, but I went back through all her records."

"Who did the surgeries?"

He shook his head. "Dunno yet. That billing is separate." He pulled up a list on his computer. "Dr. Burns is an internist. He wouldn't do surgeries, but internists charge for some things on an outpatient basis, like colonoscopies. Surgeons also remove polyps from what I can tell from the codes. All surgery, outpatient or inpatient is billed separately. And..." To my surprise, Radar's voice trailed off in embarrassment. He looked down and shuffled his feet. "I haven't been able to obtain the surgeon bills yet."

It couldn't be for lack of trying. Nothing was sacred to Radar's tapping fingers. "Why not?"

"It's a lot easier to break into the hospital database because I work here. The admitting doctor is logged by the hospital. But what the doctor charges, be it a surgeon or internist or general physician, is a separate bill. I have to break into an entirely different network for that, and some of the doctors keep those records at a separate office or home machine." He swallowed loudly and then added, "My research shows that some of the machines in those offices might not be connected to the internet all of the time."

"What if they don't even have an internet connection?" I asked.

His eyes widened. "But..." He shook his head like a dog trying to get rid of water. "If they have a private office and their own database program for storing their records and doing billing, they wouldn't *require* an internet connection." He stared at me and blinked. "But, I, they'd *want* to be connected, don't you think?"

"Let's just look at the info, okay?" My poor buddy couldn't fathom not being connected. It would probably be easier for him to do without food and water than his internet connection.

We looked back at the sheets. "These first two were in for a colonoscopy, so not only are their admitting records the same, most of the charges on the rest of the bill are identical," he said.

"Hmm. Both of those were admissions by Dr. Burns, but here's one for Dr. Staple, and one for Dr. Fox," I said. After seeing Dr. Fox in action, it was hard to imagine any doctor engaging in petty theft. Why would a person with a God-given and trained ability to save a life stoop to stealing? Wasn't their job satisfying enough?

I followed the lines of data down the page. The data was very confusing. "Who stands to gain by all this?"

He shrugged. "The hospital racked up charges for all of these stays. The admitting doctor in these first two cases," he pointed to the data, "was

Dr. Burns. But I can't see who actually charged for the colonoscopies. It could have been Dr. Burns or one of the surgeons."

"But all of these bills point to different people!"

"There are other people who stand to benefit too. Remember when these three were in and had x-rays?" He typed madly at his computer for a few moments. "The x-ray is read by a radiologist. That's also a separate bill."

"Oh, good grief. It looks like the whole place is on the take." I glanced at my watch. "I gotta get back upstairs."

He handed me an unmarked manila envelope. "I peeled off any incriminating information, including the patient name, but this gives you a history. Each sheet is marked in code, so if you get them confused, I can tell you which patient is which."

I rolled my eyes, thanked him and hurried outside to stash the envelope in my SUV before rushing back inside. As I reached the third floor, the pager system intoned, "Sedona O'Hala, please report to the nurses' station."

Whoops. Gone too long. I was already hurrying, so I hurried in that direction.

Crissa waved at me. "Oh, hey," she said. "Mr. Silva escaped downstairs again. The ER nurse caught him trying to leave the building. Can you go down and get him?"

Mr. Silva had numerous ailments, but the worst was definitely his mental instability. Maybe he still thought he was a member of Congress and had decided to catch a plane to Washington.

I hurried back downstairs, but couldn't find Mr. Silva anywhere in the emergency room area. The triage nurse was no help. "He's in that wheelchair, honey." She pointed with the end of her pen.

I looked in that direction. Sure enough, there was a wheelchair. "You mean that empty chair?"

She sighed as if I had used up the last of her patience. She stood up and leaned her rather large bulk over the counter, jabbing with the pen. "That one." Since her beady brown eyes were busy glaring at me, she still didn't notice the chair was empty.

I folded my arms and tapped my foot. "It's going to look bad for both of us when I wheel that empty chair upstairs."

She finally gave the problem some attention. Her eyes followed where she was pointing. "Oh, shit." She did the same scan of the waiting room I had already done. There were a couple of people; a kid with enough gauze around his toe to suffocate an elephant, and another lady who sat down, but then got back up and ran toward the bathroom. No Mr. Silva anywhere.

The nurse leaned back into her cubbyhole and sent a coded page over the intercom system. We definitely needed additional technicians to assist in finding him. "Maybe he's in the can," she said.

"Uh-huh."

Mr. Silva wanted to go home, a fact he made quite plain on a daily basis. My coat was upstairs so I went back to get it and informed Crissa that Mr. Silva had made good on his escape.

"Oh my God, not *again*." She started looking for his file or some other pertinent paperwork, probably the records of negligence or CYA forms.

Sure enough, when I got downstairs, "the cans" had all been checked, and there was no Mr. Silva. The police were always notified in these instances, but none had arrived yet. I went out the door, got in my SUV and circled the building before heading for the road.

About a quarter mile from the hospital, Mr. Silva was mincing his way along wearing only slippers and the hospital gown. The gown flapped in the wind. Although the police had already been notified by hospital staff, no doubt a few passersby had also reported the escapee given that he was half naked and such a strange looking sight.

"Mr. Silva!" I called out through the rolled down passenger window. "Mr. Silva, would you like a lift? It's awfully chilly out." His feet had to be getting brutalized by the gravel and dry cold. At least it wasn't snowing.

"Damn cold out here," he replied.

He couldn't see my pink striped apron from the side of the road, but he might have recognized me. "Mr. Silva, how about we go back to the hospital, and I'll sneak in some hot chocolate for you?"

"Damn cold out here."

"Yes, it is."

He stopped walking and folded his arms across his shivering body. "I was an astronaut you know. And this is what it has come to. Damn cold."

"Outer space is pretty cold isn't it?"

"No damn air there either."

I pushed the door open. He stared at the interior and could feel the warm air coming from the vents. "You won't take me back to the base will you?"

"Not until you've had some hot chocolate. All this exercise requires that you get good and warmed up first."

Apparently that was enough logic for him. Besides, a cruiser had pulled up behind me, and Mr. Silva was a little too old to attempt running. His head hanging in defeat, he tried to climb into the SUV. Before I could go around to assist, the officer came forward and helped him in.

Of all the cops in Denton, it had to be Derrick, Sean's friend. He didn't know I owned a Mercedes and with the pink-striped hospital apron, he didn't recognize me at first. "You going to be okay getting him back to the hospital ma'am?"

"Sure," I said cheerily, ducking my head.

"Sedona?" He grabbed at his cinnamon hair as though it might fly away.

I sighed. "I'm doing a stint of volunteer work at the hospital."

Boyish, normally trusting brown eyes narrowed. "Last time you volunteered, you weren't much help."

"Nonsense. You eventually got your man." It was quite unfair for him to blame me for the last debacle. In fact, if I hadn't agreed to go along as a witness, he would have been in a lot more trouble because his witness had planned on accusing him of assault.

Derrick wasn't through lecturing. "See if you can't keep a better eye on these patients in the future. This must be the sixth time this month we've gotten a call."

"Uh-huh." He shut the door firmly. I immediately drove back to the emergency room entrance where Crissa met us with a wheelchair.

"Mr. Silva, Mr. Silva," the technician scolded. "What were you thinking? It's cold outside."

"That's what I have been telling my wife here. Why she wants to go out in the cold at a time like this, I can't imagine."

Crissa grinned at me. I rolled my eyes. Wife indeed. All I needed was to be part of his imaginings.

By the time I got back upstairs, a committee had been formed and a search team organized. Mr. Silva was tucked in safely before the team had a chance to disband. Attila didn't waste the opportunity to put on a show for her audience. She chastised me for going out on my own. "You need an official from the hospital. What if he had required medical care? You aren't qualified! Unacceptable. I'm going to have to write you up."

I didn't bother to reply. She could put my write-up next to hers for allowing a patient to walk out in the first place. It was her floor, her responsibility. I was just an innocent volunteer. What were they going to do, fire me?

Mr. Silva's escape caused all of us to run behind on our normal duties. That meant I stayed longer than scheduled. Again.

By the time I got home, Sean had already called four times and left messages demanding to know what I was doing at the hospital, and what I was doing to Brenda. "She's pregnant with my first child, Sedona. How can you do this to me?" he whined into my machine.

Of course Derrick had told Sean that I had been spotted in a Mercedes hauling a half-dressed, crazy old man back to the hospital. Tattle-tale.

Unfortunately, my mom had called too and left a message inquiring about my volunteer position. Someone had unkindly brought in the big guns, probably because he knew I wouldn't return his nosy phone call. While I could safely ignore my brother and his obnoxious messages, parents were a different story. It could take weeks to smooth things over with a parent after ignoring one of them. In some cases it could be costly or require a trip home, and I certainly didn't have money to burn.

I dialed. "Mom?"

"Oh dear, how are you? I hear you are volunteering at the hospital, although I must say Sean sounded awfully upset about it. He seems to think you will get Brenda in trouble or lead her astray. Why he believes you can be a bad influence on Brenda is beyond me. Has she learned to cook yet? I really worry about my grandchildren starving."

"Yeah." I wasn't even sure which question I was answering, but she was in one of her moods where it wouldn't matter.

"It was so nice of you to teach her to cook at Thanksgiving. Are you going to help her with Christmas? You know your brother Dean is coming here this Christmas so we can't make it up there. Can you come down here? Or do you think Sean will be devastated if he is abandoned? I don't think they should be traveling with Brenda pregnant and all."

Sean would starve if I didn't cook Christmas dinner for him, but that would totally serve him right for tattling on me. "I should probably stay in town," I hedged. "Although I was thinking of going to Hawaii--"

"Hawaii? But your brother Dean is coming up to see you after he visits here. It will be the week after Christmas of course, but he does want to see you." She paused. "I don't know if he has told you," she said almost reverently, "but he's bringing a *guest*. Wouldn't it be wonderful if you also..." She changed her mind. "Are you still seeing that young man we met at Thanksgiving? He seemed very nice in a rugged sort of way. Like your father when he was younger, an outdoor type."

I didn't answer. She sighed. She knew there was no way I would talk about Mark even if she held me at gunpoint. I probably shouldn't have invited him to Thanksgiving dinner, but I had been feeling all warm and fuzzy and family oriented and hadn't fully considered the Mom and Dad consequences.

She finally prattled on again about Dean and his guest. The conversation didn't bode well for me because Dean bringing a guest meant Mom was going to pursue my lagging opportunities for marriage with even more determination.

Dad was out being an outdoor type in the greenhouse so I didn't get a chance to talk to him. Luckily the holidays had Mom wound up enough that she didn't ask for many details about my volunteer work. Sean would have to use some other avenue for spying on me.

Chapter 9

The conversation with Mom created a nagging inside my brain that could not be silenced. Saturday morning seemed like a good time to address the inevitable.

Because Dean was visiting my parents for the holidays and keeping them and himself out of Denton, Christmas would be a small affair, but it was still going to occur. Sean would invite me over, and I'd have to go and cook dinner. And even if I skipped out and went to Hawaii, I was still on the hook for dreaded presents.

What do you buy for a pregnant woman who doesn't fit into any of her clothes and doesn't want to be reminded of that fact? Sean was easy. Huntington was impossible because the man had absolutely everything. Then there was my new leather jacket that either Huntington or Mark had left as a gift a couple of weeks ago. I was almost positive Mark had given it to me, but I couldn't overlook the fact that Huntington had been pretty generous at the end of the first case when he gave me the Mercedes.

Since there was absolutely no competing with Huntington's money, I didn't try. Instead, I visited a little craft shop that sold art from every corner of the United States. American Arts and Crafts specialized in Native American crafts, and although Huntington had been outfitting his condo, it wasn't very personalized yet. Perhaps there would be something unique and special, but that wouldn't break my piggy bank.

The selection was artsy. Looking at the various dust collectors, bunnies, bowls, rugs and paintings it was hard to feel inspired.

Hmm. Then again, maybe I could kill the bird with two heavy stones, so to speak. A pair of beautiful bookends carved out of black marble resembled jagged cliffs. A slash of a smoky blue mineral, maybe quartz, ran through the front part of the stone. The bookends reminded me of Huntington, dark with a clash of sudden color that were his blue eyes.

There were other choices that might work; a bowl with a cougar running across one side or a hand tooled leather box. Nothing was quite as elegant as the bookends. As gifts went, it was expensive for my budget. I grumbled under my breath about it, but he had given me the SUV. Even fifty dollars wasn't all that adequate a gift in return for his generosity.

As I was about to leave, a row of pictures by a local photographer caught my eye. Several were shots of the various mountains in the area, and there were some beautiful springtime pictures. It was uplifting to see the flowers when everything outside was cold and bleak. One picture in particular was so very hopeful because it showed tiny, determined flowers growing despite the harsh odds of the wilderness. Maybe...well, Mark hadn't ever gotten round to inviting me to dinner.

I bought the picture anyway.

After my shopping trip, I stopped to mail packages to my parents, including Dean's gift. I also purchased a gift certificate for Marilyn, my former cleaning lady. Even though I had hired her as a necessity during the first case, Huntington had been smart enough to keep her on after the case was over.

I needed to drop off Suzy's gift, but my incorrigible best friend would not wait until Christmas to open it, so the longer I waited, the better. Feeling generous, I bought my former boss, Turbo, a little plastic Garfield for his toy collection. I had no idea what Radar was into. He played an awful lot of computer games, but that was way outside my area of expertise. Since he was an unknown but liked food, and I was too cheap to buy him a restaurant gift certificate, I added him to my cookie list.

With my shopping finished by early afternoon, there was time to tackle another unpleasant task. Until I met with Huntington, I would be scrambling about in the dark at the hospital. Mark probably could have told me a lot about the case, but he might think I was asking him as an excuse to rekindle the personal relationship. Of course I wouldn't sink that low, but either way, I didn't want to chance accidentally getting into a discussion about me having taken the volunteer position.

Just because I accepted the job shouldn't mean Mark couldn't date me. And maybe I didn't want to see someone who put conditions on our relationship before we even had one. It made no sense for me to check with Mark before taking a job. And besides, the best paying jobs I'd ever had were the ones where Huntington was paying me on the side.

Maybe neither brother would be at the condo.

Denton wasn't very big and traffic was light on the weekends so it took less than fifteen minutes to reach Alpine Hills where Huntington's condo was located.

Good old Michael was still on duty at the concierge desk. Had we been friends, or even remotely interested in pretending to be polite, I would have inquired about whether or not Huntington was upstairs. Since Michael was used to me ignoring him, he ignored me right back and picked up the phone to call and warn Huntington. Good, that meant Huntington was home.

The door to the condo was not open when I exited the elevator. I knocked on Huntington's door, but he opened it just wide enough so that he could see me. "Come in."

"Are you going to open the door, or is this some kind of fatness test?" He was sweeping his foot around like a metal detector.

"Hurry up or the cat will get out," he replied testily.

I stopped in the act of going through the opening, his wrapped gift held high above my head so I could fit through. "The. Cat."

Just then, said beast announced itself with a hiss and snarl, due either to my presence or the fact that Huntington's swinging foot had stopped it from running past me and out into the hallway.

"Hurry up!" He grabbed my arm and yanked me inside. The back of my coat barely made it in before he slammed the door behind me.

Not that I was paying any attention to my clothing. The black feline held my complete attention. I would have closed my eyes, but I knew better than to take my eyes off the enemy.

It hissed.

I hissed right back.

It waved a paw at me in a rather threatening manner. Since Huntington was now watching me warily, I just sniffed and gave the cat my haughtiest glare.

Mistake. No one can out-haughty a cat, especially a sleek, short-haired killer.

"What the hell is wrong with you?" Huntington demanded. "This time, I mean."

I turned my glare on him. "That cat doesn't like me. What is it doing here? Why in the world did you keep it?" I knew where the cat had come from. Huntington had probably kept the cat to irritate me. This perky feline had caused me a lot of grief, not to mention severe punctures and scratches when it tried to use me as an escape ladder.

Huntington grinned and didn't look that much different than a cat with a can of tuna. "He's mine now. No one seemed to want him, so I kept him."

"Great." Moving carefully and keeping a watchful eye on the enemy, I crossed the living room. I set Huntington's present and Marilyn's gift certificate down on the bar. The cat followed me. Warily, I moved away and perched on the edge of the couch.

"I changed his name," Huntington said. "I didn't want him to go around with a name attached to a criminal case."

"Why not?" Seemed to me that being associated with criminal activities fit the cat. He had a sneaky look about him, and he was dangerous to boot.

"I changed it to Shadow--Black Shadow, but I call him Shadow."

"Original," I muttered, not surprised that Huntington hadn't the imagination to name him something more creative and fitting like, "Claws," or "Killer." The right name would at least warn visitors of the cat's tendency to shred innocent humans. Even now, the cat stalked me, walking back and forth in front of the couch, twitching his tail.

"Soda?" Huntington offered from the kitchen. The magnificent chrome kitchen ran halfway along the living room with a bar separating the two. It was a perfect suite for entertaining. Huntington had recently upgraded the television on the wall away from the kitchen with a very large plasma display. A new speaker system was recessed into the walls.

Luckily the bookends were classy enough to fit in.

"No thanks. I came over to get some case details. You neglected to fill me in again." So that I wasn't the only one complaining, I added, "Radar also mentioned he could use some info."

Huntington shrugged and helped himself to the glass of orange juice that was on the kitchen table. "From what you told me the other night it sounds like you already have a good handle on some suspicious activity."

This type of discussion was part of a longstanding pattern. Huntington had a crazy notion that telling me what he suspected would ruin my ability to investigate with an open mind. I, on the other hand, wanted to know as much as possible to avoid putting my foot in something dark, dank, smelly or dangerous. I folded my arms and sat back. "I have all day."

Huntington looked disgusted. "I don't."

"I suppose I could do without the information. I survived for a long time unaware of what was going on the last time. The case took us a lot longer to solve, of course."

"There's no way you can know if more information would have helped solve the last case faster or not!"

I wagged my finger. "Au contraire. Note that we didn't make any progress until your auditor friend filled me in on what you already knew."

"You mean after you drugged me and invited him over?"

That didn't even deserve an answer, so I plowed on with my original intent. "The basics, Huntington. At least the basics." When he took another drink of orange juice without answering, I said, "After you got yourself shot, Mark said something about charges for services not rendered. Let's start there."

"I don't remember him saying that."

"You had been shot. You may have been concentrating on surviving rather than the conversation." Maybe because the look on my face implied he might be in danger of getting shot again, he doled out a few scant details.

"False charges to bills is pretty much the case in a nutshell," he said. "Of course, it's possible there is no case at all and that Crestwood just has a few too many billing errors. The errors seem to take the form of extra services which are added to the bill after a patient has already been discharged. That and perhaps we weren't digging quite deep enough, assuming that the three patient names you turned up prove to be visits that never happened at all."

"How did someone notice the charges in the first place?" Brenda certainly wouldn't have gone crawling through the files if Mark hadn't made her curious with his remark.

"The hospital board--"

"Geez," I interrupted. "Are you on every single board in town?" He had served on the last two company boards during the investigations.

"No. I'm friends with someone on the hospital board. He hired me to look into some suspicious activities."

"Oh." I got back on track before he decided to get secretive again. "So what did your friend notice?"

"His sister-in-law was in town visiting. She fell and bruised her hip so badly she couldn't walk. Dan took her to the hospital. There were x-rays, of course, and since she also bumped her head when she fell, the hospital kept her in overnight."

"Except the bill didn't match what happened?"

He nodded. "There was some sort of nonsense about treatment of ulcers and an MRI added to the charges."

"The MRI could have happened because of the fall, right?"

He nodded. "But his sister-in-law knows what one is and said it didn't happen. And there was a stack of charges related to swallowing whatever it is they swallow and then x-rays to look for ulcers. Of course, the hospital corrected it immediately when Dan called to complain."

I started to ask another question, but the cat distracted me. It hopped up on the cream-colored leather couch and inspected my leg. Mr. Shadow cat had already met me so there was no real reason for this perusal. Still, after he finished sniffing my blue jeans, he stretched so that his face was near mine. He sniffed again. Finding me lacking, he jumped back to the floor and went over to Huntington and rubbed against his leg.

Huntington smiled like a proud parent.

"You were telling me what Dan did after he got the bad bill?" I prompted dryly.

"Basically he hired me, but he's a new board member and not sure there's anything worth investigating."

A bad bill was a flag, but not a large one. Half the time I went in for a routine exam, my bill appeared inflated by at least fifty percent, but the doctor's office claimed the highway robbery was legal. "He must have had other suspicions."

Huntington almost smiled. Maybe he admired my tenacity or better yet, maybe he was impressed that I was smart enough to know I didn't have the whole story yet. Either way, he answered. "Dan worked for the Mayo Clinic in Scottsdale until he retired and moved here about a year ago. One of the reasons Dan was so impressed with Crestwood in the first place was because it was very profitable. Mayo is a not-for-profit institution. All the money goes back into the hospital for research and there are always more projects than money. In fact, most hospitals struggle to remain profitable, but Crestwood is doing very well by any standard."

"Maybe too profitable?"

Huntington nodded. "According to Dan's research, Crestwood charges an average of two to three times the price of any other hospital in Colorado."

My eyebrows shot up. "What did the chief of staff have to say about all of this? Surely he knew the hospital was charging more than other hospitals!"

"Dan is friends with Dr. Johnson. One of the reasons he was invited to serve on the board was because he and Dr. Johnson have been friends for years. After the billing mistake Dan started to probe deeper, but then thought better of it. He doesn't want to risk his spot on the board or lose friends if he's wrong."

The wheels in my head churned. "It would look incredibly bad for Dan if there was no problem at all, I suppose." But if the hospital was overly profitable...Dr. Johnson might already know why. He might even be part of the problem. "You're telling me that Dan didn't bring up his concerns with Dr. Johnson. That would mean that Dr. Johnson, the chief of staff, a man who also sits on the board doesn't know about this investigation."

"The board is paying me to investigate."

I knew Huntington well by now. This was a chess move with one hand waving in distraction. He had a unique way of stating things without telling the whole story. "The board, via Dan, hired you to investigate, but he didn't tell the rest of the board what he was doing?"

Huntington brooded for a while, no longer amused by my cleverness. This time when he answered, he completely avoided my question. "The high prices at Crestwood aren't entirely unusual. It's the only large medical facility available in the area, and let's face it, Denton is predominantly a resort town. Crestwood not only serves some wealthy visitors, it also serves a large surrounding area. The circumstances allow the hospital to set prices without a lot of comparison or competition. For Medicare, they get the standard payment of course, but for a lot of other patients, they rake it in."

Huntington was keeping secrets on this job, and not just from me. Dan had hired him, but the board was paying him for an investigation it knew little or nothing about. That meant there were even more suspects than I had imagined.

My stomach clenched. "I guess it's a good thing I'm not sickly. I don't think I want to be admitted to this hospital right now."

"You should definitely try to stay healthy for a while," he agreed.

The problem was that whenever I was involved with Huntington, my health seemed to be in imminent danger.

I got up to leave, glad for the new information, but not liking the facts. The cat took two steps in my direction. Looking down at him, I noticed four or five little black hairs on my jeans. "Marilyn is going to need special dust rags. She'll have to vacuum every surface to keep up with Shadow's shedding." Huntington's maid had her work cut out for her. Thinking of her reminded me about her gift certificate. I waved towards the bar where I had left the gifts. "I brought a gift certificate for Marilyn. Can you give it to her when you see her?"

"Sure. I'm having her come once a week." He smiled. "She likes Shadow."

I sniffed skeptically and took my leave.

Chapter 10

Generally speaking, Sundays were lazy days for me, but this time of year, there was no time to snuggle under the covers daydreaming. Christmas cooking called and, if there was time, maybe I could look up one little, important address before church.

I pulled some butter out of the fridge to soften and booted my computer. The hospital board members were listed on the hospital's web site along with a nice dossier of their very impressive accomplishments, most of which was of little interest. I was only interested in Dr. Dan…Hernandez.

Once I had his full name, his phone number and address were a cinch. Oh, the wonders of modern civilization. I didn't even have to be an expert hacker like Radar.

One quick phone call and I was in. "Dr. Dan? I mean, Dr. Hernandez?" A male voice chuckled on the other end.

"Dr. Dan will work."

"I work for Steve Huntington," I introduced myself. "He went over some background on the case we're working, and I wondered if I could meet with you sometime? I have a few follow-up questions."

"No problem," he agreed heartily. "Steve didn't tell me he would be hiring other people. Come to think of it, he didn't say much about how he would investigate."

I'll bet he hadn't. "Don't worry, sir. He has an excellent track record."

"That he does. But I'd love to talk to you. I have an appointment at three. Why don't you come for lunch, and we'll get it taken care of then?"

Guilt, and not just a little panic at how quickly things had moved, made me stumble over my answer. I had devised wild plots to convince the man to meet with me and fretted about an excuse in case Huntington found out. None of it had been necessary. Well, I was still short a good excuse for Huntington, but I could worry about that later. "Oh, lunch isn't necessary," I said hastily. "I can just stop by for a few minutes."

"Throwing on an extra fillet is no problem. Amy cooks every day anyway. She's an excellent cook. We're having fish."

Arguing seemed pointless. I needed the information, and here was an open invitation. "Well, okay. How do I get there?"

Much to my surprise, he lived nowhere near Alpine Hills and Huntington. Denton had a lot of county roads that meandered off into the mountains. Dr. Dan lived along one of those, just outside the city limits. "Okay, I'll see you at noon," I said and hung up.

Now I had to put the butter to good use, because showing up to lunch empty-handed would not be acceptable. With fish, a nice chocolate cake ought to go perfectly.

I bustled around, got the cake in the oven, showered and picked out one of my more presentable outfits. Dr. Dan probably wouldn't mind jeans, but serious investigators didn't wear them. At least Huntington never did.

Getting to Dr. Dan's house wasn't difficult. Once I was off twenty-four and on the county road there was no traffic to speak of. Dr. Dan did not live in a mansion. His lovely, brick ranch-style house sat about two-hundred yards off the road, nestled on forested acreage. Ceiling fans and what looked like track lighting adorned a very long porch. It was nicely decorated for Christmas with fake icicle lights and a stuffed Santa sitting in a rocking chair.

Since Dr. Dan was expecting me, there wasn't a wait after I rang the bell. His wife and a little brown toy poodle greeted me at the door.

"Hi, I'm Sedona."

"Come in, come in. I'm Amy. Oh my, you didn't have to bring anything! Dan is always inviting people over, and we have plenty, but my, that does look delicious." She took the cake and since the patient envelope was under it, nabbed that by accident. She looked like everyone's favorite aunt; a tad plump, warmly dressed in a sequined fleece top and matching bottoms.

"This is Pooh," she said, stepping expertly around the coffee-colored poodle. The dog dutifully sniffed my shoes to find out their secrets. "Just ignore him. His sister is somewhere around here." She used her free hand to point to a little face that peered out from under the sofa. "She's Rabbit. They aren't really related, you know, but of course we tell them they are."

True to her name, the little white dog scurried out, yapped at me and instead of running, she jumped up in the air, landed and then took a few steps and did it again.

"Heya Rabbit," I greeted the little dog. I knelt down so that both dogs could properly inspect my fingers. They discussed my qualifications by sniffing and grunting at each other before following their "mom" into the kitchen.

I left my coat on the couch and played caboose, coming in last. Amy set the cake and papers down on the pristine counter top. The kitchen opened into a wonderful dining room that was all windows overlooking a fabulous yard. Rosebushes and what looked like dormant lilac bushes formed an attractive hedge. If the Hernandez's had any neighbors, and I had seen houses along the way, the trees blocked all but the tops of the mountains in the distance. "This is beautiful."

"We like it. Let me get Dan."

She disappeared down another hallway, but reappeared quickly with

Dan in tow. As the two of them walked into the kitchen, that little saying about owners resembling their dogs came to mind. Amy's curly hair formed a dark brown helmet reminiscent of Pooh. Dr. Dan's hair was silver but had grown long enough that it curled on the ends and ran into his wavy beard. His hair wasn't as coiled as Rabbit's, but it was the right color. He had a bounce in his step much like Rabbit's hop.

Dr. Dan was engrossed in the paper he was reading as he approached. His wife tried to snatch the paper from him. "Dear, you're being rude."

Dr. Dan finally looked up. All resemblance to a playful poodle disappeared. His gaze was firm and all encompassing. He sized me up, no doubt prepared to jot down my weight, any visible moles, hair color and a battery of suggested blood work.

"Hi. I'm Sedona."

We shook hands, still watching each other warily. "So, you're an investigator."

I opened my mouth to tell him I was really a computer technician, but for the moment he was correct. "Well, yes, for now."

"I would never have guessed that."

I frowned. He sounded like Huntington, as if he doubted my abilities already. "It helps me stay undercover."

His brown eyes lit up, enlightened. "Ah, I suppose that is the case. If you went around looking like a spy, you probably wouldn't learn much."

My point to Huntington many a time. "Exactly."

"Sit down, sit down," Amy scolded. She pulled a couple of plates out of the oven. "These are hot." A fish fillet drizzled with a glaze, asparagus, and a helping of Spanish rice graced each plate.

"Wow." I cooked, but never took the time to arrange anything. Growing up with two brothers meant learning covert elbow techniques and grabbing a big portion. With my brothers, there was no time to appreciate the beauty of the food.

Once we were seated, I tried a bite of everything. The fish was excellent, and I told her so. "Could you give me the recipe?"

"Oh, of course. It's just a lemon butter sauce, but we can't eat it too often because we're watching our cholesterol." She directed a mindful look at her husband, but he just gave her a playful smile.

"Tell me how the case is going," he said.

"I brought a few patient bills along with me." They were still under the cake plate, so I left them for later. "Basically, we're tracking some records and keeping an eye on certain patients as well as looking for charging patterns. But I wanted to ask you a few questions."

"Go ahead, but like I told Steve, I'm pretty new to this area. My sister-in-law's bill could have been a one-time mistake."

"It's possible. What I wanted to know is, who stands to benefit from overcharging?"

He took a few bites of food and chewed for a while before answering. "The hospital, of course, and the shareholders. There's also a bonus plan for the hospital administrators for reaching certain revenue goals. Some of the doctors could benefit. Most doctors use the hospital facilities, but charge separately for their work. Of course some doctors, like those in ER or those handling general hospital calls, are on salary. Those on salary could order extra tests all day long, and it wouldn't fatten their personal paychecks. But the hospital benefits."

"Are you a shareholder?" I dared.

"Me? As a board member, it's part of the compensation."

"Do the other employees get stock options?"

"Sure, the doctors certainly do."

Similar to a computer company, it was mostly the managers and executives who got the perks. "So any or all of them could benefit from profits in some way or another." I was surprised to look down and see that my fish was already gone. "This was really a delicious meal."

"I'm glad you liked it." Amy lowered her eyes guiltily, and it wasn't until she pulled her hand back up from under the table that I realized she had been giving the dogs a taste. I smiled. Her eyes darted to her husband. He hadn't missed it either.

He tousled her hair as he pushed back from the table. "Let's go into the living room, and you can ask more questions there. Is that dessert I see?"

"Sedona brought it," Amy said. "Not," she emphasized to her husband, "that we need it. You two run along. I'll bring the cake out. Would you like coffee or tea?"

"Tea would be excellent." Talk about service. I wondered if they would consider adopting me.

On the way through the kitchen, I snagged the medical records and handed them to Dr. Dan. "Here are a few examples of the things we've noticed. It could be nothing at all, mind you, but these three patients have similar charges. They all happen to be..." I stopped myself before saying old. Dr. Dan was retired and age references would be putting my foot in it. "Well, they might not always pay a lot of attention to the billing."

He laughed softly and looked over the bills. "Hmm. Looks to me like a typical exam for checking the colon. The barium enema," he pointed to a line on the medical record, "is a dead giveaway on this one." He frowned over it for a while. "But the results are missing."

"What results?" I asked.

"The medical record doesn't say whether or not the BE found anything. Something must have been abnormal because the patient stayed overnight." He looked at the billing date and shook his head. "I would expect more doctor notes and an x-ray report. Polyps must have been found because there are also charges related to a colonoscopy. If there was a tumor or large mass, surgery would be warranted, but I can't determine what was found."

He looked at the other two bills and then went back to the first. "The patient may have been told no solids before the barium enema. Because of that, some patients don't drink enough and get dehydrated. That could be the reason for the fluids, but why an overnight stay unless the patient was kept for another reason?" He handed me back the bill. "Is this the last page of the medical records or just the dates that match this billing?"

Since Radar had packaged the stuff, I didn't know. "There might be more. I'm not sure."

"These three bills are remarkably similar, but more so because the results are missing than the fact that the tests ordered are the same. There are multiple billing codes here, but no detailed explanations or findings. If a patient came for a colon cancer screening, these don't look quite as I would expect." He looked up at me. "An ulcer check was the procedure added to my sister-in-law's bill. Do you think this one," he held up the last bill, "is an add-on also?"

"Possibly." I didn't want to tell him that the cause of suspicion was that Brenda believed the patients hadn't been in *at all*. It could be a billing mistake. Someone could have accidentally entered the admittance code for what should have been an outpatient x-ray. But that was the whole point. If there were lots of "mistakes" of this type, it implied more than incompetence.

Dr. Dan tapped the sheet he held. "In a hospital this size, I'm not sure three similar bills are indicative of a problem. Four, if you add my sister-in-law."

Dr. Dan's wife chose that moment to bring in generous servings of cake. It was a good distraction although Dr. Dan kept staring at the files as we all dug in with enthusiasm.

While I ate, I thought long and hard about how Huntington treated me. Dr. Dan was the one who had hired Huntington, so Huntington should be the one explaining things, but he rarely bothered. Reluctantly I said, "We're not sure the patients were actually in the hospital on those dates. Therefore we don't know that they received any of the services listed."

He paused mid-swallow and looked up. "Ah."

"We'll have to catch it in progress of course, but in the meantime… look, I have to protect the people helping me on this. Faulty memory could be playing a part here too." Brenda could be credible and competent on the witness stand once she wasn't dressed as an elf, or God forbid, a bunny, but it would be a lot better to find proof that didn't require her testimony.

He waved me silent. "I understand. That's precisely why I hired Steve. The last thing I can afford is to have government officials subpoenaing records and causing all kinds of trouble."

"At this point, everything is a bit confused. We need more than a patient or two making claims. On a witness stand, at least two of these people would look...frail."

He corrected me. "Old and muddled."

"Muddled," I agreed, still afraid to bring age into it.

He laughed. "They'd look pretty old too, trust me."

"Okay, okay." I had to laugh myself.

I finished my cake, and as I stood up to go, Rabbit barreled out from under the Christmas tree. She grabbed my pant leg with her little teeth. Her growl was almost as threatening as a mosquito. Amy was just coming back from the kitchen with the fish recipe on an index card. She scolded right away, but I held up my hand. "It's okay. My parents have dogs."

I crossed my arms and looked down at Rabbit. "Ahem." I pushed my leg in the direction she was pulling. She growled and pulled some more. I didn't bother to try and get away from her. "Listen, you little squirt, you let go of my pants or I will dangle you over the garbage disposal by your tail."

She tilted her head to study me better. Then, with a little yap, she let go and wagged her tail happily.

"A likely story." I patted her on the head.

"Thanks for the info." I shook Dr. Dan's hand solemnly. "I might have some more questions."

"Call anytime. Come on over. Bring cake."

"Oh," his wife gasped. "Let me have you take some of that back with you!" She scurried off to the kitchen, the two yappers on her heels.

I looked at the good doctor. We understood each other. I was gone before she made it back to the living room.

By the time I got home, barely twenty minutes later, there was a message on my answering machine from Dr. Dan. He asked me to call him back so I complied. "Hello, Dr. Dan?"

"Hi Sedona. I was thinking about those medical records you showed me. It occurs to me that unlike the bill for my sister-in-law there is a way to check and see if work was actually done for these patients. It ought to confirm whether or not the patients were in on those dates."

"How?"

"There should be physical x-rays for all of these patients."

My brain churned. "You're suggesting that if I were to somehow obtain the hard copy of the x-rays, that would verify services for that date?"

He sounded troubled when he answered. "I'm not suggesting anything. I don't even want to know how you would go about obtaining old x-rays without proper permissions." He paused then and took a deep breath. "Well, that isn't really fair is it?"

"Don't worry about it." If Dr. Dan had wanted to be involved, he wouldn't have hired Huntington.

"This is very difficult for me," he said. "I have the utmost respect for those who have chosen this profession. It's harder than ever with the cost of medical school, the hours away from your family and the sacrifices. I can't tell you how many patients think we're raking in the cash while they are in pain, and sometimes, despite all our training, we can't even help. To think that someone is giving us all a black eye--it's just wrong."

"Every profession has its bad apples," I said. "The computer industry has the same troubles. Just because there are a couple of lousy engineers who don't care about their design doesn't mean there aren't an awful lot of professionals who take pride in their work."

There was silence and then a grunt. "Nobody's life is at risk if your computer doesn't boot, is it?"

Messing with a person's health and their health records was a lot more serious than poorly written software. "Well, no. But don't worry. I'll look for the x-rays."

After I got off the phone, I thought about the problem. As a volunteer, I was allowed down in records. The storage room was located in the basement near where Radar worked, but it was kept locked. Unless I was sent down there to retrieve old records, how could I obtain a key?

Of course, I knew someone with the ability to get in. And this was exactly the sort of task he was good at too.

Chapter 11

Monday morning, as soon as breakfast trays were distributed, I buzzed by the nurses' station and told Crissa I planned to spend the rest of the day in x-ray.

"Did you schedule it officially?" she asked.

"No, not yet. I'm not sure about working down there. Tell Attila I had a special request for help so I went." I wasn't sure how long it would take me to find out what I needed to know.

Crissa didn't look convinced. "She doesn't even like the fact that I work two of my shifts down in ER. I don't think she'll buy a "special request" excuse."

"Okay, just tell her I went down to x-ray if she asks. If the work goes well, I'll ask the volunteer coordinator to schedule some permanent time down there." It probably wouldn't go that far. If I couldn't get the key to the storage room today, I'd call in someone with special skills.

"Okay," she agreed reluctantly.

Despite the disapproval, I went looking for Holly. She was sitting at the desk, sorting some x-rays.

"Hello," I called out. "I came over to see if you can use a volunteer for a few hours. I'm Sedona from upstairs." I pointed to my volunteer apron in case she had forgotten me and mistook me for a nut off the street.

She turned, the x-ray light above the desk creating a halo behind her head--and making it obvious from dark roots that blond was not her natural hair color. With her fair skin, I never would have guessed. "Hi! Yeah, I remember you, the code brown. Those x-rays turned out well since she was all cleaned out."

My smile slipped a bit. In my opinion, people here threw bodily functions around a little too casually.

"You really want to learn this stuff?" She flicked off the lights on the x-ray tray.

"I do, but if you don't need me right now I can come back."

"Are you kidding me? The only reason I ever leave on time is because I run out of approved overtime hours. They'd rather pay a tech a couple of times a month to help me catch up because it's cheaper. Having a volunteer would be perfect. I worked two extra hours yesterday, so I'm scheduled to leave here early and go to The Pavilion."

"They have x-ray machines over at The Pavilion?"

"Yup, and it pays better. There are four or five doctors over there. It's easier for them to take x-rays there rather than schedule patients to come over here. I moonlight over there a lot. All the doctors order x-rays for one reason or another, plus Dr. Staple runs his sports practice from there."

"I thought Dr. Staple was a surgeon?"

"He is. But his private practice is sports medicine. A lot of doctors start out with a hospital career, but if they want more control over pay and hours they have an outside office. He can't do big surgeries privately unless he goes into cosmetic surgery and that means a lot of expensive equipment and time."

"Oh, I didn't know that."

Turning to business, she asked, "Have you done this before?"

"No."

"Then let me show you how to load the x-ray cassettes. I'll teach you to develop later."

We went in the dark room. "This drawer is full of the unexposed film. Never open the drawer until after the lights are off and the red light is on otherwise you'll expose this entire drawer." She opened the long metal drawer. "The larger films are in the front." She demonstrated how to put the thin sheets of x-ray film into the cassettes and place them in the pass box.

There was a knock on the door. She looked at her watch. "Show time! Nothing like a live example, huh?"

Out we went. A skier from ER with either a bad sprain or a broken ankle awaited. "Good," she whispered. "This will be an easy one."

She entered his name, the doctor's request and other information into her computer. Since she had already loaded a cassette with fresh film, she pulled it out of the pass box and loaded it into the x-ray machine. I helped position the patient, a young guy who was very stoic.

Holly took the x-ray. "Okay, let's develop it." Inside the dark room, she turned on the red light, retrieved the cassette and demonstrated. "This flashcard has the patient information on it. Slide this little door open and it exposes the flashcard information right onto the x-ray. Once you've labeled the x-ray, you process it." She slid the film into the machine for processing. "That's it!"

"What if I forget something?" It seemed likely.

"If you forget to put the patient info on there we can always label it with a sticker. Sometimes when it gets really busy, I forget to take the old flashcard out and end up flashing the new patient with the previous patient's information, but when that happens I just cover it up with a sticker that has the right information."

"So every x-ray is marked with the patient data?"

"Yup."

Dr. Dan was right. If I could find the x-rays, they would have the patient name and date right on them. The only question was, did the x-rays exist?

Holly pulled the films out and kicked the drawer that contained the fresh film. "Be very sure the drawer with the unexposed film is closed before you turn on the light."

I nodded dutifully and asked, "When everything is all done, does the x-ray come back here? Where in the world do you keep them all?"

She waved a hand. "Not in this tiny space, that's for sure. They go downstairs." She laughed. "Don't worry. I won't make you go down there. The place is dusty as hell and filing these things is a pain in the ass. We usually hire a temp worker to come in and file them periodically."

"Oh." I had been about to volunteer myself even though filing paperwork was foreign to my nature. Maybe I could filch the key. It had to be around here somewhere.

By lunchtime, I managed to find out that every one of the x-ray technicians had their own key to the storage room, including the part time guy. If there was a spare hanging on a ring somewhere, it was well-concealed, and Holly didn't mention it.

Dispirited, I told Holly that I had to help back upstairs in the afternoon and went down to visit Radar. On the way, I checked the storage room door. Locked.

"Hey, Radar!" I called out as I opened the door so that he wouldn't accuse me of sneaking up on him.

He still jumped out of his chair and looked a bit panicked. When he saw it was me, he settled down.

"What is up with you?" It had to be his proximity to the morgue. I know I wouldn't like working in a cavernous basement next to that room.

"Nothing." He sat back down after making sure the wheeled chair hadn't ended up in the next county. "What's new?"

I gave him a quick update on my visit with Dr. Dan. "Those sheets were the entire billing?"

He nodded.

"Dr. Dan seemed to think the records were sparse. He also mentioned that the doctors charge separately, like you discovered. Are we going to be able to see which doctors actually billed those three patients?"

His shoulders slumped. "The hospital doesn't keep a database of the doctor billing. It looks like most of them use a personal billing system."

"So if they aren't connected to the internet, we're out of luck. You can't tunnel in if there is no tunnel."

He perked up. "I didn't say that. I *can* do it from their personal machine. Heh, heh, heh."

"Yeah, uh-huh." Right after he and Mark broke into the doctor's house or office. I wanted nothing to do with that plan, not unless we could pin it down to one doctor. "I gotta get back upstairs. I've been down in x-ray all morning, and I'm sure that will make someone irate."

Sure enough, Attila must have figured out that I missed the morning work, because she checked on me all afternoon. Of course, Dr. Fox was on the floor at least twice, so she might have been stalking him, but it was hard to tell the difference.

Schedule or no, by two-thirty, I was through. I made sure none of the patient lights were on and headed home. On my way out, I took the stairs, cutting through the hallway near the ER.

As I turned the corner out of the stairwell, I saw Mark. A smile started across my face, and I felt lucky for about half a second.

Mark had his hand on the wall so that he could lean over attentively. He was smiling down at Crissa. With her fluffed blond hair and dainty face, she looked more like a pixie than a professional.

Mark must have sensed movement as I changed my mind about going down the hall because he looked up and froze.

My face was blank; I ordered it to be so. There was no reason for me to be jealous. It wasn't as though we had managed a single date. Of course, the fact that I knew what that spectacular twinkle in his eye could do to a woman's insides turned me absolutely green. Seeing him standing there in his jeans and shirt, his muscles rippling as he brought his arm down to Crissa's shoulder....I didn't know whether to be angry or hurt or crawl away and hide.

When in doubt, go with hide. It seemed I had been mistaken about hospital romance. Crissa looked like she would have been more than happy to find an available closet. I had better not fumble into the janitor's closet again. What with Dr. Fox, Attila and now Mark, there would be a line waiting.

I was out the door and halfway to my car when Mark caught up. He walked beside me until we reached the Mercedes.

"Hi." I was determined to be casual and unconcerned if it killed me.

He sighed. "You see why I can't date women I work with?"

That was incomprehensible. "Uh, no."

"You wouldn't have seen me here working if you hadn't taken the job."

I shook my head. "If I was dating you, I still might have wandered in to visit Brenda. Even if you didn't work at the hospital, if you go around flirting with every cute woman you meet, it would be a problem sooner or later, job or no job. Trust me."

"It's part of the way I get information," he said patiently.

I shrugged. "Whatever. You could probably find another way most of the time."

"I could. But there are times I have to be someone I'm not."

That was certainly true. I had witnessed his fine acting skills several times in the brief time I had known him. "So what does that have to do with dating?" I didn't want to sound desperate, but I still didn't see why he thought we couldn't work together and date.

"Look, I don't like it when women I date are involved with Steve. It never works out." He stared over my head, not making eye contact. Behind his head, the windows of the hospital winked in the sunlight. Was Crissa watching out one of the windows? What had she thought when Mark came after me?

Wary in my own right, I asked, "Involved with Steve?"

He looked accusingly at my SUV. "It isn't as if he hasn't given you enough hints."

Dumbfounded, I stared at him. "What are you talking about?"

"Steve would be more than happy to start something. Or continue it or whatever. So if you think you have to date me to get his attention, you're wrong." He turned and stalked off.

His comment infuriated me. My brain on fire, I launched myself after him, intent on holding my ground until he stopped and explained himself. He stopped abruptly just as I reached him.

I ran smack into his back and careened on impact. With an amazing lack of grace, I fell onto the tarmac.

He had forgotten about my tendency to act first, think later. "Shit, Sedona." He reached down and picked me up, setting me on my feet. He was going to brush me off, but I smacked his hands away.

"Just what," I demanded, "are you talking about? Are you actually implying that I would go on a date with you to get to Steve? *Are you nuts?* If I wanted to go out with Steve, why wouldn't I just ask him?"

"Women always want Steve. You can't walk away from what he has to offer."

"I can't?"

"You took the job, didn't you?"

My temper was already sparked. "I work for Steve, Mark! And I don't work for him because I'm lying in wait hoping he will ask me on a date. Just how desperate do you think I am, anyway?"

"Women always want Steve." He was amazingly stubborn on this point.

"Whoopee." As arguments went, it wasn't very persuasive, but I was tired of standing around in a public parking lot arguing a topic that had a history I didn't understand.

We watched each other warily for a few more seconds before Mark finally said, "You're saying I'm the one who has a problem."

I flapped my arms. "How can I have a problem? I don't even know what you're talking about."

"You're not dating Steve."

Two deep breaths. "We've had this discussion before. I'm not dating Steve."

"Maybe we should try this again." He waited for my reaction, but I was still peeved so I just stood there. "Are you free Saturday?"

I shook my head. "That won't work. I'm making Christmas dinner or lunch or whatever over at Sean's." Generously I offered, "You're welcome to come if you want."

Since he had been to dinner at Sean's for Thanksgiving and met my illustrious family, his hesitation was understandable. "Do you volunteer every weekday?" he asked.

I shook my head. "I decided to take Wednesdays off." I had fully intended it to be a day for working on the case, but mentioning the investigation right this moment didn't seem like a very good idea.

He smiled. "Perfect. Wednesday then?"

After an appropriate pause so that I didn't sound too eager, I said, "Sure. What time?"

"Steve says you like that Anthony's place."

Hmm. Was he fishing for information again? "I guess. I didn't really eat there."

His eyes narrowed. "That's not what Steve said. He mentioned taking you there. Said it always goes over well."

Maybe it did with Steve's usual dates, but ours hadn't been a date, not really. "He did take me there, but he didn't stay long enough to eat. After the two guys with guns chased him out of there, I decided it would be rude to finish both his and my entree in front of the waiters and staff so I had it packed to go."

Mark started to frown and then laughed. "Okay, whatever. I'll pick you up at nine."

"At night?" That was way too late for me to be eating. By ten I'd be in real danger of falling asleep in my soup.

His next words stopped that worry. "No, Wednesday morning. I know a great place to go driving."

As I watched him walk away, I figured even if it was ten at night, I would be able to think of *some* reason to stay awake.

Chapter 12

The insanely busy work routine at the hospital made it a real pain to keep running out for lunch. Since food, medication and baths ran by the clock, so did the chores. Unlike the computer industry, people really did notice when I wasn't back in time to help with a particular job.

It was time to outsmart the lunch thief so that I could bring my lunch with no fear of it going missing. Tuesday morning, very carefully, I labeled my brown lunch bag with a printed sticker: "Lab Specimen. Do not contaminate." Sure, all of the samples were supposed to be in the lab fridge, not the nurses' station, but would the lunch thief really want to check inside the labeled bag? And my leftover stew was unidentifiable enough to be unappetizing and questionable.

It was a solid plan. I'd be able to park my lunch in plain sight and not worry about it.

I smiled all through breakfast trays and then managed to sneak down to do some case work. Admittedly, the case work had a personal twist to it as well. Working in a hospital had made me realize that volunteering didn't include health insurance. I hadn't been particularly worried since I was relatively healthy and flat out hadn't thought about it. I'd eventually get another real job, right? Besides, if I got hurt working for Huntington, it would probably be terminal. Life insurance would probably be a better investment.

The hospital insurance billing office was happy to tell me which health insurance policies were easiest to file and which offered the broadest coverage. Hopefully, the list would provide clues as to which companies would be easiest to bilk. For myself, the information looked promising until I did the math. Carrying health insurance would cost me half a house payment. If I used every dime Huntington paid me, I might be able to afford it. I recalculated. No, I'd still have to sell the Civic.

Sheesh. I'd better stay healthy or just die. Dying was a lot cheaper.

On the way back to the elevator, I spotted Radar standing in the hallway with Attila.

What was he doing on one of the regular floors? I waved, but he didn't look my way. Attila didn't either. She hovered over Radar in an almost protective stance.

I wandered closer.

Radar held a magazine, staring down at it as if it held some sort of death threat or fatal disease. I almost turned around, but then I heard what

Attila was saying. My mouth dropped open. I stopped dead in my tracks, one foot in the air.

"I simply can't decide between the black teddy and the red for New Year's eve. Which do you prefer?" Her "sexy" voice was the crumbling of concrete. She flipped her long black hair over her shoulder and put her free hand on her hip in an artful pose.

Yikes. Was she really standing there hoping Radar would picture her in the red or black teddy???

Of their own accord, my feet began shuffling. They might have been short circuiting as my brain tried to decide whether to interrupt the conversation or let Radar handle it. The problem was that Radar looked like he was suffering from more than a single fried circuit. He wasn't moving at all. I wasn't even sure he was breathing.

Well, hell. I stepped forward. "Radar, there's a problem with one of the computers. Dr...Evans...can't log in and get..." My mind went blank. "Uh, I think it's an emergency."

Radar didn't move. He stared down at the catalog, either hypnotized or dead. Attila jumped back a few inches. Maybe after he made his selection, she had been planning on carting him off over her shoulder. She had the muscles for it.

"Radar!" I grabbed the catalog and tucked it under my arm. Attila didn't like that one bit.

She snagged it, leaving a long claw mark from her fingernail on my arm. There went my plan to blackmail her.

In less than a heartbeat, Radar awoke. His eyes bulged, and his chest deflated. I had been right about him not breathing. When he sucked in a breath, it was like the hissing of a balloon. He started walking, almost knocking me over.

I followed him.

The minute Attila was left in the dust, I pushed him sideways into an empty procedure room. "Radar, are you all right?"

He finally looked at me. He still looked pasty, but then again, he was an engineer. His eating habits ranged from not eating for days to gorging himself in a few sittings. Maybe he was having a heart attack from bad health habits. Or maybe he was having a heart attack because of Attila. "Should I order Chinese?" Food was the only solution I could think of.

"She..." he gulped and sucked in more air, wheezing again.

"How long has this been going on?" It would seem this one occasion was more funny than dangerous, but I had been sexually harassed on the job enough to know that the evil perpetrators worked quickly and constantly, taking every opportunity to push their agenda of belittlement and embarrassment.

Of course, it was weird to think that Radar was in a harassment situation even though I had witnessed it. I didn't know men were ever treated that way.

Radar's eyes scanned the area wildly, a trapped animal praying for an open window.

"My guess," I sighed, stepping back now that he was responding, "is she's been bugging you since you've been here." I shook my head, still trying to grasp the concept. "It's close enough to lunchtime. Wanna go for Chinese?"

"Will you marry me?"

That was too much. *"What?"* I entered the modern ages and asked one guy to lunch and this was the response I got? Wait until I told my mom. If she only had guessed. Then again, since marriage was high on her achievement list, she might think the strategy deserved consideration.

"Do you think she'd leave me alone if I was married?" His eyes still bulged with the not-enough-air-in-here look.

He hadn't even heard my question about food. Unbelievable. He was in critical condition. Turning him around, I marched him out the door and down the corridor.   Maybe with some food, his brain cells would fire properly again.

On the way out, I lectured, "Marriage is hardly the way to solve this, Radar. That's not the way to deal with it at all. Trust me. Harassment happens to women all the time. You've got to get a grip, buddy." I shook his arm to emphasize my point. He followed along, not saying a word.

If I could have explained it to the police, I would have taken the ambulance. The poor guy was in shock. He needed emergency rations. I settled for breaking the speed limit and running two yellow lights.

The sight of the restaurant brought a little color to Radar's face. We hustled inside and our dear friend, Mrs. Chang, sat us down. I asked for "the usual." She would have brought it anyway, but she must have sensed the mood, because she didn't tease us about ordering Peking Duck, her usual banter.

"Radar..." How to start? "Listen, it isn't like she grabbed your ass or anything. You--" His face flamed red. He eyeballed the door, and my mouth dropped. Okay, this was serious stuff. In a tiny, disbelieving voice I asked, "She grabbed your ass? Women do that sort of thing?" I sat back. Well. This was a whole new dilemma.

Radar swallowed so hard it had to have hurt. "Has it happened to you?" His voice was barely above a croaking whisper.

Silently, I nodded. "Well, sure. Couple of times. Happens to every woman who works for a living. Even my best friend Suzy, and she wasn't in the work force very long. Used to happen in college too. I guess you expect it there." I was babbling. Had this been Brenda or any of my female friends, I would have had all the answers. You deck the guy. You smash his face in.

Failing that, turn into the biggest, fattest bitchiest creature that he never imagined existed.

"I guess you can't punch her. Wow. That's too bad. It's usually the most effective." So was stealing a man's toupee, but she didn't have one, unless she wore a wig. "Does she wear a wig?"

His eyes bugged out again. "What? Why?" Our food came. He automatically started shoveling. Around his second or third bite, he asked, "How the hell would I know?"

I recognized the defensive anger and knew it wasn't directed at me. "If you knocked a wig off in public it might embarrass her so badly, she'd leave you alone."

Now he eyed me like I was the dangerous one. "What?"

"I did that once. This guy goosed me, and I knocked his toupee off. He never got within striking distance again. You can't very well punch her lights out because you'd look bad since you're a guy. I was trying to think of another avenue."

His mouth started to hang open, but he clamped it shut before food spilled out. He choked and had to drink some of his tea. After he finished chewing, he took a deep breath. "You stole some guy's toupee because he groped you?"

"I didn't steal it! What the hell would I want with a slimy toupee?" I served myself a very generous helping of fried rice. "The point is that you have to do something drastic. These types of people make it their personal objective to try and make you feel like nothing more than a sexual object with no brain." I waved my chopsticks to make my point. "It usually starts out innocently enough. They compliment you. They stand close and tell you your perfume is heavenly, even if you aren't wearing any. Whether you respond or not, politely or not, it escalates. They trap you in an office. They make lewd suggestions. Then when you, out of the kindness of your heart, tell them to knock-it-off or you will shoot them, they accuse you of leading them on." I sniffed disdainfully. "As if."

Radar watched my waving, poking chopsticks warily. "I guess you have a lot of experience with this type of thing."

That wasn't the point I had been trying to make. "After that, the grabbing and rubbing start."

His face got red again.

"Well, that's the way it happens when guys harass women," I amended, assuming that Attila had more imagination than to contemplate rubbing up against a guy in public.

"Works the same, minus the perfume thing," he muttered.

It was my turn to try and keep food in my mouth. "She grabbed you, *and* did the rubbing thing? That is pathetic! Disgusting!"

"You're telling me? She came down to the basement, pretending she had a question. She tripped," he made little quote marks with his fingers, "and sat in my lap!!! What am I gonna do?"

Since marrying me wasn't the answer, I didn't remind him of that idea. There was no point in going to human resources either. He'd be laughed out of their office. Those people didn't take it seriously when a dainty, defenseless female complained that the big bad wolf was at the door. What would they say if Radar walked in and complained? Oh, that was not a good resolution, not at all.

"Does the lab door lock?" I asked.

He glared at me. "Yeah. But it's supposed to remain unlocked during work hours. She has come down there several times to check. Mostly I get a call to come and look at some problem machine, which I'm not even supposed to do. I was hired as a contractor, and Huntington told me no one would even know I was working in IT. Somehow people found out and they call downstairs and ask for help. After I go up to look at a problem, she shows up like she knew about the call ahead of time."

"Ohboy." He was right. It was exactly the same as when a guy harassed a woman. You never knew where they would be lurking, but like a roach, when you least wanted them around, they popped out of the woodwork. "You're going to have to do something really mean," I said. "Something that hits where it hurts so that she'll leave you alone."

"How about pointing out that I don't like women who can bench press more than I can?"

"Not bad. But you have to find a way to say it so that it really digs. You have to make sure she knows that she isn't woman enough for you. Not successful enough, doesn't make enough money, too much of a loser." Given Radar's brains, I added, "She's not smart enough for you, and you have to prove that. She has to be so insulted around you, she stops trying to, ah, you know."

"And how do you propose I go about doing that?"

The how was a lot more difficult than identifying the problem. I considered what little we knew about her. "She's obviously pretty hung up on her personal appearance. And Crissa told me that she's very interested in getting married."

He looked frantic, so I went with idea number one. "You should make the mistake of assuming that she's fat, not muscular and tell her you don't like fat women." He grabbed his tea like a lifeline and shook his head in disbelief. He was either worried about getting decked by Attila or the thought of telling a woman she was fat was out of reach.

There was no easy solution. We finished our meal in silence. As we left the restaurant, Mrs. Chang reminded us that she wouldn't be open for Christmas. That reminded me that I was supposed to have brought Radar some cookies for Christmas.

"Oh hey, I'm baking cookies for Christmas, but they're going to be late. I'm scheduled to work on Christmas Eve and Christmas. So if it's okay, can I bring them in Monday?"

"Cookies? Tomorrow, Monday through Sunday, January through December, whenever." The thought seemed to cheer him greatly.

"You don't have any family in town, do you?"

"No, but I'm leaving for San Jose tomorrow morning. Oh. I won't be back until Monday."

That was precisely why I had asked. "Okay, Monday." I had two batches in my freezer so all I had to do was make another batch or two and bake like a maniac.

"Listen, Radar." I hesitated to give him advice, but who else would do it? "I guarantee that Attila doesn't see herself the way you do. None of the men who pester women think of themselves as jerks. They think they're awesome studs. They're freaks who think women enjoy some sort of hunter and hunted game, or they flat out don't care. The ones who don't care are the really dangerous ones."

He gave me a side glance that told me I might be the freak.

"Seriously. You have to take the power away from her. If you try to be gentle about it, it's going to fail." It was easy for me to think of ways to make a guy keep his distance, but Attila was a different story. She would keep score, just like a man would, but she was also quite capable of smashing prey that dared to defy her.

I didn't envy Radar and his problem. All I had to deal with was overbearing doctors and a few weird personalities, heavy on the weird.

Back upstairs, the call lights blinked like a Christmas tree gone mad. The first one I answered was Mrs. Starksy. The poor thing had saved her cookies again, and Dr. Burns had nabbed them on his rounds. Maybe I should bring her some cookies and disguise them as...well, that probably wouldn't be too appetizing.

It took me almost an hour to get the rest of the lights to stay off. I took sheets to the laundry and finished making up some beds. With only a few minutes left on my regular shift, I checked the fridge. Sure enough, my "lab specimen" label had worked. I sighed. Too bad I hadn't actually needed my lunch today. Maybe if I'd left the bag unlabeled, Mrs. Starksy's cookies wouldn't have been stolen.

Then again, Dr. Burns didn't seem likely to pass up any available snack.

Chapter 13

It snowed overnight, but Wednesday morning dawned cold and clear. Colorado was a beautiful place, even covered in snow. I didn't love snow, but if I was going to be in a nice heated vehicle, I could enjoy the view.

Mark showed up at nine driving his gray Lexus SUV.

"Nice wheels." I remembered the SUV from Thanksgiving.

He grinned. "This one is mine. The others I drive are Steve's. He keeps a few on hand."

I had noticed. Huntington rarely showed up in the same vehicle twice. I knew very little about cars, except that this one was a hybrid. It was sleek even with snow tires.

I climbed in and handed him his Christmas present. There was more than a little red in my cheeks, and it wasn't from the cold. "Merry Christmas," I mumbled, making a big play of studying the fancy navigation system and brushed aluminum accents. He smiled down at my package so I added, "It's nowhere near as great as this awesome leather jacket." I was wearing my new jacket, but then, I hadn't stopped wearing it since he left it for me. I don't know how I knew it was Mark who had left me the jacket, but I knew.

"It looks good on you."

He peeled back the paper from the framed photo I had purchased. A sudden urge to babble nearly overwhelmed me, but I clamped my lips closed and stared at the dash.

The picture was a forested setting that promised hope and an adventure, yet there was an air of peace about it. The frame was natural wood, light with a dark grain running through it. Something about the jagged lines reminded me of lightning--and Mark.

When he didn't say anything, I peeked over at him. He was staring at the picture in amazement, his eyes wide.

The picture was nice, but he looked inappropriately stunned, as though he had never seen a decent photo before. "You don't like photographs?"

He shook his head as if to clear his thoughts. "No. I mean yeah, I do. This is great. It's..." He looked at me. "Really nice. Did you take it?"

"No. I saw it in a little shop, and it looked like a gorgeous place to hike. I love the springtime because it gets warm again and everything is so beautiful."

He looked down at the picture again.

Maybe he thought it was a strange present. I hadn't known what to get him.

"It's really nice." He leaned over and grazed my lips. "Merry Christmas."

I couldn't breathe quite right so I just nodded. He glanced at the picture one more time, and then set it on the back seat before starting the car.

We took highway eighty-two out of town and drove for a long while. He took one or two of the county roads, stopping once to put chains on.

By the time we were deep in the forest boundary, I was totally sold and enjoying myself. From the top of a rise, I could see almost as much horizon as my one helicopter ride. "This is incredible."

"Haven't you ever been here? It's something to see in the spring and summer."

I shook my head and drank in the view.

"It's one of my favorite areas," he said.

Near the top of the mountain, he pulled onto a forest road almost completely obscured by all the snow. Before we went too far, he pulled off to the side and drove the SUV around in a large circle, packing the snow enough that we could get out without trouble. "Come on, I brought snow shoes."

I stopped partway out of the truck. Uh-oh. That would be the part of snow that I didn't like. I could walk forever on dry land, but put me in snowshoes or on skis, and I was like the cartoon where the guy ran into a tree and came out cut in half on the other side.

"Uh..."

Mark didn't notice my discomfort. He handed me a pair of flat shoes and went back to get another pair.

I stared at them, but they didn't disappear.

Rats.

I put them down and gave it my best shot, but while strapping on the first shoe, I fell over.

Mark smiled and leaned over to pull me up. I almost took us both down.

"You ever done this before?"

"Once," I replied tersely. He let me go. I over-corrected, my arms windmilling.

"Hey!" He grabbed my arms and held me still. "Stop. Just stop. No wobbling. Don't try to move or bend or breathe."

I held my breath. Miraculously, I stopped swaying.

"Okay, I'm gonna let go of you, and you just stand there."

He did. I did.

"Good," he grinned. "Do you think you can pick up a leg?"

I shook my head, mutely miserable. It would have been better had we gone skiing. I could at least point skis downhill and outrun anyone who might be watching. Since I couldn't stop reliably, if I beat the competition down, I could crash without any witnesses.

"You don't know how to do this at all, do you?"

I hung my head, completely humiliated. Little tears from the cold pricked my eyelids. "Let's get this over with." No doubt it would turn out like all my previous athletic dates, an embarrassing disaster.

"Here's a better idea." Mark leaned over and unhooked the straps. He then proceeded to lift me up and set me down on the hood of the Lexus. It was nice and warm. "Hungry? I brought lunch." It was kind of early, but I wasn't about to turn the offer down. Anything to keep me off the walking tennis rackets.

He went around the back in his snowshoes without any trouble. While he didn't look graceful, he looked better than I was ever going to.

"Got some fried chicken at the grocery and potato salad." After he took supplies out of the back and set it on the ground on top of a blue cooler, he moved me from the hood to the back. He pulled out sodas.

Food I could do. The chicken was cold, but absolutely wonderful. We sat for a while and stuffed our faces. It was never too early or too late to eat.

"I should have asked if you like snowshoeing," he finally said, licking his fingers.

I shrugged. "I'd have come anyway."

"Yeah?" He looked at me with what was probably supposed to be an evil leer, but it was really just a sexy, come-hither smile.

"It's a nice day," I pointed out. And so his ego wouldn't get too big, I added, "I would have told myself I could learn or something."

He laughed. "And can you?"

I made a face. "I doubt it. It was looking pretty hopeless there, don't you think?"

He finished his soda and collected the remains of lunch. "I bet we can figure something out."

With food in my stomach and feeling more comfortable with Mark, I had no choice but to try. If he wanted a graceful, athletic girlfriend, well, maybe he'd better ask Crissa out. Or Attila. I bet she could not only snowshoe, she could probably win a race in the things, especially if a rich doctor was the grand prize.

Mark helped me strap the shoes on this time. I didn't try to move. Not moving wasn't necessarily good because I was standing by the tailgate, and it was going to be hard for Mark to close the back door unless I moved.

"Okay," he said. "If the snow isn't powder, you just slide your foot ahead like you're on skis. Only you have to pick your feet up a little, sort of like you're waltzing. Glide forward."

It looked easy when he did it. I watched his hands mimic the glide, and then tried the motion. I didn't fall over right away so I took another tentative "glide."

"That's it!" He shut the door, walking around like he had been born in the things. "Besides, what I want to show you isn't that far."

It had better not be. I wasn't likely to last very long. He stood next to me, and we edged forward. If I leaned slightly forward, my balance was better. The snow where he hadn't driven wasn't packed. I eyed the first drift distrustfully.

"Now you're going to have to pick your feet up higher."

"Yeah." I studied the problem. Something always seemed to go wrong when I lifted my foot because the back of my shoe wasn't connected to the tennis racket and then the thing swayed down and before I knew it I was tangled. I watched Mark stomp around athletically.

"Here." He stood in front of me off to the side. "Just take one giant stride. Like you're going up stairs, but stepping over something in the way."

"But the back of the shoe falls down."

"Just ignore that. You let it drag as you move your foot forward."

The first step nearly capsized me. With one hand on a tree and the other in a drift, I asked, "You're going to dig me out when I'm buried, right?"

I dared take my eyes off the evil snow and found he was laughing at me.

"Sedona, I swear! Just walk in the things. This isn't a life or death matter."

"Says you. I could die in one of these drifts." Or die from embarrassment.

"I'll dig you out," he promised, still laughing.

Resolutely, I started walking. Stomping. Gliding.

Eventually, two falls later, my lips clamped against the cold and a couple of whimpers, I made it to an overlook.

"Was it worth it?" Mark asked, breathing hard himself.

It was God's beautiful country, and it was breathtaking. The trees were decorated in ice and snow, and the valley below was carpeted in white. The view looked vaguely familiar, but I'd definitely remember if I had stood on this precipice in such a crisp breeze with this spectacular a view. I cherished the heat stored up inside my jacket from the brief but strenuous hike. I felt alive...clumsy and exhilarated at the same time.

"I was planning on coming here today even before you gave me the picture," Mark said.

I started to ask what he meant, but then...There were no flowers or green grass...no wonder it seemed familiar! "Oh my gosh!" The scene was exactly the same as in the photograph, only the season was winter now instead of spring.

I looked up at him and he smiled, his cream-coffee eyes drowning me.

It was probably really hard to put an arm around someone with snowshoes on, especially when she was wobbling, but he managed it.

"I was going to bring lunch out here."

My gaze snapped back to the view. "That would have worked if you didn't need me to help carry it."

He squeezed me in a half hug. "I had been hoping you could carry the sodas." There was laughter and teasing in his voice.

"That would have been a disaster."

"Probably."

Since he didn't seem to be done teasing me, I asked plaintively, "If I can't make it back are you going to leave me here?"

He didn't say anything for a while. He looked pensively across the valley below us. "You fit here. Kind of untamed and beautiful, like the spring flowers in the photograph. You have to take a photo and leave the flowers undisturbed because they belong to the wilderness, but you want to take them home because they're too beautiful to be left in the wild."

I was afraid to look up, but afraid not to. It was simply the nicest thing anyone had ever said to me. Since I couldn't risk hugging him without toppling over, I tilted my head onto his shoulder and pressed hard.

He must have understood the gesture because he moved his hand a bit, letting me lean into him.

We stayed that way for a long time with nothing disturbing the quiet except for the occasional bit of ice or snow falling. There were little movements by a bird and in the valley, I glimpsed a coyote or maybe a fox. I don't know how long we stood there, but I resented the chill creeping across my legs, because it meant the moment was destined to end.

Mark squeezed my shoulders and pointed to the crown of a tree below us. "See the hawk? Halfway down, to our right."

My eyes searched the landscape and quickly spotted the bird as it beat its wings for balance on the end of a branch. It finally gave up flapping and decided to fly, screaming a battle cry. The sound echoed.

Watching it spiral higher and higher, I wished I could fly. "Wow," I said.

Mark nodded. "You ready?"

"Okay."

He propped me back up, and when he was certain I had my own balance, he stepped away. I had to make a wide turn to face the direction we had come, but heading downhill was easier than uphill. Since I was following him, I didn't have to pay attention to anything but keeping my balance.

Halfway back, I quit reaching out for the trees. It still wasn't pretty, but I made it.

At the truck, he opened the back again. I sat down gratefully. Despite the energetic exercise, my nose was cold and the tips of my ears would have shivered if they were able. "Whew."

He ruffled my hair. "See. Not so bad, not so bad."

"Uh-hmm."

Mark shook the shoes off and put them in the truck. He pulled one last item from the food bag. "Hot chocolate," he said holding up a giant thermos.

My eyes widened. "Did you make it with real milk?" I barely dared hope.

He looked puzzled. "Of course. How else do you make it?"

Okay, that was it. I was firmly and completely head-over-heels in love. I might have been able to resist his other charms, but the hot chocolate put me right over the top. The fact that it wasn't the powdered stuff mixed with hot water was absolute proof of his intelligence.

They say the way to catch a guy is through his stomach. Well, men didn't have a monopoly on that particular market. It was indisputably the direct path to my heart. Mark had just provided a most excellent lunch, taken me to a fabulous place with a view, and now he was offering my very favorite drink, bar none.

He unscrewed the lid, poured some and handed me the cup. "I'm not sure I've ever seen anyone quite so ecstatic over hot chocolate."

"You," I declared, "are awesome."

He looked pleased. "Oh?"

He sat down next to me with his own cup. I snuggled against his side. He could find out later just how awesome I thought he was. For now, things were just perfect.

Chapter 14

The snow lingered in the mountain passes much longer than it did around town. We were lucky that this year there had already been some good dustings with heavier snowfall at higher elevations. Springtime was going to be beautiful. I couldn't think of anything I'd rather do than go back to the mountains with Mark.

As Mark drove back into town, we chatted about the case. I updated him on my visit with Dr. Dan. "What do you think about checking the patient files for x-rays?"

Mark glanced over at me. "I can take care of it."

"Good. When do we look them up?"

"You can't come with me."

"Why not? Two could find the files faster than one!"

"Two can get arrested faster than one also," he pointed out.

It wasn't absolutely necessary for me to go, but that didn't stop me from arguing for it. "I helped the last time you took me along."

He raised his eyebrows briefly. We both knew that my "help" had been more accidental than planned.

"Please?" I tried.

He smiled. "Why?"

I hated working with only partial details. In the computer business, it paid to be there, working right in the thick of things, watching the machine do its thing, or fail to do it as the case might be. Sometimes it was a little clue, sometimes it was repeating the test with slight differences until you found the one time it failed, but in all cases, solving problems didn't happen by sitting at home thinking about them. Then too, it didn't seem right to hand it off to someone else, even if they were as obviously competent as Mark. "If we went during the day, I could cover for us and claim to be looking for a record."

"And get fired."

"I'm not even getting paid!"

"Nothing to lose, nothing to gain," he said. When he pulled into my driveway, he made no move to get out, so neither did I. "This is what I mean about mixing work and play."

I didn't see the problem. "You mean because you don't want me to go look in the files, you don't want to date me?"

"I mean--" he blinked and shook his head. "I don't want you to get hurt."

I shrugged. "Even if you were just a coworker helping on this case, I'd ask to go."

"What if it were my brother going?"

That had nothing to do with anything. "Mark, the first time I met you, I insisted on helping. Ask Huntington. I always want to know more about what is going on and be involved, not just pick through scrap clues he throws my way."

"What if I gave you a complete report when I finished?"

I grinned. "It would save time if you took me with you."

He shook his head, but laughed. "Let me go home, unpack this stuff and pick up a few things. Then we'll meet for dinner and talk about it, okay?"

I smiled and leaned over to kiss his cheek.

"What was that?" he growled.

"Depends," I said as I opened the door. "On whether or not we're dating." It could have been a thanks for a wonderful day. Or maybe it was encouragement. Hmm. Or maybe I was being a naughty tease.

* * *

Break-ins combined with dinner dates were not my forte. After Mark dropped me off, I studied my wardrobe carefully, but had no idea how to dress up for dinner, yet be prepared for the hospital basement in the dead of night.

I settled on black jeans and a black, long-sleeved jersey knit top. Not very sexy, but with my leather jacket, maybe I'd look cool. Luckily, I had black sneakers because white ones simply would not do.

Before I had a chance to waffle further, the phone rang. It was Mark. He had to cancel dinner, but promised to pick me up at ten.

"Okay," I agreed. Before I could ask any nosy questions, he said good-bye and hung up.

I stood with the phone in my hand, pondering. Would he really show? Or was this the start of an excuse? Would he show up *with* the files and tell me he had already done the job?

I sighed. "Men."

My interest in making cookie dough for the freezer was minimal. Dinner, which had been so promising only moments before, had completely lost its luster now that I'd be eating alone.

I grumbled my way into the kitchen and started on the cookie dough.

By the second batch, I was in the groove, mixing and tossing ingredients like a chef--until I poofed flour across my black shirt and pants. Perhaps I should have worn an apron.

I was too nervous to eat a real dinner. Raw cookie dough was more satisfying than anything else I had on hand anyway.

With four batches of dough in the freezer, I still had time to spare. If I napped now, I'd be more awake at ten. Napping was usually something I could do standing up, but with my mind racing, I couldn't fall asleep, not even with the alarm clock set.

Thumbing through tv channels, I mused about how lucky I was to be almost dating someone like Mark. Compared to some of the other supposed successful people out there, he was a fabulous pick. Dr. Fox was obviously a great surgeon, but an even bigger flirt than Mark. The way he carried on, his original marital troubles probably involved "other opportunities." Besides, he had a daughter, and he was too old for me anyway.

Dr. Staple was also very handsome and a successful doctor, but he didn't think the rest of us deserved to exist. Maybe he equated bilking insurance as his due. He showed little to no respect for the nurses. He didn't even like his elderly patients much.

All in all, Mark was a very good catch; not that I had done any real catching yet. Of course, there was the fact that he tended to lurk around unsafe places after dark. No, I couldn't hold that against him. Wasn't I responsible for the upcoming nighttime activity that sort of involved breaking and entering? Was it for a good enough cause? Or were we no better than whoever was bilking the hospital? For that matter, Dr. Fox didn't necessarily look to flirt with women; some of them--namely Attila--begged to be flirted with, or...worse. Or was that better?

It wasn't until a knock on the door woke me up that I realized I had fallen asleep. I had been in the middle of trying to take a donut from Huntington's cat to give to the ever-starved Dr. Burns. Vague memories scattered back to dream world; Attila holding Radar hostage with a stethoscope and Crissa yelling at me about being a thief either because I had a date with Mark or because I was about to break into the hospital.

But Mark was at my door, not Crissa's, so I crawled out of my recliner and scurried to let him in.

Chapter 15

The hospital did not look the same at night. It took on a much spookier dimension, resembling a towering brick threat rather than a place of refuge. The basement didn't have any windows, so unlike the front and sides of the building, the entrance at the back was darker and quieter. Not that lights would have helped, because the heart knew when it was nighttime. Or maybe the heart knew when it was doing something it shouldn't be doing, so it pounded especially hard.

I had expected Mark to want me to wear my apron so that if anyone spotted me, they would assume I belonged. Not even close. He gave me lab clothes that matched his own loose-fitting dark green ones. "If they see either of us, the clothes will be right, and the faces will just be faces. If they happen to have seen you before, you'll be even more familiar, and no one will recall that you usually wear a volunteer apron."

"You know," I said, "the hospital is kind of small. There's probably only," I had to stop and do the math in my head. "Three floors, approximately two nurses each, three shifts, technicians…only two hundred or so people working here. I bet most of them know each other."

"Then let's not get seen," he said. "Unless you want us to go in as ER patients and sit around until we get a break to sneak downstairs."

I shuddered. "No thanks. Have you seen the prices they charge?"

Of all the doors in the place, we had to use the one located down a flight of old metal stairs right next to the loading dock for the morgue. Mark's ring of metal picks answered the call in less than two minutes. I had planned to time him, but it was too cold out. No sense in peeling layers off my arm to check my watch.

The door led into the wide open hallway. Only auxiliary lighting was on, but that was typical down here even during the day.

"Which door?"

"Not that one," I hissed as he started for the ice room. "Come on."

We floated past Radar's door to the one almost directly across the corridor. "This one."

Mark broke into the storage room quicker than he had unlocked the outside door. As soon as we were in, he turned on the lights.

"Should we do that?" I asked. "What if someone comes in?"

"Someone forgot to turn the lights off," he said with a shrug.

I pondered that. "Where will we be?"

He looked over his shoulder and grinned wolfishly. "Hiding."

Good idea.

Like a big library, the rows of shelving had ladders attached that slid back and forth. The latest year was in the front row. That would make hiding a little difficult because we'd have to duck back into a different row.

The tags for the year of service were color-coded and little tabs with the medical numbers stuck out on each folder. I started to hand him the cheat sheet with the social security numbers on them, but he must have memorized them. Pretty impressive since I could barely remember my own social security number.

I sneezed. The dust of the ages was stored down here with the files.

As Mark pulled the ladder to the appropriate spot, it squealed like a stuck pig. Chills ran across my brain and down my back. "Ugh."

He handed me the first of the files. I checked it while he repositioned the ladder to search for the next file. The x-rays were present, dated and documented. He handed me the next one. As I took it, I thought I heard a door slam. The doors in the basement and to the basement were big and heavy.

"Any reason for someone to come in here at night?" Mark asked.

"How would I know? I've only been working here for a couple of weeks!"

When in doubt, hide. Mark was at the light switch in a heartbeat, while I headed to the very back of the room. There was no way of knowing what year someone would look for because the files were kept seven to ten years.

Just as the lights went out, I heard a key in the lock. Miraculously, Mark managed to make it into the aisle with me before the lights went back on.

My brain had a deja vu moment. Why did I keep finding myself smashed between shelves with this man?

I could hear another ladder being moved. Unbelievable. Who would need to be in here at this time of night? Of course if someone came in the ER and had a history, I suppose the doctor might want to look up old x-rays. Who else could it be?

I looked at the ladder for our row. If I climbed it, would I be able to catch a glimpse of whoever had entered? What if they were facing my direction?

The other ladder being used by the mysterious someone screeched as it was moved again. It then creaked as someone stepped on the rungs. Okay, using the ladder to spy was not a viable option.

Mark looked at me. I pointed up. He shook his head side to side, but not really in a decisive, "no."

I shrugged, slumped my shoulders and looked defeated.

He shook his head and rolled his eyes. Then he squatted down and motioned for my feet. Him lifting me up wouldn't be high enough; sitting on his shoulders might not even do the trick.

Still, we had to look at the guy, didn't we?

I put a leg around and half sat on his shoulders. When he stood, it wasn't enough. I was going to have to stand on his shoulders and hope that if we toppled over, whoever was in here would be spooked enough to run rather than investigate.

I grabbed the nearest shelf to maintain my balance. The old building had numerous creaks and rattles joining in what sounded like someone stepping off the ladder or climbing higher.

Time to get moving.

Using the shelves for balance I carefully edged my way up. What would I do if I was seen? Duck back down and hide?

Sudden movement was out of the question. So was sneezing. Being that close to the dusty shelves made my nose itch. Really, really itch.

I caught a glimpse of the back of a blond head and a lab coat before a female hand opened the door, held it with her body and hit the light switch without turning.

The door closed just in time.

I sneezed. Mark sneezed.

I lost my balance.

I grabbed onto the shelving and sneezed again.

Mark sneezed again, and my left foot slipped off his shoulder even though he was trying hard to steady me. "Eek!" I dangled, grabbing onto the files that were packed in tighter than sardines. In the meantime, I breathed in more dust.

Close packed files saved me. I found purchase with my fingers just long enough for Mark to get a hold of me.

"Slide down, I've got you."

He didn't really, but since gravity was winning, I let go and his hands ran along my legs and halted at my waist. He lowered me to the floor with a grunt.

I sneezed again. "Ah-choo!"

"No kidding. Who was it?"

I shook my head, not that he could see me in the dark. "Not sure. It might have been Holly from x-ray, which would make sense if she got called in. But Crissa is blond too, and she works ER sometimes. If she worked tonight, maybe she was sent for some older records." I thought some more. "It wasn't Attila because she has black hair."

"Attila?"

"Sally. The head nurse." I shrugged. "I don't know every blond in the place, and since I don't work nights, there could be people I've never even seen." I tried to decide whether or not I needed to sneeze again before adding, "Whoever it was, she was already leaving so I only saw the back of her head. She had a lab coat with the collar sticking up. I couldn't even tell if her hair was long or short. I think I saw a ring or two when she reached for the light."

"Wedding ring?"

"It was shiny...It could have been the key ring hooked around two of her fingers. It looked large." I sighed in disappointment.

"Let's check the rest of the files and get out of here."

I nodded. He pulled a flashlight from his pocket. As soon as he switched it on, I   picked up the files we had already retrieved, and then waited while he turned the main lights back on.

He quickly found the next set of files and handed it to me.

It too had several x-rays stuffed inside. Ugh. People were not very pretty inside.

"Okay," he said. "They all look legit."

Brenda must have been wrong. There were x-rays for all three of the patients. They had to have been in the hospital on those dates. Maybe they had come into the ER or she had forgotten seeing them. I certainly couldn't remember which patients were in and on what days. I didn't even remember half of their names once they were gone.

Mark gestured for the file so he could return it to its place. I stood and stared at the x-ray. I had seen the pictures about three times, once when he first handed it to me, and then again while I was waiting for him to find the next file. I was no expert, not by a long shot.

"Sedona?"

I extracted one of the x-rays from the second file. I held it up to the light, along with the first x-ray. The basement lights were almost as bad as no lights at all. I couldn't tell diddly and that was what was bothering me. "Let's take them. I want Dr. Dan to look at these." It was probably a complete waste of time, but someone with more knowledge needed to inspect them.

Mark said, "That one in your hand is darker than the other one."

"The settings are never identical so the shots aren't either." At least that was what my limited training led me to believe.

"Fine, take them. Let's go." Once Mark was moving, he didn't slow down. We got to the door. He turned out the lights. Then he listened.

No sound. He opened the door less than an inch and paused to listen again. Going out was more nerve-wracking than getting in.

Out in the hallway, he walked quickly, wasting no time. Before we exited, he glanced back. I didn't. I didn't want to know if anyone was waiting at the stairs or elevator to watch us depart.

Chapter 16

Thursday morning was Christmas Eve. It felt strange to be making lunch and going to "work," because the computer industry shut down for the holidays for at least two days and sometimes for two weeks. Even in college, the school and most related student jobs shut down for the holidays. People like Brenda kept the world running while the rest of us took a break.

Since Brenda and I were both working this year, Christmas dinner would have to wait until Saturday. I wasn't feeling warm and fuzzy Christmas thoughts as I packed my lunch into a brown paper bag and carefully pasted on my anti-theft label.

Luckily, when I got to work, things started out on a positive note. Two extra, unused specimen labels were sitting on an abandoned cart near the elevator. I put them in my apron pocket for later use, feeling quite pleased.

Dr. Burns was at the nurses' desk about to go on rounds when I came out of the break room. I hoped he hadn't seen me put the bag in the fridge because he was my prime suspect. Luckily, he was distracted by the box of donuts sitting at the nurses' station. I watched as he pulled out an oblong chocolate covered mass of calories and ate it while studying the chart in his hand. He asked Brenda to look something up for him, all the while eating.

He wasn't like Radar, stuffing his face. He stood there and gazed off into space, thinking deep medical thoughts and chewing slowly. He reached in and took a second donut. If he stood there long enough the whole box of donuts would disappear.

"You like donuts?" I asked, disrupting his reverie.

"Huh?" He looked down at his hand. "Donuts?" He blinked little round eyes and pushed his glasses into place leaving a smudge of chocolate icing on his nose. Wisps of thinning hair floated around his head. He studied the donut, turning it from side to side. "These are very bad for you," he pronounced gravely, setting the donut back in the box. He wandered away, studiously reading his electronic pad.

My mouth dropped open in disbelief. Brenda grinned. "He does that all the time."

"Eats donuts?" His half-eaten one sat on top of untouched ones.

"Leaves food around. Takes food from one place or another. Some of the patients get awfully upset with him."

I could imagine. For a guy complaining about the lack of healthy features of donuts, how exactly did he think he got that round bulge around his middle? Or maybe he didn't notice that either.

Dr. Staple chose that moment to come around the corner. "I need a cup of coffee."

I ignored him. Dr. Staple acted like we were all internal organs that he had removed and as the surgeon, he could now poke at, order around or discard us at will. He stood there reading patient notes while waiting for coffee. Brenda either chose to ignore him too or more likely hadn't heard the request in her rush to go complete her chores before the doctor began his rounds. There was no one else around to play fetch; too bad. I wasn't going to do it.

I headed away to start my morning chores, but moving drew the attention of the hunter, turning me into prey. Dr. Staple said, "Hey, you're new around here, aren't you? I remember you from the other day."

Surprised at the friendliness in his voice, I stopped. "Uh, yeah."

"What was your name?" He stretched out a hand. "I'm Dr. Staple."

I actually stuttered, I was so taken off-guard. "Se...Sedona. I'm a volunteer. I went on rounds with you the other day."

"That's what I thought. Do you clean offices?" He stroked the cleft in his chin with a happy smile.

"Offices?"

"We could use some volunteer help over at The Pavilion."

"You're asking me to volunteer to do *cleaning* work?" Who in their right mind would volunteer to clean? I mean, as a volunteer here, my cover story was that I was considering a related profession. Volunteering in a hospital setting was required by several nursing and doctor programs. Why would anyone offer to clean a doctor's offices for free?

"What's the difference?" he asked. "You shovel shit here, you shovel shit there. I guarantee you, the mess isn't nearly as bad at our private offices. My nurses keep things in tiptop shape. But we could use some extra help with filing and cleaning the bathrooms at night."

"Don't you have a cleaning service? *And* a file clerk," I amended in case he didn't realize that the two jobs might be considered separate by most people.

He shrugged. "The cleaning service tried to raise their rates again. What do they think we're made of, money? All we're talking about is removing some garbage and wiping things down. How the hell they can charge the prices they do for an unskilled job is beyond me."

"You think such a service should be free?" Apparently he did or he wouldn't have asked me to volunteer.

"Okay, fine," he groused, his pale blue eyes snapping with irritation. "I can see paying you minimum wage. But if you're willing to volunteer here, why not there? What's the difference?"

Just because I wasn't a legitimate student didn't mean I didn't empathize with those who were. "The idea, Dr. Staple, is that by working here, I get experience with patients. I actually have the opportunity to learn things such as first aid and CPR." A moron could have inferred that cleaning his office wouldn't provide any of those opportunities. Leaving him no time to respond, I stalked off to make beds or throw bedpans or have a fit of some kind. Geez, he was a real piece of arrogance.

I was halfway through making a bed when Brenda snuck in the room. "You okay?" she whispered. "You gotta be careful, Sedona. He can make your life miserable."

My mouth dropped open. "By doing what? I'm kind of at the bottom of the food chain here. I change *bedpans,* for crying out loud! And I'm not getting paid to do it!" Huntington's side salary didn't count because he was paying me for something else entirely.

Brenda shrugged. "You don't want to work for him, even if he does pay you. I know he's good-looking and all that, but that's the third or fourth cleaning service that has quit over there. He has a hard time keeping nurses working in his office too. The other doctors at The Pavilion don't have problems, but he goes through personnel like water."

I had already figured out that working for Staple was not a helpful career move. "Yeah, okay. Thanks."

She zipped away. I appreciated her effort to save me. It made it easier to ignore the little voice in the back of my head that noted how working at The Pavilion would readily provide access to all kinds of doctor records. I could check out five different doctors in great detail or let Radar in a back door to do so.

I grabbed some sheets and took them down the hall. It was best that Huntington not find out about Dr. Staple's offer. He'd probably demand I take the "job."

To make up for my lax dedication on the case, I decided to visit Dr. Dan during my lunch break. I had intended to wait until after Christmas, but if following up with him on Christmas Eve wasn't showing my commitment to the case, I didn't know what was. Besides, I was nervous about hoarding stolen x-rays. As crimes went, it had to be right up there with mugging a little old lady, pitiful and desperate.

I drove carefully so that I didn't get pulled over with the stolen goods.

Luckily, Dr. Dan was at home. Rabbit and Pooh were thrilled to see me, despite the holidays and lack of treats. "Hiya fellas," I crooned, giving the toy poodles an enthusiastic greeting. The little dogs had a yapping contest and didn't quiet down until Amy lured them into the kitchen with dog biscuits.

I followed Dan to his home office where he looked over the x-rays and then searched the patient folders. "This one is missing the radiologist report. I assume this is the whole folder?"

We had taken the entire sleeves because I didn't want anything to get mixed up. Unlike Radar, I hadn't even tried to cover up patient names or data. These files had to go back, intact. "That was it. I didn't take anything out."

He frowned. "The x-rays are real, no doubt about it. These two are a tad light, but very readable. This one looks like a typical barium enema shot. This other is a barium swallow for the ulcer patient. Maybe the missing radiologist report for the first one ended up with the internist. He might have asked for it before doing the colonoscopy because it looks like the patient was going to need one." He held the x-rays up to the light again. "There were some obvious polyps on these so they would have to be removed.

"I wonder..." Dr. Dan stared off into space. "Didn't the bills for these patients have an overnight visit?"

I nodded.

"There's no obvious reason these patients had to stay in overnight," he said. "Not right after the BE because it takes a while for the barium to clear the system before either a colonoscopy or surgery is done. I could follow up on that."

Uh-oh. "I wouldn't go around asking questions."

"Why? Don't want an old man interfering in your fun?"

I shook my head. "No, I don't want you asking the guilty party the wrong question."

"How about I talk to the chief of staff? Henry--Dr. Johnson and I have been friends for years. We went through our residency together. He is one of the best surgeons I know, and he knows the work of almost every person in that hospital."

I waved my hands. "No, no, that's the point. We don't know who is benefiting from all of this. What if the chief of staff has told five people to try and get the hospital extra business? Run up charges, we can use the profit?"

Dr. Dan shook his head vehemently. "I trust Dr. Johnson as much as my own Amy! The only reason I didn't go to him with this mess is because he would be extremely hurt by it. This hospital is his baby, it's his life."

I didn't mention that people with "babies" really, really wanted them to be a success, so I took another tack. "What if the chief of staff isn't guilty but he mentions it to his wife? And she tells a friend? And the friend knows the radiologist?"

He tilted his head. "That could happen, I suppose."

"Even if the radiologist wasn't guilty, it could still have some nasty consequences. We certainly don't want people getting all bent out of shape unnecessarily. That's the reason Huntington doesn't like to tell me things. See, I'm over here talking to you. And if you talk to a source, before you know it, the entire hospital knows who I am, and why I'm there, and we have a real mess."

He looked at me with his serious doctor gaze, not at all softened by his gray hair or fluffy beard. "You sound like this has happened before."

"It did, once." I didn't mention it had been Huntington's fault.

He indicated the x-rays. "Can I keep these for a couple of days? I assume whatever work was going to be done to remove the polyps has been done, and they won't be needed by anyone."

"I guess so." I didn't like it, but none of the patients were currently in the hospital. If Dr. Dan didn't think anyone was going to want them, he could study them indefinitely or at least until I was done volunteering.

I didn't have any spare time left by the time I got back to work, but I went to see Radar anyway. I raced to the basement and barely remembered to make sure he hadn't locked the door before barging in. "Glad you didn't fly home yet," I panted.

"I leave tonight," he replied. "What's up?"

I sat down and took a couple of quick breaths. "Just an update. I went to see Dr. Dan and showed him the x-rays from the patients in question."

"Where did--" He stopped. "I don't want to know where you got the x-rays, do I?"

"They were in storage," I claimed innocently. I proceeded to tell him what Dr. Dan said.

"So the x-rays prove the patients were in the hospital on those dates."

"I think so, but the radiologist report was missing, and I thought it might be a good idea to pursue all the angles."

He sat down and did some typing. "We already know the admitting doctor wasn't the same for each of the patients and neither is the radiologist. " He ran his finger an inch in front of the monitor. "One radiologist was Carter," he said. "The other was Dr. Burns."

"Dr. Burns is an internist, not a radiologist." I thought about what Holly had told me. "But I think that the doctor looks at the x-rays too. Maybe the records are mixed up."

"Lot of mix-ups and unexplained people where they don't belong on the records, huh?"

"That reminds me. I wanted to ask you, who from x-ray was working last night?"

He slanted his eyes at me. "What makes you think I can get that information?"

I pointed at the computer. "It's part of the hospital computer system. If it were at The Pavilion or elsewhere it might be hard to get, but since it's here, it will take you, what? Less than a second to get it?"

He grinned, wiggled his fingers and then asked, "What time?"

"Around midnight. Sometime after midnight."

"Heh-heh-heh."

I ignored his glee.

After more typing, he came back with, "No one."

"What do you mean, no one?"

His finger traced up and down the screen. "Nope. No one is scheduled that late." More typing. "And according to this, no one was called in." Before I could protest, he held up his eureka finger. "Sometimes it takes a while for a called-in employee to get entered into the database. I have to cross-check payroll and time sheets to be certain."

"Is nothing sacred?"

"Not really." He seemed very smug about it too.

"Someone was called in," I muttered. "Do you think someone from ER might retrieve records from storage?"

He shrugged. "How would I know?"

It didn't seem likely. Wouldn't old records wait for the attending physician? It hadn't been a doctor down there. The only female physician at the hospital was Dr. Evans, and she was not blond by any stretch. "Look up Crissa...Sheldon, I think her last name is. She is the only other person I know with blond hair likely to be down there."

He did some typing. "Nope. Looks like she's on days all the time."

Knowing he couldn't look up time sheets according to "who is blond and works at night," I gave up on that angle. "We've got incomplete medical files, overnight visits that don't make a lot of sense and messed up entries in some records." It could really be simple incompetence. It was hard to imagine anything else. Doctors, the ones who stood the most to gain by adding charges, were busy enough already. They put in long hours and had lives to save.

Then again, not all engineers applied their talent to positive uses. Radar was talented, but his specialty hadn't always been turned in an admirable direction. He was able to do something that ninety-eight percent of the population couldn't do and luckily, because of Huntington, he was applying his skills to a worthwhile cause. But not every hacker would get hired by a Huntington. And maybe not all doctors were completely dedicated to saving lives either.

Chapter 17

Friday morning before heading into the hospital, I called my parents to wish them a Merry Christmas. My brother, Dean, answered.

We chatted for forty seconds. He wasn't sure when he was coming up to visit me. He hemmed and hawed and acted evasive, but brothers were strange creatures anyway.

Mom was chirpy and happy, but since Dean was standing right there, she couldn't gossip about his "guest."

Dad was Dad; he thanked me for the garden gadgets I had sent and seemed especially happy with the bat guano. "You know it's a better fertilizer than anything else I've tried," he told me for the fiftieth time. "Plants grow like crazy in the stuff!"

Dad viewed guano as manna from heaven. "Hoard it," I advised. "It's hard to find." I didn't mention that it was also extremely expensive. He probably knew anyway.

"I only use it to start seeds or on troubled plants," he said. "I hear that elephant dung works almost as well. I can't wait to try some. It has to be easier to buy. Think about it! One elephant, and I'd be in business!"

"Uhm," I hadn't a clue about where to find a willing elephant to give to the cause. "I guess so."

I hung up and drove into work. Attila had scheduled a team building event that was supposed to be a "Christmas gift" for our health. Since it was snowing, I figured her "gift" would be canceled. A postponement would leave my lunch break open so I could attend Christmas Mass. It certainly didn't make sense to walk around the frozen pond outside the hospital in the bad weather.

What was I thinking?

Attila gathered us downstairs in shifts starting at eleven. "Today we are not only going to team build, we are going to make progress on being healthier and losing weight! My team will be in *great* shape, setting an example for everyone else." She looked as if she might beat anyone who didn't participate.

Did she have to be such a fanatic? "Is Attila a weight-lifter or something?" I whispered to Brenda.

Brenda asked, "Who is Attila?"

"I mean Sally."

Brenda didn't have a very well-rounded sense of humor. She was also a lot more respectful of other people than I was. She sniffed and looked down her nose at me. "Sedona!" When I didn't respond she added, "Yes, Sally lifts weights. She even does those competitions. You know, the body building contests where they pose in a bikini."

I grinned. I couldn't wait to tell Radar. He would be soooo pleased. "But why do we have to get dragged along on her get-in-shape hobby?"

"We get paid fifty cents for every pound we lose," Brenda explained, even though I had heard the lame explanation at the pep rally.

"It's cold out," I complained.

"I know, but we have to team build and trust me, it's a lot better than the last idea they had."

How could that be? We didn't even have umbrellas and a slushy sleet drizzled in our faces. "I doubt it."

Brenda said, "No, really. The last director of nurses--see, Sally is just temporarily assigned to the job--anyway the old director, her name was Martha, picked the last team building exercise. She's on leave at the moment while they investigate." Brenda leaned close to my ear. "She suggested a séance in the morgue downstairs, to you know, build morale."

My eyes goggled. "*What*?"

Brenda nodded. "Truly. She had us all go down there one afternoon. It was supposed to be one of those hold hands, get real close and comfortable with the people you work with. But unfortunately, that day the mayor's mother-in-law had died. Martha, the director, didn't realize there were reporters in the hospital."

I groaned. "You guys didn't actually get caught in the act? Why didn't anyone protest?"

"I wasn't too keen on the idea, I can tell you that."

I wasn't too keen on walking in drizzling snow either. It wasn't making me feel close to other employees nor was it likely to make anyone skinnier. At least two people walking ahead of us were eating Oreos out of their coat pockets. "So what happened?"

"Well, when Martha ordered us down there, three of us claimed we had to go to the bathroom. Not that we knew about the reporters. We thought we'd be able to think of a good excuse if we put our heads together, but in the end, we all went. We got down to the morgue, and there was Martha with a big black hood over her head. The reporters had followed us, thinking something was going on, but not really knowing what. Then Martha lit candles and started chanting. The reporters took pictures and ran."

"What did the mayor say?"

"Oh, that made it even worse. Now the mayor is in a big divorce battle."

"Why?"

"He made a big stink over the séance. Got caught on tape saying he didn't want to hear what his mother-in-law had to say when she was alive, and he sure didn't want to hear from her after she was dead. His wife was absolutely appalled. He'll probably lose the re-election too."

Now there was a loss. Although I couldn't blame the man for saying what he did. It might well have been the only honest comment the politician had ever made.

After getting miserably cold and grumpy to boot, we headed back upstairs. I happily noted that my lunch trick was still working. Brenda had her lunch in her locker. We sat in the break room and ate lunch together.

We were just finishing up when Dr. Evans wandered in. She grabbed a soda from the machine and perused the snack machine.

I thought about Dr. Staple and his cleaning crew problem. "I hear you might need some cleaning or filing help over at The Pavilion." While I wouldn't willingly help Dr. Staple, Dr. Evans was a nice lady. If she was in the lurch over the cleaning service, I could pitch in temporarily for her--and it would get me inside the building.

She turned to me, her eyebrows raised. "Don't tell me. We lost the cleaning service again."

Apparently she hadn't known. "Dr. Staple mentioned something about it. I can't really clean the whole place or anything, but if you need temporary help I could probably do filing and cleaning on Wednesdays until you find something more permanent."

Her lips pressed together, and her face looked like it might self-combust. Very succinctly she said, "*I* don't need filing help because *I* don't have a problem keeping staff." She slammed her Sprite down on the table. "That man is in charge of hiring the cleaning staff." She jabbed her finger out toward the nurses' station even though Dr. Staple was nowhere around. "*He* is supposed to hire a cleaning service because he fired the first one we had and drove out the other two." She paused. "Now the other three."

Brenda swallowed nervously. I babbled for the both of us. "Oh. I, uh. I guess I don't want to work with him either, but thought if you needed some temporary help, I could do it for a little while."

Dr. Evans smiled grimly. "Honey, no one wants to work with that man except the drug sales people. Dr. Staple thinks he deserves to have the world put him on a pedestal and since the salesmen are the only ones willing to put up with his attitude, they are his only friends." She grabbed her soda and took a long drink.

One of the call lights came on. I got up to go see what Mr. Potts in three-fourteen needed.

Before I cleared the doorway, Dr. Evans called out after me, "Do you need a job?"

I needed a life. "No, I'm okay, really." There had to be a better way to get inside the building. "Maybe you could each hire your own cleaning service, like you do for filing."

Dr. Evans opened her mouth and started to speak. She closed it. "There are still the shared hallways and the entrance. Lord, that entrance is huge. It's one of the things I loved about the building." She smiled then. "I'd even pay my person to do the hallway and front to avoid this crap." Before I could utter another word, she patted me on the shoulder and went around me. "Brilliant. That's a great idea."

I looked over at Brenda. The call light was still blinking. "I better go see Mr. Potts. What does she mean about the drug salesmen?"

Brenda shrugged. "Oh, the salesmen for all the drug companies try to get the doctors to prescribe their drugs over a competitor's product. So the happy little salesmen come by, take the doctors to lunch, give them tickets to sporting events, and hold conferences in places like Hawaii. As if getting information on a new drug in Hawaii somehow makes it more effective for a patient."

Hmm. I hadn't known that, but I did find it interesting. "Aren't all drugs different? Aren't some better than others?"

"Sure," Brenda agreed. "But some of them are equally efficient. And if a drug is effective, the doctor could prescribe the cheaper one, unless said doctor has decided he likes working with, say, the representative who takes him to lunch four times a week. Then he may prescribe that drug. It's no skin off his nose. He isn't paying for the drug and usually the patient isn't either. Insurance is picking up the tab so no one is paying any attention."

"But don't the insurance companies complain? Don't they ask why the doctor couldn't prescribe the cheaper drug?"

"They can complain. But the doctor can say he's tried the other stuff, and it had too many side-effects or whatever. That's why when I go to the doctor, I always talk over all the prescriptions. Of course," she lowered her voice to a whisper, "I wouldn't go to Dr. Staple anyway. He might be a good surgeon, but I bet he's responsible for some of his patients' high blood pressure. I know he makes mine go up."

"Yeah. He is pretty high and mighty." I scurried away to answer the call light. The longer I worked here, the more it resembled a computer company. Instead of pushing a particular drug, computer vendors bribed managers with lunches to get them to buy specific computers.

The medical industry was just sick. Of course, accepting lunch in the computer business wasn't illegal, and it probably wasn't in the medical industry either. It was a far cry from overcharging or claiming a patient was hospitalized when the patient hadn't been. But giving a patient a more expensive drug didn't seem all that ethical either.

Maybe I should let Dr. Evans or Staple hire me. We were going to need access to doctor records somehow. But cleaning?

Surely Mark was a better way in than me having to clean, especially for Dr. Staple.

Chapter 18

Christmas was a complete disaster. It had nothing to do with the fact that we celebrated two days late, nor my extra activities. Even worn out I could instruct Brenda on warming up a ham and slicing potatoes. Everything proceeded smoothly until Mom and Dad called.

We had just finished eating. I was comfortably sleepy and contemplating going home when the phone rang. Brenda hopped up and answered it. Maybe its proximity to the dining room was the reason I could hear my mother yelling, her Irish temper going full steam.

Sean looked at me and jumped up to get the phone.

"What now?" I muttered, trying to decide between another helping of the main course or extra pie. The dessert selection was pumpkin pie rather than chocolate pecan. I vastly preferred the chocolate, so I was tempted to eat more ham and potatoes.

Brenda rushed back in from the kitchen. "Oh my gosh, they are married! Your mother is beside herself."

My parents had been married for ages. "What are you talking about?"

Brenda sat and fanned her face. "Your brother and his…"

That thought was so mind boggling, it took a minute to compute. "His…my brother Dean?" I finished chewing the last potato I had stolen and nearly choked. "They got married today?" That didn't make sense and as the implications hit, my eyes widened. "You mean, they showed up at Mom and Dad's and sat around and had Christmas two days ago and just now got around to telling them?"

Brenda nodded. "It was a surprise."

"Oh, I'll bet it was." And I bet they had waited this long to tell my parents because Dean hadn't found an appropriate time to tell them sooner. "Ohboy."

Brenda glanced over at the kitchen and decided it would be a while before Sean could join us. "You should open your gift now. I'll show you all of mine too."

We retired to the living room by the tree. I was on auto-pilot as I unwrapped my gift. Brenda "oohed and aahed" over the recipe box I had gotten her. It was filled with a bunch of recipes from me and Mom.

Brenda had been to the store and gifted herself more "costumes" for work. When she lifted one of them up to show me, I was too tired and stunned to cover my horror. "You aren't really going to go into work as a bunny?" She put on a strange little hat with *ears*, long ones that flopped over.

"Isn't it great?"

"Brenda, don't you think--"

"You've met Attila," she interrupted. "What would you do? Would you just tell her?"

I squirmed uncomfortably. "Well, yeah, probably."

Brenda sat down and pulled off the cap. Sean came in from the kitchen looking grim. The droopy rabbit ears flopped over Brenda's knees. "You...you would?"

I chose to ignore Sean even though he looked like he was going to burst at any minute. "Look Brenda, Attila is going to have to face facts sooner or later, and you have the right to be pregnant."

Brenda's eyes filled with tears.

"Brenda--" Oh, dear.

"You think I'm a stupid coward, don't you?" Her eyes brimmed over, spilling tears down her face.

How was I supposed to answer that? I loved my sister-in-law, but the woman was walking around wearing felt hats and a cape two days out of the week. She now had rabbit ears hanging over her knees and sat next to a box holding some sort of clover tiara.

"Sean got me this great sweat top for the bunny costume," she sniffed.

"Wear the sweatshirt! Just maybe not...the hat."

It was the wrong thing to say. "Do..do..waaaaah!!!" Off she ran into the bedroom.

Sean folded his arms and hissed, "Thanks a whole lot, Sedona. You're a great sister." He waved a hand towards the bedroom. "Now look what you've done. And on top of that I've got to tell her that *our* child might not even be the first grandchild. How could you?"

I sat there and blinked, thankful that we had already eaten because I was suddenly feeling a bit queasy. "I...but..." There was no one there to hear my protests. Sean slammed the door to their bedroom. I looked down at the little box I had not yet opened and pulled the lid off.

A hand-carved frame whose border read, "For My Aunt Sedona" sat inside. There were little carved flowers and a delicate teddy bear etched along the sides. "I'll just leave now," I said to the empty air.

Chapter 19

Mondays weren't my best days anyway, but after my weekend, my feelings toward my fellow man, sickly or not, were not charitable. Due to my sulking, I arrived late, which left me with no time to sneak down and talk to Radar in the hopes that he had found a way to hack into the doctors' database files without me working at every doctor's office in town.

The first person I saw was Brenda, which was strange, because she didn't work Mondays.

I greeted her tentatively, wondering if she was over her snit. "Hi. I thought you only worked on Thursdays and Fridays."

She glared at me and sniffed. "Paul called in sick so I was called in. As if I need the stress. I'm going to have to work his shift, my two days this week, and tomorrow if he calls in sick again. *This* is exactly what I mean about Attila. I'm positive that shrew is guilty of helping those patients overcharge insurance companies."

"You are?" This was news to me.

"She has to be. She is mean and cruel. I'll bet she is doing it for the hell of it, not because she pockets a dime."

"Oh." While I didn't disagree with Brenda about Attila's personality, being an ogre wasn't illegal. None of my old bosses had been arrested and most of them had been complete jerks.

Brenda hissed into my ear, "This is precisely why I can't tell her about my pregnancy. Then she wouldn't schedule me to come in."

"I thought you said you didn't want to come in?"

"Exactly. But she would make me pay by noting I wasn't a team player and that would affect my raise."

"Uh-huh." There was no point in continuing the conversation. Brenda didn't have any actual proof against Attila; if she had, she would have gleefully told me.

I started distributing breakfast trays. Brenda was on her rounds, pushing the medicine cart. We both entered the first room together.

"Mrs. Trin, how are you?" she started. Brenda was in front of me, blocking my view of Mrs Trin. She abruptly left the med cart, rushed to the bed and put her hand on Mrs. Trin's neck.

I was barely two steps inside holding a breakfast tray in each hand.

Brenda ordered, "Hit the code blue button."

I nearly dropped the trays. The code blue button meant there was an extreme emergency…like someone wasn't breathing.

Brenda moved to start CPR.

I backed up and hit the button with my elbow. Then I stared at it, not quite believing. We had been drilled with the location and the procedures for a "code blue" several times in training.

The intercom dutifully blared, "Code Blue, room 318, Code Blue."

My CPR training hadn't even been scheduled, never mind completed. I wasn't of any help to Brenda unless she wanted to tell me what to do in-between trying to do it herself.

I moved from the doorway to the other patient's bedside, put the breakfast trays down and pulled the privacy curtain.

The patient whispered, "What is going on?"

"Nothing to worry about, of course." I set up her tray as if everything was normal even though there were uncharacteristic noises coming from the other side of the curtain.

I peeked around the curtain, wondering if I should leave.

Crissa skidded into the room, focused and serious. She pushed the code blue crash cart into place. Another guy took Brenda's place near the head of the bed and put a tube down Mrs. Trin's throat.

Dr. Burns entered the room, moving his plump form very quickly compared to his usual meandering gait. Brenda grabbed the clipboard from the side of the crash cart and reported, "When I came in, she made a short gurgling noise. By the time I reached the bed, she was not breathing and there was no pulse."

I had never seen Dr. Burns in action, unless you counted his eating habits. In his element now, he was even more efficient and focused than Brenda. She might be ditsy and completely unable to cook, and he might be a man on a mission to eat every stray piece of food he found, but this was their world and they knew it well. Dr. Burns never hesitated, and for once, he completely ignored the breakfast trays.

"Epinephrine, one milligram," he ordered. He picked up the paddles from the crash cart.

When he said, "Clear," I pulled the curtain tight. This, I did not want to see.

Apparently, Emma, the patient behind the curtain with me, was a lot more curious than I was. "What is happening? I can't see!"

"We have a pulse!" Brenda said.

"Is she going to be okay?" Emma whispered.

"Uhm, of course." The voices counted. No one said "clear" again, and I did not hear the snap of the defibrillator.

Now seemed like a very good time to make a graceful exit. "I'll be back," I whispered without promising when.

I picked up the extra tray and scurried into the hallway. The big cart with all the breakfast trays had been pushed out of the way. I very carefully maneuvered it so that I could continue to pass out trays. I wasn't sure what else to do.

Every time I came out of a room, I peeked down the hallway. Amazingly, none of the other patients seemed aware of what had happened. I supposed that was why they called it in code. It would be a lot more upsetting to have the intercom blare, "We have a dead one, let's resuscitate!"

After a while Brenda wandered down the hall.

"She make it?" I asked.

Brenda nodded. "Yup. She'll go to the unit for a few days. That reminds me. I wanted to tell you this morning that Mr. Prescot in four is going into surgery after all. He's on clear liquids from now on. Double check his tray before you give it to him, will you?"

"I can handle that." I grabbed the next tray. Funny, in previous jobs, I had been to a lot of meetings where tech managers acted as if they were dealing with life and death problems. The real thing was a lot different. No one stood up and pontificated. No one showed off or tried to outdo someone else by shouting out every technical fact they had learned since birth. These people concentrated on the immediate survival need without wasting precious seconds.

By the time I finished doling out trays, making beds and restocking supplies, I was exhausted from the nervous adrenalin of doing nothing to help during the emergency. Brenda didn't look perturbed in the least. She was simply doing her job and appeared normal. Correction, she looked normal for Brenda. She was wearing a striped flag-like outfit in celebration of the New Year. This costume was definitely a winner because no one would notice her pregnancy while she walked around looking like a cross between Lady Liberty and a cartoon president.

I sighed. At least her nurse's jacket covered most of the silly thing, and she wasn't wearing a top hat.

Since my nerves were shot, I figured I more than deserved some peace and quiet. "Psst, Brenda. I'm gonna be gone a little longer than usual for lunch, 'k?"

She raised an eyebrow, but I zipped away before she could ask why.

I headed for the basement and Radar. Luckily, he hadn't left yet. "Hey, you planning on eating today?" I asked.

He looked at his watch. "It's barely eleven-thirty."

"So? Are you hungry or what?"

"I could eat."

I had planned on Chinese, but Radar suggested Italy's Canal. Having been there once with Brenda on Radar's recommendation, I was enthusiastic. It had great food.

While we were walking through the parking lot and arguing over who was going to drive, I noticed Dr. Fox get into a fancy white Porsche with a slim, short blond. I was delighted to see the blond was Crissa.

For my own selfish reasons I hoped she really, really liked Dr. Fox. And I hoped Dr. Fox stayed interested in her for months, or at least until the case was solved.

One thing was for sure--short, blond hair wasn't black and there was no way it was Attila being treated to Dr. Fox's attentions. "Is Attila still bothering you?" I asked Radar.

He frowned. "I have a plan for that."

"Sounds like a yes. I don't know if it will help any, but she also throws herself at Dr. Fox. Maybe you can mention him and make her feel guilty about hitting on you. Or if you get really desperate, you could break into his computer account and send her fake love messages from him."

His eyes narrowed. "Is the guy an asshole?"

That was a big flaw in my plan. "Not that I know of."

"Then why would I do that?"

I shrugged. "He handles her attentions pretty well. She has him on a pedestal. A tad different than the way she treats you."

"Thanks, but I think I'm handling it."

That made me curious. If he thought my plan wouldn't work or wasn't advisable, I hated to imagine what he might have come up with.

Radar's cell phone rang as we approached his car.

I waited patiently on the passenger side, but he waved at me, walked over and handed me the phone. "Huntington," he said.

"Hello?"

Huntington talked so fast I could barely understand him.

"What? Dr. Dan?" At first I thought Huntington was complaining about my trip to give Dr. Dan the x-rays, but it was much worse than that. "What do you mean, his head bashed in?"

"Amy called me," Huntington said. "Dan was out walking. We can't take him to the hospital. This attack is bound to be connected. Can you bring the doctor who sewed me up when I was shot?"

"Are you crazy? Is Dr. Dan breathing? Is he able to talk?"

"He's breathing. Erratically. He hasn't been conscious since Amy found him."

"You call 911 this minute," I ordered. "Dr. Taylor is probably working today in the ER, but I can't just kidnap him!" Actually my scruples weren't that high, but by the time I got Dr. Taylor out there, it might be too late. "The ambulance will bring him to the ER, and Dr. Taylor will be the one to treat him when he arrives!"

There were millions of other questions to ask, but I wanted Huntington off the phone and calling 911. I grabbed Radar's arm and ran towards the hospital. "*Now*, Huntington," I yelled. "You can't expect Dr. Taylor to look at a head injury out in the middle of nowhere. What if it's really serious!!!" It certainly sounded bad.

I tossed the cell phone to Radar and hissed, "We've got to steal the ambulance!"

Radar was running beside me, but came to an abrupt halt, his arm pulling free of my grip.

"Come on," I urged, slowing to look over my shoulder.

"I...my...Steal an ambulance? You can't do that."   His head tilted. He was thinking pretty hard, but it wasn't going to do him any good. There was no way to get an ambulance to Dr. Dan by computer, no matter how good Radar was at hacking them. The guy "stole" information all the time, and now borrowing an ambulance was a problem?

"We've got to do this! Dr. Dan is hurt!"

"What's the address?" he asked.

"Country road 24. Dr. Dan lives out there."

"Dan who?"

"Hernandez, come on!"

There wasn't time for twenty questions. I skidded around the corner and in through the emergency room doors. I slowed down and tried to look innocent, but that was hard to do while walking at a slow run and praying.

Just past the exam room, I spotted a white lab coat draped across a chair. Perfect, especially since I had left my volunteer apron upstairs. I kept right on walking, but put the lab coat on under my outdoor coat. The white lab smock hung well below the bottom of my coat.

I hadn't been to the little break room where the ambulance crew sat, but I knew where it was. Holly had told me the name of one of the guys, but I couldn't remember it. She had also told me he was good looking. As soon as I rounded the corner, I could see for myself that one of the guys was pretty polished.

"Emergency out on country road twenty-four!" My announcement came out in half a pant.

Radar finally wandered in behind me. Even in my harried state, I could see that he looked suspiciously smug.

"I need--" I stopped because I could hear the radio squawking. Huntington had listened to me. Thank God, because these guys didn't look gullible enough to let me drive off in their ambulance. "That's the one," I shouted. "Let's go!"

There were three guys and one lady. Two of them scrambled. The good-looking guy glanced over at me as we ran out the door, but I helped myself to the back of the ambulance anyway. "I know the guy," I said. Maybe they'd assume I had treated the person before.

Thankfully, the ambulance crew hurried. If there had been time to argue with me, they probably wouldn't have allowed me to hop inside.

The radio inside the ambulance squawked and the driver, the good-looking guy, responded to it while driving.

The guy in the passenger seat looked back at me. He was young, maybe only a few years out of high school. His short-short haircut did nothing to disguise the size of his big hook nose. There wasn't likely to be a hair style that would help hide that nose, but for my money, growing his hair out like Radar's and draping it over his face had to be a better solution. "We aren't allowed to take passengers," he informed me in a nasal tone.

With a nose that big, he should sound like a clear, beautiful trumpet rather than a cell-phone underwater. "Don't worry, I know the guy, and I got a call before yours came in." I held onto a strap and huddled on a sturdy looking ledge. "I work here." My voice was barely audible over the noise of the sirens.

Hook nose looked very disapproving, but he obviously didn't know what to do about me. I was used to drawn eyebrows and lips twisted in disgust. That's what brothers were for. They trained you to ignore people that looked at you as though you were weird, unhinged or ugly.

Every time the driver turned a corner, the truck swayed and bobbled. The shocks either needed replacing or these vehicles could use some redesign for stability. A person could get injured riding back here. It was no wonder they had to strap patients down. "Can you go any faster?" I asked. Huntington had already wasted enough time. What if...

I didn't want to think about what if.

The driver answered my question. "No, contrary to what everyone believes, we can't drive like lunatics. We have to slow at intersections, and we still have to remain safe. What's the deal with where we are going?"

"Head injury."

"Where exactly do you work?" he asked. "I'm John by the way."

I didn't want to introduce myself. It was far better if they didn't know me or remember my name. "Sedona," I mumbled, hoping he couldn't hear me. "Upstairs," I said louder. My jeans weren't common wear for most doctors or nurses on duty. It was marginally possible I was an intern of some sort. There was no point in smiling and acting friendly. I was too worried about Dr. Dan and scared that maybe the ambulance driver had called and requested cops at the scene to arrest me.

As we approached Dr. Dan's house, I saw flashes from cop cars in the congestion a few hundred yards up the road. The forest's edge came all the way to the pavement in that spot, leaving little room to park.

I needn't have worried about getting arrested. The ambulance attendants were good at their job; they were all business--theirs, not mine.

I crawled out of the back, and spotted Huntington standing over a prone Dr. Dan. Huntington's shirt was spattered with blood. His call to 911 had unfortunately brought the police, but they looked more interested in Huntington than me. If I was a policeman who knew both of us, I would have zeroed in on Huntington too. It was in his nature to be guilty of something, whereas I prided myself on being an innocent bystander.

Dr. Dan lay unmoving on the ground. Amy sat with a very bloody and limp Rabbit in her lap, tears streaming down her face. The little dog wasn't even whimpering.

"Oh no!" I didn't know where to start. I moved out of the way and watched the dog and Dr. Dan's chest in turn, trying to discern whether or not either was breathing.

"Amy?" I wanted to ask what happened, but she was in no condition to answer. The ambulance attendants got Dr. Dan onto the stretcher. Amy looked around blankly when they moved him.

"Let me take the dog," I said. "You need to go with Dr. Dan." I tugged on Huntington's arm. "Can we take the dog to the vet in your car?" Couldn't he see the dog needed help too?

"I can't leave," he grated out. "These guys want to ask me questions." He glared at me as though it was my fault. Given his bloody shirt, it was obvious why the cops weren't inclined to let him walk off.

"It's good that you called 911. I'm not sure I could have gotten the ambulance guys here on my own," I said.

"I didn't call them. I assumed you did."

"Oh." No wonder Huntington was angry and surprised by the rather hefty response. Radar's smug face came to mind. It hadn't occurred to me to call 911 and report the accident from the hospital, but Radar was into logging things anonymously. I bet he had done it.

I scanned the area and spotted a green jaguar convertible. Since policemen didn't drive such cars to accident scenes, it must belong to Huntington. "Can I have the keys? I need to get Rabbit to the vet."

His eyes shut. He took a deep breath, but he reached in his pocket. The policeman next to him kept his hand on his gun. I skimmed over the faces, but didn't see Derrick or Adrian, the only two policemen I knew on the force. One of them could show up at any time so the faster I moved, the better.

A little lady I didn't recognize ran toward us from up the road. Like Amy, she was probably in her sixties, but she carried a bit more weight, and she ran with a slight limp. Her hair was in disarray and instead of neat brown curls, hers were gray, black and yellow-white. She was dressed in a purple sweatshirt with a giant white cat embroidered across the front.

"I've got a towel!" She waved a large blue cotton bath towel. "Here we go."

John helped Amy climb in the back of the ambulance next to Dr. Dan. Dr. Dan looked awful, his head covered with blood. He had not done any moving on his own.

I transferred poor Rabbit to the towel. The little poodle squirmed slightly and licked my fingers once.

"Okay, I've got him," the lady said. "Henry has Pooh up at the house, and he's bringing the van. We'll get Rabbit taken care of." She called this reassurance into the back of the ambulance as the doors slammed closed. She sprinted away toward a dark blue van that was pulling out of a driveway a few yards up the road.

Huntington held his hand out for the keys. Instead of returning them, I asked, "Do you think I could take your car back to the hospital? I..." I didn't want to say that I wanted to keep an eye on Dr. Dan in front of the policemen so I trailed off into silence.

Huntington snapped his teeth on his reply. "Fine."

There was no point in giving him any additional time to think about it or consider how he would get home without the Jag.

I hurriedly stowed myself inside and pulled away.

Ambulance rides might be smoother if they were all sports cars instead of giant vans, but I wouldn't mention that to the drivers. In fact, it would be better if the ambulance drivers never saw me again. Hopefully they would forget I existed.

Chapter 20

If not for a couple of red lights, I would have beaten the ambulance back. Half the police were at Dr. Dan's so I was generous when stepping on the gas.

I parked, took off the lab coat and ran inside, my heart beating fast more from worry than exertion. Surely Dr. Dan would be okay.

To my dismay, Dr. Taylor, the ER physician, spotted me as I draped the borrowed lab coat back across the chair. I froze, trying to decide whether to run away or ask him about Dr. Dan. He stared at me with a puzzled expression, but no doubt due to examining an "attacked" patient, he placed me quickly. "You!" He pointed his finger straight at me and then curled it into a "get over here" message.

I was already pointed in that direction anyway. "Is he okay?"

"How is it I managed to forget where I knew you?" He steered me inside one of the empty ER partitions. There was no real privacy. "Do you want to explain what is going on? This had better not have anything to do with that friend of yours who was working on something around here."

"I think it does," I said, making hushing motions with my hands. "Is he--" I had to force the words out around a throat that didn't want to work right. "Is he going to be okay?"

He shook my arm. "I'm shipping him out. I've ordered an MRI, but it doesn't look as encouraging as I'd like. I could probably admit him. Is there any reason I should let him be treated here?"

"Oh no. Probably not a good idea." Dr. Dan had been the one who hired Huntington in the first place, and with me talking to him about the case recently…he had mentioned wanting to ask some questions. But I had talked him out of that, hadn't I? "Oh Lord," I muttered. Dr. Taylor glared at me one last time and then stalked into the next partition. Since he hadn't said I couldn't, I followed.

I swallowed hard when I caught sight of Dr. Dan on the bed. His head was now swathed in bandages, IV lines ran from his arm, and a monitor for his heart or his head was by his side. If his wife, Amy, hadn't been holding his hand and talking softly, I wouldn't have recognized Dr. Dan at all.

It was almost worse seeing him in bandages than lying on the ground all bloody.

"Amy?" I said tentatively, wondering if she would rail at me and send me away.

She didn't respond except to continue crying. I put my arm around her, carefully keeping myself out of the way. "Dr. Taylor said they will send Dan to another hospital. It's a good idea." I wanted to convey that Dr. Taylor was one of the good ones, and that everything else would be okay, but I didn't know all of that, especially the last part.

Amy rubbed at her cheeks without removing her little round glasses. "He was out walking the dogs after we ate lunch. Pooh came back barking like crazy without Rabbit. I knew something was wrong." Her hand clutched mine, and her whole body shook. "I found him just lying there!"

"Did you see anyone?"

She shook her head. "I called Steve and then Marge, my neighbor. Rabbit--" she sucked in much needed air and tried again. "Rabbit was hurt too," she sobbed quietly.

"I know." My own eyes teared. That wasn't supposed to happen. In training we had been instructed to keep our composure at all times.

"She's a fierce little thing, you know. She must have tried to help and whoever did this--" Her hand clutched hard. "Her head looks just like his."

"Your neighbor took Rabbit to the vet," I said.

Amy nodded. She gallantly tried to regain control, holding her fist against her mouth.

"While Dr. Dan is getting ready to fly out, let me go get an update on Rabbit for you." My mouth was dry, my heart was hollow, and if I didn't get away from this room, I was going to burst into tears.

Amy told me where she thought Rabbit would be taken.

I hurried out to make the call.

The news wasn't horrible, but it wasn't great either. "Mostly a large cut on her scalp that we sewed back together. Her leg is badly bruised, probably from being kicked. The bruised leg seems to be what kept her still, and that's a good thing."

"Will she pull through?"

The lady on the other end hesitated. "She is licking hands and responding well. Hopefully there won't be any long term damage."

To my dismay, as I finished the call and made my way back through the ER, Huntington came through the doors from the waiting room. He spotted me. The muscles in his jaw spasmed at least twice. He had changed clothes, but his black hair was out of place from the wind. He wasted no time confronting me. "Is there somewhere we can talk?"

"Yes, but let me update Amy first. She's in with Dr. Dan."

"How is he?"

"I--they're shipping him out." I turned and hurried behind the partition. I gave Amy the report on Rabbit. "You'll be flying with your husband. Do you need me to pack clothes? What about Pooh?"

"Marge will take care of it. She already has Pooh, and they have a key. I'll have them send anything I need."

I didn't ask what hospital Dr. Taylor had recommended. I assumed it would be one of the Mayo Clinics or one that Dr. Taylor trusted. I grabbed a piece of paper from a drawer and wrote my name and phone number. "Call me and let me know how to get in touch with you. And if there is anything I can do to help, please don't hesitate to call. I can pick up Rabbit when she's better or take care of Pooh."

"Thank you. You can call my cell. I can't guarantee I'll answer, but I'll talk to you when I can." She rattled off a number.

I wasn't ready to deal with Huntington, but I knew he was waiting. The server room in the basement was the only place that would be deserted. No one except Radar was ever in there, and he should get the update anyway. As I steered Huntington to the basement level, I asked worriedly, "Where's Mark?"

Huntington replied, "I called him so he knows what is going on. It's best if not too many people look interested." In other words, as usual, Mark wouldn't come into the hospital unless he had some sort of cover.

Radar was surprised to see me and even more surprised when he saw who followed me in.

Huntington didn't start berating me about Dr. Dan, but then, I hadn't mentioned my last trip out there. I started with what Amy had told me and that Dr. Dan would be going to a larger hospital.

"Because it's bad or because we can't let him stay here?" Radar asked.

"I think more the latter, but I'm really not sure. Dr. Taylor asked if this had anything to do with the investigation. I think he was already considering sending Dan out anyway."

Huntington nodded sharply. "If anyone else asks, it was a bad head trauma, and Dr. Taylor wanted him out of here because his chances weren't looking good, period."

I winced and prayed that it would turn out to be entirely a cover story. "I guess we should tell his wife not to give too many updates."

"I'll call her when they get there."

"You know where they are going?" I asked.

He nodded. "I checked with Dr. Taylor while you were in talking to Amy. Unofficially, he's giving him a good chance. He won't be putting much on the chart just in case."

Confession time. "I went to see him a couple of days ago." I waited for the explosion.

"I know," Huntington said. "Dan called me yesterday evening, all in an uproar about us young people running things. I told him the same thing that you apparently told him--stay out of it and let us take care of it. He said he thought he could be more help to us if he did a little poking around himself."

I stopped pretending to study my shoelaces. "And did he? Poke around?"

Huntington paced. "Why else would he have been attacked? He's in a jogging suit for crissakes and was out in the middle of nowhere. It isn't likely anyone thought he'd have a wallet stuffed with cash to go walk his dogs. His neighbors are ranchers or retired. The place isn't full of hoodlums, nor is it a ritzy enough neighborhood to draw thieves in droves in broad daylight."

"He didn't say who he planned on talking to? He mentioned something to me about checking with the radiologist."

Huntington shook his head. "I have no way of knowing who he talked to or if he even talked to anyone at all. Someone is serious about this though. Let's hope he didn't mention any of our names if he talked to anyone."

"He seemed to understand my concern about the wrong people finding out. What made him change his mind?"

"Who knows?" Huntington exploded. "You ignore my advice all the time! Why do you do it?"

I almost grinned, despite the situation. "Because you're not always right," I said.

Radar rolled his eyes and offered, "I'll do some checking on the radiologist's records. See what I can find."

"I've got to get back upstairs." It wouldn't be good if anyone besides Brenda noticed I had gone missing. There was no sense in calling more attention to myself.

"Keys?" Huntington put his hand out.

"Oh, yeah." I dug into my jeans pocket for the Jag keys.

"I think the Mercedes should be more than enough for you."

I had no clever reply so I ignored the comment and hurried back upstairs, just in time to spend a half hour helping Mr. Parks take his afternoon stroll around the hallways. Afterward, I helped Crissa with a sponge bath and delivered two patients to x-ray before heading home.

Mark was waiting for me when I arrived. I pulled into the garage and tried to compose myself. For some reason seeing him made me feel more emotional than I had before.

He very carefully kept his distance. "Do you see what I mean about working with someone on this stuff?" His voice sounded like he had a cold, but my dad's voice got that way whenever he was trying very hard not to yell at me.

"This situation calls for some food," I mumbled.

"What?"

"I'm hungry."

The worry in his eyes eased the tiniest bit. "Do you really think that food solves everything?"

I nodded emphatically. "Just about."

He contemplated that for a while. Finally he took a deep breath. Some of the tension went out of his shoulders. "Okay, what do you have to eat?"

"Cookies?" I offered.

He laughed. "For a start." He followed me inside, but then he had to, because I had reached out and captured his hand. It was warm and alive... and not bleeding.

"How did you get in this business anyway?" I asked. "Seems to me you're in at least as much danger as I am." Maybe more considering his late-night activities.

"How do you think?" He grinned, but there was a seriousness behind the question that let me know the answer mattered.

I put some cookies in the toaster oven and started some hot chocolate. "I can't begin to imagine how anyone would get into these investigations. Maybe you were caught burglarizing some fantastic art out of the Smithsonian and as penance, the government forced you to apply your skills protecting stockholders or something."

He chuckled. "That's a good one." He laughed harder. When he finally stopped he asked, "Do you have anything besides hot chocolate? Like maybe a beer?"

I stared at my refrigerator. "I doubt it."

"You don't know?"

I sighed. "You've met Sean, remember him?" After he nodded, I explained, "He eventually takes almost every scrap of food or drink I own out of my fridge. So, although I purchase beer or wine occasionally, it is doubtful there is any left." I checked. There should have been a bottle of wine that Suzy gave me for Thanksgiving, but it was already missing. "Sorry. How about hot chocolate?"

"It will do." He must have been thinking about our trip up the mountain because he caught my eyes for a moment. Suddenly, I couldn't breathe. We stared at each other until I was forced to let out a pent up breath. "You still didn't tell me how you became involved in this."

"Don't you assume I work for Steve, like you do? Swept along by my older brother's lead?"

I shook my head. "I doubt it."

"You doubt I've been swept along?"

"I doubt you work for Steve," I corrected.

This seemed to amuse him. "Really? It's what most people assume."

"I don't think you work for anyone. Not even your brother."

I served the hot chocolate, which was almost as good as the stuff he had taken on the picnic. The cookies were very hot, but I slid them onto small plates anyway. We sat down at the table. My place wasn't big enough for a real dining room; the little white-washed oak table off the kitchen served instead. We could see out the window into my small backyard, but there wasn't anything to look at, especially in the winter.

He sipped his drink and gave it his approval. "Steve was CEO for a small company that was doing quite well. One of his directors skimmed quite a bit of money when Steve wasn't paying attention. The director then skipped town leaving behind an absolute mess."

My eyebrows about left my face.

He nodded soberly. "It was quite a blow for Steve. No one had managed to make him look that bad in all his thirty years. He had clawed his way to the top in record time and then was summarily fired. Worse, he was blamed, even though no one could publicly tie him to any crime because there was no tie. He had been truly duped."

"Oh my," I said. "That couldn't have gone over well."

He grinned at my understatement. "You could say that. This was in Pennsylvania. I was already in Colorado, but Steve hired me to find the guy. I was running my own private investigating firm."

That was almost a disappointment. I thought of Mark as a secret agent, possibly CIA, working through people who didn't even know he existed. "What happened after you found the guy?"

"We evened the score. And my brother decided on a new career."

"So you're a private eye?" I was a little skeptical. He didn't obey laws very well, and I was pretty sure that private investigators could get in a slew of trouble if they didn't.

"Not anymore. Steve and I opened our own company. We do exactly what you see us doing. We hire out as a security operation to investigate internal issues."

"And it's lucrative."

It wasn't a question, but he laughed at me and answered anyway. "Extremely so, but then my brother knows the environment. Despite the fact that he got ripped off by his own employee, he actually understands the bottom line very well and knows how much these guys can afford to pay."

"He seems to do okay in that arena," I agreed. "So Steve has set out to prove to the world and his old buddies in the CEO chain that it can happen to anyone--and he won't be fooled twice."

Mark's eyes twinkled. "Pretty much. Now he's earned a different reputation, and his old friends come calling."

"Does he want back in?"

Mark lost his sense of humor. "Would it matter to you?"

"What," I asked in exasperation, "is your hang-up with Steve?"

He drank his hot chocolate.

I waited.

He finally responded, "Nothing."

"Uh-huh." I took his cup and rinsed it out with mine. He stood up and put his jacket back on. The atmosphere was suddenly awkward. Nervous, I noticed that the message light on my answering machine was blinking. Since I was stalling, I pressed the button.

To my surprise, Dr. Dan's voice came out of the machine. "Sedona, I've been looking through those x-rays again trying to sort through the things that didn't make sense. I found something." His voice cracked, he was so excited. "Since the patient notes were missing, I took a close look at the x-rays to see what treatment was indicated. You aren't going to believe this. The x-rays from two of the patients are exact duplicates! The patient name is the only difference.

"I laid the x-rays out and noticed that the lightest set of x-rays for patient Brown is exactly the same as the set for patient Olsen. The whole set isn't in both folders, but it leads me to believe that perhaps one or two real patients were run through, duplicates were made, and the duplicates were stuffed into these folders to make it look like real x-rays were done for these patients. You were right. It's quite possible that the patients listed on these folders were never in the hospital. Look, I know someone I can ask about this."

I held my breath. Mark and I stared at the machine, willing it to provide the name.

Dr. Dan continued, "Call me when you get home. By then I should have some very interesting answers."

There was a very, very loud click as the machine stopped.

Who had he called?

"Phone records," Mark muttered. "We're going to have to get them."

"What if he met with the person? Whoever bopped him didn't do it over the phone!"

Mark shrugged. "I have to start somewhere."

He drew me in for a long, thorough kiss. It was different from before, less of a rip-your-clothes-off and more…significant. It was as if he was reassuring himself that I was still alive and all in one piece. His right hand started at the back of my neck and worked down, his thumb grazing the side of my breast and then both hands spanning my waist and holding on.

When he pulled back and looked at me, I didn't know what to say. Intelligent conversation was out of the question.

"Be careful," he whispered. He touched my lips once more, gently.

I had a funny feeling in my heart. Like maybe I mattered to him. The real Mark, not the one who broke into buildings or flirted with hospital employees.

After he left, it was a long time before I fell asleep. My feet tingled. My lips tingled. I was exhilarated…and scared. I was pretty sure life would be less complicated if we stuck to raw passion and left feelings out of it.

Chapter 21

Volunteering was becoming a little too much like a real job. There were people at the hospital I did not want to see, the pay was lousy and there was no chance of a raise. I went in anyway, but avoided the front entrance near the ER where Dr. Talylor might be, and took the stairs. All the way up, I regretted taking them. It was way too early to exercise.

When I got to the third floor, I found another reason I shouldn't have taken the stairs.

"Did you get your free bagel?" Brenda asked. "The sign was by the elevator inside the double doors near the ER. Free bagels and coffee this morning in the cafeteria. They'll even toast it for you, but you'd better hurry. There weren't too many left."

I took her advice seriously. I grabbed one of my lab specimen stickers and put my lunch in the fridge. Hurrying back out to the front of the nurses' station, I noticed three call lights blinking. Out of the corner of my eye, I saw Attila heading toward me with the tall, handsome Dr. Fox in tow.

The lights blinked. My stomach growled. Would she notice the lights while hanging onto Dr. Fox?

I sighed. The lights were like a hockey game, and unfortunately, there were a lot of goals being scored today. Grumbling, I slugged off to see what the patients needed.

By the time I finished answering call-lights, breakfast trays had arrived. Unless I stole food from the patient trays like Dr. Burns, I could forget freebies.

I started on the first load, right about the time Attila barreled out of the nurses' station, a lunch bag held high. "This is a violation! Who put this in here? Why hasn't this been taken directly to the lab?"

I stared in dismay. Admitting the lunch bag was mine would not only get me fired, it would alert the thief. My name wasn't on the bag, and now seemed like a good time to forget about the little food container and call it a loss. Worse, I wouldn't be able to use the lab specimen stickers again. Attila was bound to check every refrigerator in the place now that someone had committed a "violation."

"Rats." Geez, getting food and keeping it around here was a pain in the ass.

After staring up and down the corridor, Attila strode away, taking the offensive bag with her.

Brenda hung up the phone and said, "We've got a new admit in the

ER. Crissa has her hands full and asked if you could bring the guy up. I told her you were standing right here and would be happy to help." She grinned.

"Okay." I left the breakfast trays and headed for the ER.

The new patient was waiting in a wheelchair with a duffel bag draped across his lap. He clutched it tightly. I picked up the paperwork from the nurses' station before approaching him. "Hi, Mr. Vin. I hear you're coming upstairs for a visit." Under all circumstances we were supposed to ignore the fact that entering the hospital was not generally considered a great thing by most people.

My happy greeting didn't fool him. Most of the whites of his eyes showed. "They can't do this to me! I don't need to be here, I tell you!"

The gym bag he held bulged on its own and almost fell to the floor. "Uh…" I glanced at his name again. "Mr. Vin. What's in the bag? Pets aren't allowed."

Why was he being admitted? Animal bite? Insanity?

"I am fine, I tell you. They gave me antidote, I want to go home!" He clutched the bag to his chest. The movement from within got worse.

The ambulance driver I had so hoped to avoid passed through the side hallway, headed back to his own area. I was too desperate to keep quiet. "Hey, John? Did you bring Mr. Vin in? What's with the bag?" I tried to keep my voice down, but Mr. Vin was now struggling up out of the chair.

John stopped and reversed course. He gently pushed on Mr. Vin's shoulders. "What's going on here? You need to go upstairs. Do you want a blanket?"

"No! I want out!" Mr. Vin did not calm down. He actively struggled against John, hitting and kicking. In the scuffle, Mr. Vin's bag fell on the floor.

I innocently pushed it out of the way with my foot.

It rattled.

That was not funny. It *rattled* and didn't stop.

John, holding one of Mr. Vin's arms, froze. He looked at me, and I looked at him. I knew that rattle. "Uh," I swallowed, "what did you say you were here for, Mr. Vin?"

John choked out in horror, "Snake bite."

I didn't have to ask what kind.

"I am collector," Mr. Vin shouted. "I demand to go!"

Dr. Taylor came out of the doctors' lounge. "We discussed having you in overnight." He had to raise his voice above Mr. Vin's shouting. Doctors were very focused people. He dealt only with Mr. Vin, completely ignoring the rattling sound. "We want to make sure that the snake bite…" the word "snake" must have penetrated his doctor brain. He blinked rapidly before switching his gaze to the duffel bag.

Dr. Taylor looked up, spotted me and frowned.

I ignored him. There was no way he could blame this incident on me. "Does anyone have a hoe? Or a large rock or a computer monitor? Something *heavy*?"

John turned on one heel and shot between partitions.

No one else moved. We all stood there listening to the hypnotic rattle.

John reappeared quickly with an apron-like garment. It was nothing more than a cleverly disguised strait jacket. Good. At least Mr. Vin wouldn't hurt himself or anyone else.

Sadly, it wasn't going to help with the snake. No arms to tie down and no way to tie down the fangs.

John managed to pin Mr. Vin to the wheelchair. In the meantime, the bag got testier. It came up off the ground as it pushed in one direction and then the other.

It either wasn't zipped well, or Mr. Snake created a hole. To my utter horror, the snake slithered out. "Ohboy." The thing was maybe twelve inches long, a baby really, but all twelve inches were angry and dangerous.

I decided against the computer monitor because it was still connected to the actual computer and too heavy for me to lift and get over the snake.

Crissa came out of a partition wheeling a patient on a gurney. She walked backwards, completely unaware of the danger.

The crash cart was the only other movable object nearby. I grabbed an end and started steering. "Quick," I shouted in a loud whisper, hoping any nearby patients wouldn't hear me. "Somebody help me with this!"

For some reason, the snake didn't coil; maybe because it was winter and should have been hibernating. Then again, maybe it was on the run because its owner was crazy, and the snake was interested in escaping.

I was interested in road kill.

It took two tries to actually run over the head. The first run slowed it down by squashing part of its body. At that point it decided to coil. Luckily, we were able to drag the wheels back over the head before it got going. The term "we" was relative; Dr. Taylor was the only one who actually tried to help, and he almost knocked me over.

Once John saw what I was doing, he jumped away, dragging the wheelchair with Mr. Vin. He plastered himself against the wall and looked like he might climb up onto the chair with Mr. Vin.

Crissa had no idea what was going on until I almost hit her with the crash cart. She turned. Her mouth opened, ready to blast me for being careless, but then her green eyes widened as she spotted the writhing snake tail under the wheel of the cart. She let out a little scream. The patient bed she had been pulling careened into the wall.

In a single heartbeat, Crissa scurried up onto the nurses' station desk, completing the four foot jump in a single bound. The admitting clerk on the other side of the desk, a large black woman, had her arms around her knees and her feet balled up into the chair where she sat. There weren't any other high surfaces available unless she wanted to join the patient on the bed or try and share the top of the desk with Crissa.

Good thing the patient wasn't being wheeled anywhere in a hurry. He tried to sit up, looking around in dazed confusion.

Crissa blinked and came back to life. "Don't worry, sir. Everything is fine. Just ran our carts a little too close. We'll mosey you along." It would have been a lot more convincing had she not been clutching her blond hair with both hands and calling her reassurances from the top of the desk.

I reached out and halfheartedly pushed the patient backwards away from the snake.

Crissa had no choice but to come down from her perch. She did a good job of staying far away from the serpent. She was no dummy either; yanking the bed toward her, she went backwards in the direction of the x-ray department.

After the bed disappeared down the hall, I moved the crash cart carefully. I did not want to find that the snake had flattened but not died. If it got away, I couldn't work here anymore, because it would remember me. No doubt it would pop out of a cabinet or drawer someday and attack me.

Mr. Vin saw the results and let out a screech that convinced half the people present that I had run over him, not the snake. "That is mine! You cannot kill! I am collector!"

I didn't point out that he shouldn't take his collections out into public, especially after they had bitten him. I gasped with relief because the thing was very, very dead.

Mr. Vin didn't stop screaming, even though John hurriedly rolled the wheelchair away.

The smashed snake lay there, mangled.

I waved my hand at it. "Shouldn't someone clean this up?" Several pairs of eyes looked at me.

All of the feet connected to the eyes backed away, except Dr. Taylor's. He stayed put, staring at me intently as if he were going to say something incriminating.

"Dr. Taylor, room one," a voice hailed from down the corridor. "Stat."

I didn't mind that he had to leave. "Does anyone have a trash bag?" I asked.

The admitting clerk, still balled up on the chair, reached down to a side counter where a large pot of coffee rested. Leaning precariously, she opened a drawer, emptied a coffee can into a filter paper and handed me the can and lid.

I stared at it and her for a while before taking it. "Thanks." I didn't mean it, and she knew it.

With the side of the crash cart, my foot and the can, I managed to sweep the body of the snake into the can. I held it away from my body and headed outside.

Where to get rid of it? If I left it in the open people would freak out when they saw it. It could cause an accident.

I stared down at the can. It could actually be mistaken for a live snake. Even dead, it was still a snake. A scary snake.

Hmm. Maybe…Mr. Snake could help me out.

I made sure the lid was on very, very securely and then put it in the back of my SUV with the tire iron on top of the lid. Of course it wouldn't slither out of there, it was dead. I searched for something else to put on top, but my SUV was woefully unequipped for snake transportation.

"I need a new job," I told myself.

Back inside, I discovered it was my lucky day. Now that the snake was removed, a janitor was willing to mop the floor of the tiny smear that was left. "Good thing. I wasn't going to do it."

I hurried upstairs.

Brenda immediately waved me over. "Look out," she whispered. "Sally is after you."

"Attila? Why?"

"Something about you killing one of the patient's pets."

How in the world had Attila already found out about the incident? It had just happened, and I hadn't been gone that long disposing of the snake body. "Brenda, it was a snake, for God's sake! What did she expect me to do with it?"

Brenda's eyes narrowed suspiciously. "Really? Crissa didn't mention that when she told Attila." She rolled her eyes in sudden panic and looked around to make sure that Attila wasn't bearing down on us. "I mean *Sally*."

Hmm. Either the telling had morphed already or Crissa had left out important details on purpose. Maybe she really was jealous over the Mark incident.

Brenda's eyes widened suddenly, and she scurried away like I had the plague. The second I took my first step down the hall toward relative safety, I heard my name cawed out. "Sedona O'Hala! Mizz O'Hala!"

Oh, for pity's sake.

"I understand you upset one of our patients." Attila looked me over with an evil eye so threatening, I shuddered.

"Really?" I blinked rapidly. "Which one?"

My stall tactic halted her for a moment. She recovered quickly, drew herself up and began listing Mr. Vin's complaints. Sure enough, there was no mention of the fact that his "pet" was a venomous snake. "You cannot kill patient pets! We could get sued. I really think you should reconsider volunteer work. Perhaps there is some other good deed you could do."

"Uh-huh." What was she going to do, fire me? I stood there while she explained that she was going to write me up again, and then I walked away, relieved. At least the patient on the bed who was rammed with the crash cart hadn't complained. I felt bad about him getting caught in the crossfire.

Crissa certainly hadn't wasted any time reporting me to the head nurse. It would seem to me that the snake part was pretty damn important. Geez. How many people were walking around thinking I had run over Fido, someone'sdifferent cute poodle?

When I had a bad day, it was always a good idea for me to change course as soon as possible. I took one step in the right direction. I told Brenda I wasn't feeling well and left.

That didn't mean that I played it smart when I got home.

Chapter 22

Instead of going directly to bed without passing go, I made myself breakfast, lunch and dinner when I got home. Feeling only moderately better after eating, I called Amy, but she didn't answer her cell. I left my number and my best stuttered good wishes. Maybe Huntington had an update, but rather than call him, I dialed my parents to find out if they had recovered from Dean's news.

I shouldn't have bothered. Why was it that when one sibling was in trouble, all children got the cold shoulder?

"Hello, Mom? It's Sedona."

"Yes, I know." My mother's voice was on the frosty side. "Just because I don't get invited to the important events in my children's lives doesn't mean that I don't recognize their voices."

"So, Happy New Year!"

"You had best talk to your father."

Uh-oh. That meant that she was barely keeping her temper. It had been a few days since the news, but apparently she hadn't calmed down. My father's mixed heritage, a bit of American Indian from my grandfather mingling with European genes from my grandmother, had somehow produced a blessedly calm demeanor. Nothing much riled Dad, except maybe my mother.

She must have been on a real tear because Dad sounded strained.

"Sedona," he sighed. "Thank God it's you. If either of your brothers call here again soon, I swear I'm having the phone taken out."

"That bad?" I wondered what Sean had done to get on the "don't answer," list.

"Unbelievable! You heard that Dean is married? And, and..." Dad seemed unable to express himself. I could picture him gesturing, waving his hand at the ground. He always did that when angry, stumped or otherwise frustrated. It probably had something to do with the fact that he was an agricultural scientist; it was usually plants that caused his frustration.

"What is her name?" I asked to break the stuttering.

"Married," my mother shrieked in the background. Dad said forcefully, "Her name is Anne. Anne O'Hala." Mom shrieked again.

"Uh, Dad, we might want to wait until she's calmed down to talk about this."

"She may as well accept it. It's done. So's the baby." There was no shriek this time, but a rather deadly silence.

"Isn't Mom happy about the baby? I mean, she bugged Sean about kids all the time. I'm not even married, and she hints about me having kids as soon as I do get married."

"You would think so, wouldn't you? But apparently grandchildren don't count if you don't go to some silly ceremony and stand there and cry like an idiot."

I heard pots and pans in the background. "Dad--"

"She's going to have to get over this and so is Sean."

At least that allowed me to change the subject. "Why is Sean upset?"

Dad mumbled something.

"What?"

"Dean's baby is due about the same time as Brenda's."

I digested this information slowly. "Didn't you and Mom notice when Dean and Anne arrived that she was pregnant?"

"You know I've seen enough cows in that state growing up on the ranch." The pans banged louder. "Your mother thought she was fat and dressed funny."

I closed my eyes. "What do you mean *funny*?" I did not want to hear that both my brothers had married women who went around dressing as bunny rabbits. My family wasn't perfect, but I used to think we fell within the "normal" range. Apparently not. I thought of something else. "So, is Mom mad because Anne is pregnant or because she didn't notice it?"

"Both," he said. "And upset with me because I didn't mention that I thought Anne looked pregnant."

I heard Mom yell, "You sit and talk about any other rude topic and right at dinner, too. Now all of a sudden you're too polite to bring up something this important?"

"Don't answer that," I advised. "You aren't going to win. You know how Mom hates to look foolish."

"And she was being very welcoming," Dad said. "Even hinted at how nice it would be to have a new daughter-in-law and how marriable Dean was."

Ohboy. And now Mom felt like seven kinds of a fool. "So why is Sean upset about the baby being around the same time? What difference does that make?"

"What?" Dad asked absently.

"Sean? Why is he upset?" I was losing Dad's attention and fast. No doubt he was keeping one eye on my mother. Her temper tended to flare and then cool quickly. But while it was hot, it was a good idea to keep one eye out for flying objects. Not that she would ever hurt anyone; there just might be a few things that Dad might want to put out of reach temporarily.

"Sean?" he repeated. "Oh, yes. Some nonsense about they announced it first and by God how could Dean waltz in and take Brenda's moment."

"Where is Dean now?"

Another long pause and then a sigh. "He went back home. Too much excitement for Anne."

"I thought he was coming up here?"

"Well, yes, but he and Sean had a rather big hashing on the phone, and things were in quite an uproar..." I knew Dad was waving at invisible plants again. "But I think he'd had enough for one trip."

Imagine that. "I'll call him at home."

"You do that. Give him our love."

"Tell Mom I'm still single, will you?"

He grunted. "Not sure that will help. Good-bye."

Now I had to call Dean. I dialed very, very reluctantly. "Dean?"

"Hi."

"I understand congratulations are in order." I plowed ahead using my new "happy for the patients" voice. "Not only for finding a wife, but for the little bundle of joy that will be joining you soon."

"Don't you have any complaints? No problems with the timing? No problems with when you were told or not told? Perhaps--"

I cut him off. Dean loved to lecture. Maybe that was why he became a teacher. The students *had* to listen to him; I did not. "Dean!" I shouted into the phone. "When are you coming for a visit?"

There was a moment of silence. "We were coming up there after Christmas. But things got tense."

"You probably should have hinted," I said.

"I did."

"Really." I did not believe him. Dean was very articulate, to the point of being boring. If he wanted Mom to have an idea, he was certainly capable of getting his point across. "Maybe you could make it up here for spring break. I'd love to meet Anne. Dad had nothing but good things to say about her." It would have been more accurate to say that he hadn't said anything bad about her, but even I could be tactful when I tried.

"What did Mom say?" he asked.

"She didn't say anything," I admitted candidly. "She wasn't in the mood to talk so she gave the phone to Dad. I'm sure it's the surprise though, not that she has a problem with Anne."

"Why can't she get over it already? It's my life and my decision." He started ranting about the unfairness of it all.

"Dean!" I shouted again. "I only called to say congratulations. Mom will calm down in due time. You know better than to worry about her."

There was a long pause. "I should have told them."

I wanted to ask why he hadn't, but that would make him mad again. To my surprise, he offered it up anyway. "We had to get married during the school year. She was pregnant, and we didn't have time to plan a ceremony and wait for Mom to get all excited and make a big deal out of a wedding. It was better to show up with everything taken care of rather than sort a lot of loose ends."

Ohboy. I wish he had not told me that. Now, if Mom or Dad started wondering about when the wedding versus the baby had happened and they asked me, I was going to be in trouble. "Dean, I think it's great that you found someone wonderful and are married. Do you know if it is a girl or a boy?"

"It's a girl."

"Excellent." I made a few comments that I was pretty sure were in line with what a sister was supposed to say and then hung up the phone only a little bit sooner than was probably polite.

"Sheesh." Now to avoid any telling conversations with Mom and Dad, and I'd be fine.

When the doorbell rang, I only answered it because I was hoping it was Mark.

Whoops. Wrong Huntington.

Chapter 23

Huntington barged in. "I thought you were going to blend in better," he sniped without preamble.

"I am blending in. Trust me, unlike the last time, no one has blown my cover." A nicer person wouldn't have reminded Huntington that he had blown my undercover status on the last case, but I had used up all my "nice" with my family.

"That isn't what I meant. Do you have to go killing people's pets in the ER?"

"I could have let the *snake* roam the hospital."

He paused in his pacing. His head tilted. "That would have called less attention to you."

"Okay," I promised nastily. "Next snake, I leave it alone. Won't touch the thing."

He watched me carefully, waiting for the punchline that didn't come. "It was really a snake?"

I nodded.

"Probably better if you kill it in private next time."

The man could not cut me any slack. "Fine! I'll lure it into the woman's bathroom, no problem." I flapped my arms. "What do I look like, a belly dancing snake charmer?"

He looked me up and down. "No, not really, but it would be interesting to see you in such an outfit."

I started to answer, but had nothing to say. Absolutely nothing. I clamped my mouth closed. I think my face may have gotten red.

"Are you dating Mark?"

I blinked. "What?"

"My brother."

I rolled my eyes. I knew who he was talking about. I didn't know the answer though. Or did I?

"What are you smiling about?" he asked.

"I'm not."

"Yes, you are," Huntington said. "You have one of those very small grins, like you're pleased with yourself."

"I don't have a smile like that."

"Yes, you do. And you have one for when you're not going to answer my questions because you're mad, but this isn't that one."

I crossed my arms in front of me before I realized doing so was definitely my "I'm-not-going-to-answer" signal.

He laughed. "Okay, it's none of my business, but you do look happy about it."

"How can I look happy about it when I haven't even said I was dating him?"

Huntington shrugged. "It's the look in your eyes lately when I mention Mark."

I didn't know what my eyes looked like, but the mention of Mark's name did make my stomach flip-flop. "Hmph."

Huntington took a step closer. I held my ground, but just barely. "You're going to drive him crazy." He laughed softly and squeezed my shoulder. The gesture reminded me of Sean, kind of an unemotional hug. Huntington was never easy to read, but it was minutely possible a tiny glint of regret flicked in his blue eyes. I wasn't certain how I felt about that, but he cleared it up with his next comment.

He stepped back, smiled and said, "Amy and Dan made it to the hospital. I won't tell you where they are, but he's stable."

Huntington was drop-dead gorgeous, but he had never pretended to trust me--with information or input even though he was paying for that input. His off-and-on attention span where I was concerned made me feel like second place or maybe even third, but never first. There was no doubt he would make a wonderful catch, but where Mark left me breathless, Huntington usually left me thoroughly annoyed. "Of course you won't tell me," I said.

Huntington wrinkled his brow. "Why would you need to know?"

"Never mind. Please let me know if you hear any more news, would you? I'm going to call and check on Pooh and Rabbit again. I know Rabbit made it through okay, but that poor little dog."

Huntington nodded. "I took care of the vet bill. Rabbit and Pooh are with the neighbors."

Despite all of his annoying qualities, he was a responsible and good-hearted person. I was grateful for that because the neighbors might not have been able to pay the vet bill, and it simply wouldn't be fair if Rabbit hadn't gotten the best treatment possible. "Poor thing."

Huntington abruptly began pacing again. "Remember how I told you to go to Hawaii when things heated up and got dangerous during the last case?"

I knew what was coming. "Yes."

"Mark is going to buy you a ticket."

"Mark?" I figured Huntington would be the one to ship me off for my own good. "Tell him to plan on flying there with me then."

Huntington glanced back over his shoulder, his hand on the doorknob. "I didn't tell him to get a ticket for himself. I need him here." He opened the door, and then closed it behind him.

I pondered the closed door. So did Huntington think Mark was going to buy me a ticket because Huntington suggested it? Or was the whole thing Mark's idea?

Men.

And how was I going to explain to Mark that I was mad at him for buying me a ticket to *Hawaii*??? I didn't want him making decisions for me, even if they were for my own good.

This dating stuff was complex, very complex indeed.

Chapter 24

I used my day off to get caught up. Dr. Taylor wasn't in when I called so there was no way to get an update on Dr. Dan through him. I tried Amy's cell phone again, but she didn't answer. I had promised a lot of people cookie treats but hadn't made a single tray.

After arranging ingredients, lining up the tins and getting two batches in the oven, I called Amy's cell phone again.

Thankfully this time she answered, but not so thankfully, the news wasn't good. "He was doing okay, but then pressure built up on his brain. They had to drill. He woke a couple of times after the surgery, and the doctors said he responds to light and other stimuli." Her voice was beyond weary. "The doctors said this could go on for a while before they can get a good assessment. The good news is that he is breathing on his own, and all his reflexes seem to be working."

"Is there anything I can do?"

"Marge and Henry have the dogs. They picked Rabbit up. Oh," she paused. "I forget when that was. They're keeping the dogs at night, but Pooh kept trying to escape and go home, so they take both dogs over there to sniff around once a day."

"I hope Dr. Dan will also be sniffing along soon."

She chuckled a little. "I think not. His sniffing is what started this darn mess. It's caused so much trouble, hasn't it?" Her voice trembled. "It's funny, we left Scottsdale to move somewhere quieter and now…It just makes a body wonder."

"I'll call as soon as I have any news at all," I promised. "We'll find whoever did this and stop them."

She sighed. "Of course."

When I met Amy, she had been nothing but perky smiles. Now, all I could hear in her voice was fragile regret.

I finished up a few batches of cookies and went calling. I stopped in at my friend Suzy's and then went looking for Marge and Henry. Inspecting the place where Dr. Dan had been attacked couldn't hurt, and I needed to see for myself that the dogs were doing okay.

There was still a floating yellow trail of tape at the scene of the crime. I stopped the car on the side of the road, half off the pavement. The tape was the only sign marring the peaceful countryside.

The trees did a remarkable job of blocking noises. Only the sound of shifting branches kept me company as I got out of the car and walked around.

Thankfully, there wasn't a lot of blood or gore. Unfortunately, there wasn't much else either. I could clearly see Dr. Dan's house from the road, along with his neighbor's further up. There was nothing but trees on either side of the road. Unless a car had happened to drive by when Dr. Dan was in danger or Amy had looked out the window at the right time, no one would have seen a car pull off the side of the road near where Dr. Dan walked.

I stood next to the spot where he had fallen. From here, tucked slightly back, my car was probably still visible from the houses, but Dr. Dan and the dogs would have been behind a couple of large trees. If the driver in the car had been someone Dr. Dan knew, he might easily have stood there waiting. Given where the yellow tape floated, Dr. Dan must not have walked over to the vehicle because he had been well off the roadway when he fell.

I looked into the pines, wondering if someone had counted on his walk and waited in ambush, making no noise moving across the bed of pine needles. Doubtful. The dogs would have announced the attack. It had to have been someone Dr. Dan knew. The person had stopped, walked over and attacked, maybe while Dr. Dan was distracted.

Had he turned to scold the dogs? Had the dogs done their little attack greeting routine as they had when I visited, causing Dr. Dan to lean over to grab a collar?

It would only take a second of distraction for someone to gain the upper hand, especially if Dr. Dan viewed the person as a friend.

There were no answers waiting in the forest that smelled more of Christmas than danger. Despite the tranquil setting, I was spooked.

I got back in my car and drove up to the house near Dr. Dan's. It was a lot like the Hernandez's; ranch style, only with a smaller porch and a single flower urn. Telltale barking indicated it was the right place. I knocked and introduced myself in case Marge didn't remember me.

Pooh vouched for me with his enthusiastic barking.

Marge accepted the cookies and ushered me in. Today she sported a green sweatshirt with birds stitched on the front.

"The dogs are doing wonderfully. Is there word on Dan?" she asked.

We didn't want too much news to get out, so I said, "He's about the same." My eyes caught sight of the injured Rabbit. "Oh no! She looks awful!"

"A whole sight better'n she did when we took her in," Marge declared tartly. "Let me set these in the kitchen. If I leave them where these rascals can get to them, they'll be gone in a heartbeat, injury or no injury."

She stepped down the hallway and left me to play with the dogs. "Rabbit," I whispered. "How are you?" The plastic cone around her neck made her look pathetic even without the bandages.

From behind me, Marge said, "We've owned dogs and real rabbits and birds and you name it. Trust me, I know what to feed them all. These two are a piece of cake. We keep Rabbit inside for now except to let her out to potty. Pooh still gets his walks."

She smiled at me while I tried to pet Rabbit. The dog wouldn't sit still. She kept trying to rub the satellite collar off against my leg.

"I don't suppose you saw who stopped to talk to Dr. Dan?" If Marge had seen anything pertinent, an arrest would have been made and surely Huntington would have called me. Well, almost for certain.

"Lord no, I only wish I had! We take walks too, but we weren't out that afternoon. I was at the grocery and saw the police cars on my way home. Stopped and there was poor little Rabbit in as bad a shape as Dan. I zipped home to tell Henry to get ready to take Rabbit to Terrence, our boy."

"Your son is a vet?"

"Yes, yes. That's where all the critters came from over the years."

"That's great." I gave Rabbit a gentle pat. "I won't stay. I just wanted to check on them and thank you for helping out."

She waved the dishtowel. "Lordy, no need to thank us. We're the ones who talked Amy and Dan into moving here, and Henry was thrilled to pieces when Dan joined the board at the hospital. Gave it the prestige Henry's always wanted it to have."

My gaze flew to hers. "Henry...works at the hospital? He's on the board?"

She looked puzzled. "Well, surely. Henry is the Chief of Staff at the hospital."

"Oh! Dr. Johnson? I didn't know that. I knew Dr. Dan was on the board, but not..." I was babbling so I stopped.

She laughed. "Sometimes I'm so involved with it, I forget there is anything outside of the hospital. I used to be a nurse there." Her eyes twinkled. "That's how I met my Henry, of course."

I forced a smile. And these would be the people who Dr. Dan had decided against confiding in, at least at first. Had he changed his mind? The fact that Henry was on the board and lived a few steps away from where the attack had taken place...meant nothing, really.

I thought of something else. "I left some files with Dr. Dan. Do you think we could go over to his house and look for them? He had me drop them off from the hospital a few days ago. We could call Amy and make sure it's okay with her."

"Oh, it's not a bother, not at all. I have the key. Let me get it."

Marge didn't look the least bit suspicious and that bothered me. What if someone else came by and asked to go inside? I knew the answer. She'd let them right in, especially if they worked at the hospital and she knew them.

We walked over and took Pooh with us. Pooh sniffed at everything and nothing. As we walked, I had a very reassuring thought. Surely Pooh and Rabbit wouldn't hang out happily at Henry and Marge's house if Henry was guilty of attacking Dr. Dan. The dogs were too smart. Rabbit had tried to defend against whoever had hurt Dr. Dan. She wasn't likely to forgive and forget.

Marge unlocked the front door and we both wiped our feet before entering. Pooh went crazy, running around barking and sniffing everything.

"I took their food bowls from here so they'd feel at home. I'm going to run back to the pantry and get the extra bag of dog food as long as we're here."

Pooh followed me into the study. I scanned the desk, but there was no sign of the files. The shelves were so full of books there wasn't any place to store the x-ray files. A quick check of the drawers didn't reveal any x-rays or folders either.

"Did you find what you needed?" Marge joined me, a small bag of dog food in her arms.

I shook my head. "No, I thought the files would be right on his desk. We went over them a few days ago."

Pooh sniffed at a spot in front of the desk. I leaned over to pet him and studied the clump of mud on the carpet. Surreptitiously, I checked my shoes, but they weren't muddy. Plus the mud on the carpet was dried. Marge hadn't come in far enough to dirty the rug. I looked around.

For the most part, the house was spotless. Except the carpet. There were two other smudges near the doorway of the room.

A muddy carpet wasn't enough evidence to prove someone had already retrieved the x-rays. But Dr. Dan couldn't have taken them with him. Of course, he might have hidden them before he took the dogs out, but why?

And there were no signs of a break-in, so unless someone had a key...I didn't like where my thoughts were leading me. I gave Marge a rather sickly smile. The dogs wouldn't be so friendly with someone who had attacked them. They just wouldn't.

I followed Marge out. As we walked back to her house, it occurred to me that I hadn't actually seen Henry around the dogs.

Without going inside again, I said my polite goodbyes.

Chapter 25

If Dr. Dan had spotted something in the x-rays, there was only one good place to find clues. Holly had indicated that she could use volunteer help. I called Ellen, the trainer, and left a message telling her I wanted to switch.

Before starting my shift, I dropped off Radar's cookies. "Sorry they're a little late."

"Who cares?" He took two out of the container and started on the first.

"Did you ever find out for sure if anyone was in at night last week working in x-ray?"

He nodded. "I checked pay records. Bottom line, no one was called in that night."

"But I saw someone!" It probably hadn't been Holly. Maybe it had been one of the staff getting a file for a doctor.

He held up his eureka finger. "After Mark called me about the duplicate x-rays, I did some more checking on our favorite three patients." He smirked happily while he typed. Within moments, a new screen came up, displaying a black background and what looked like two lung shots, side-by-side.

"These CAT scans aren't the originals. I had to scan them into software and write a program to manipulate them. It's not perfect yet," he said apologetically.

"Mrs. O?"

"Mrs. O and the other two. All three of them have this same scan in their electronic file. All three have been charged for it."

I stared at the screen. Radar did some quick tapping. "Check it out." The picture on the left moved over the picture on the right. There were blurs in some places, and even a squiggle that must have been rogue data, but *the scans were of the same lung.*

I stared, my heart beating faster. This must have been how Dr. Dan felt when he realized the x-rays were duplicates.

He rubbed two fingers together. "You want to see the bills that go with this type of thing?"

I shook my head. MRIs and CAT scans didn't come cheaply. "Duplicate x-rays. Duplicate scans--expensive scans."

"That much loot is gonna make this scheme very worthwhile for someone."

"Duplicates of electronic files are probably easier than x-ray files. You could do it if you had the originals."

"Heh-heh. Obviously."

"But for x-rays, there has to be a limited number of people with the expertise to create duplicates. I have no idea how someone did it, but it's obvious Dr. Dan was on the right track. I'm going to volunteer in the x-ray department. Maybe I can learn enough from Holly to figure out how duplicates are made."

Radar made a cutting motion across his neck. He accompanied the motion with disgusting gagging noises. "If one of these technicians is guilty of going after the loot, do you really want to ask them nosy questions?"

"I'm being careful," I told him crossly.

He shrugged. "Watch your back. I don't think you want to end up in this hospital."

He was right about that. "Who is working today?"

"Holly. The Gerald guy works shorter shifts, all mornings or late evenings once in a while. I took a look at the department meeting notes. He does the patient scheduling. Looks like he only does x-rays if the need arises while he's on duty."

"Thanks. You told Mark and Huntington?"

He smiled. "Of course."

Without wasting any more time, I headed to x-ray.

Holly looked up from her computer when I walked in. "First patient already?" She glanced behind me.

"No, I thought I'd take you up on your offer and volunteer down here. I'm officially changing my schedule."

"Really? That's excellent! Crissa was scheduled to help down here today, but she switched her days because she is going skiing with "someone special'." Holly rolled her pretty hazel eyes. "That left me completely short, because I had set a bunch of stuff aside for her to do."

"I wonder who could be so special?" I hoped it was Dr. Fox.

Holly yawned. "Who knows? None of my business. I'm married, and I assure you my husband isn't likely to suggest I take a day off to go skiing with him."

"You look kind of tired. Did you have to work last night, and then come in this morning?" Radar would have made gagging noises at my not-so-subtle attempt to get information out of her.

"I never work nights. No way could I stay awake. I'm on late morning or afternoon shifts here, but I do work a lot of hours. I worked over at The Pavilion this morning." She yawned again.

The yawn caught me, and I was forced to join in. "Well, if we can stay awake, I can help with the x-ray development you taught me the other day."

She grinned. "I'm almost done checking the patient schedules. Let me finish and then we can get started."

I could hear Radar gagging in the back of my mind, but I asked anyway. "Do you ever have to send copies of these things to other hospitals?"

I held my breath, but my question didn't seem to raise her suspicions at all. Rather than jump up and bash my head in, she responded calmly. "Sure, all the time. I just got a call from that skier who broke his leg." She reached for a stack of x-rays and grabbed two out of the pile. "I made copies yesterday." She held them up. They were washed out and a couple looked crooked.

"Those are the ones we did?"

"Heavens no." She pointed to a machine over in the far corner. "It's a special type of photocopy. We use that whenever we get requests from another hospital rather than give up the originals. I almost forgot I was supposed to send these."

I was stunned and had a moment of hope, but the shots, from what I could see, looked nowhere near as good as originals, and not anywhere close to the quality of the ones in the patient folders I had taken to Dr. Dan. "You can make copies any old time you want?"

She shrugged. "Copies are good enough if another radiologist needs to look at them for comparison to a newer shot. I think this guy only wants them to hang on his wall."

I studied the x-ray, but it wasn't likely to be confused with an original. Even to my untrained eye, it didn't look as sharp as the ones in the patient folders. "Do they always come out that faded or can you make them better?"

"If it were important, I might darken them some, but honestly, this guy won't care. I'm sure he's after war stories."

I wished Dr. Dan were around or that I had been able to find the x-rays in his home office. Maybe the ones in the folder had been photocopies, but wouldn't he have noticed that right away? On his phone message he sounded like he thought they were duplicates because the two were sitting next to each other, not because the quality varied. One of them had been light, but not this bad.

Maybe Holly waited until she had a cooperative candidate, a patient who didn't mind waiting on the table for long periods of time. Then she could shoot a few extra prints with a different name on each one.

That theory held up right until we had to do x-rays of a patient who had taken a barium enema. It was far worse than a bedpan episode. We're talking reverse fill, clog the pipes with white smarmy stuff, try to keep it corked and take pictures.

Barium slime leaked everywhere. Dr. Burns went in and out of the x-ray room working with the patient, but he didn't eat a scrap of food either, not that there was any around.

Holly ran back and forth as much as Dr. Burns. It was all I could do to keep up with the development of the slides Holly put through the door.

We did eight shots, only one of which we had to do over. When that was finished, since I was low-woman on the totem poll, Holly had me clean the smarm off the x-ray table while she, "organized the x-rays and made sure everything was in the computer."

My love of technology took a fast right turn and went down the toilet, so to speak. I was going to demand a pay raise from Huntington.

If memory served, some of the x-rays I had given Dr. Dan were of this lovely BE procedure. But I couldn't figure out how the duplicates were done. The technician couldn't do every single shot twice because, my God, the patient wasn't likely to wait calmly, and the doctor had been present for half the procedure.

Still, I noted the patient name so that I could give it to Radar. If this patient stayed in overnight like the other suspicious ones had, Radar could find out right away.

Things got very busy when a car accident victim rolled in. He was extremely difficult to x-ray. His ribs were broken, two parts of his leg, and something didn't look right in the shoulder shot either, but with the collarbone where it was, everything looked strange. He groaned and whimpered. I was glad to be behind closed doors doing the development.

Holly wasn't fazed by all the excitement. She took pictures, and I developed.

Lunchtime was late, but quiet.

Holly was such a nice person. She could easily explain how a duplicate could be made. If I told her what I was looking for…but what if she was the person Dr. Dan had called?

Sadly, nothing I had seen today helped answer any of my questions.

Chapter 26

I hadn't seen Mark since Christmas. I never did much on New Year's anyway, but since I didn't have the week off, the holiday was even less important than usual. I was pretty much ignoring the holiday until Mark showed up after work on New Year's Eve.

"I meant to call yesterday," he mumbled. He had flowers, a big arrangement of dried wildflowers that he could almost hide behind.

"Where did you get this?" I tried without any success to get the dopey smile off my face.

He blinked and looked embarrassed. "Ah, uh."

"Did you make it?" I couldn't believe it. It didn't fit his bad-boy persona, not at all.

"My mom made it."

"Oh!" It was my turn to hide behind the flowers. I was thoroughly touched. "These are fabulous. I didn't know you had a mother." It was a stupid thing to say, but guys like Mark didn't...I mean, I couldn't really see him riding up to his mother's porch on his motorcycle and getting flowers from a delicate little lady. He was way too mysterious to have a mom.

He was also very amused. He laughed. "What is that supposed to mean?"

I shrugged. "I don't know. You and Huntington, you don't seem like..." There was no way to explain it. "You're independent. Removed from society, like you're outside of it all. A mom means, that, well, you're normal or something."

He roared and the happy sound filled my living room. "Normal? I like that." He gave me a kiss hello, but was still chuckling. "Normal," he said thoughtfully, staring down at me.

Whenever he looked at me like that, it was impossible to breathe. We were caught by each other, neither wanting to move, questions that needed to be answered and something else, the beating of passion, drawing us close again.

The flowers crinkled when he reached for me. The sound stopped him, and he took a deep breath before closing his eyes. "I don't think you're very normal. And I've met your mom."

I had no idea what that meant. "I need a vase." I stood there, not moving for a while. We watched each other.

Then, like a robot, I made my way to the sink. I dug out a white vase that had once held cut flowers and arranged the bouquet. Mark's mother had tied them well so they stayed together beautifully. "These are awesome."

"I should have called before stopping by," he said. "I could say I was in the neighborhood, but I guess the flowers make it pretty obvious I was headed here."

I smiled. "It's not a problem." Because that sounded a little too enthusiastic, I added, "I wouldn't want to give you the impression you're the *only* guy in my life, of course. I am very busy with all my other dates." I looked around. "I had best get rid of any evidence too."

He smiled. Mark was the only one I was seeing. He knew it too, assuming he had gotten over his ridiculous ideas about Huntington.

"I don't want you to think I take you for granted because I didn't call."

"It's okay." I hadn't really expected him to stop by for New Year's Eve, but I was glad he had.

"Are you free for dinner tonight? I completely forgot about New Year's. It's been a while since I dated anyone and had to pay attention to that sort of thing."

My foolish grin came back. He had just admitted we were dating!

"What's so funny?"

"Nothing. I'm an idiot." I looked up at him. He was so damn sexy. I took a deep breath. "Do you want me to fix dinner?" I had already eaten, but he didn't need to know that.

"Do you have any food?"

"Hmm." That was a problem. "Steaks would be good."

"You have steaks?"

"No, but they would be good for the occasion. I can make a chicken casserole, but that isn't very exciting." I checked the freezer. "I have some egg rolls from Happy Family Chinese."

"Good start."

"How about clam linguine?" I always had pasta and canned clams in the cupboard.

Mark said dubiously, "Goes with the egg rolls."

I pulled ingredients out of the fridge. "We could skip the egg rolls. I have some frozen garlic bread instead."

"We could go out for Chinese. Then you wouldn't have to cook at all."

I checked my watch. "New Year's is a pretty big holiday. It will be packed."

"Everywhere is crowded on New Year's Eve."

I had a sudden, brilliant idea. "You know, it might not be crowded at The Pavilion." I focused on mincing garlic with more attention than was really necessary.

"The Pavilion? Is that a restaurant? I thought it was the name of the doctor's office across from the hospital."

"Well, no it's not a restaurant. Just the doctor's office." I peeked covertly in his direction.

"I doubt the food there would be very good then."

"No, probably not." I started water boiling for the pasta. "Holly mentioned that they have an x-ray machine over there. The setup has to be more private than the one at the hospital. I'd like to take a look at the quality of the x-rays. I'd also like to see if there are any duplicates lying around in anyone's office waiting to be put to use."

"You sure know how to throw a New Year's party, don't you?" But he was grinning.

The linguine didn't take long at all. I snacked on an egg roll since I had already eaten dinner, but Mark went after the linguine and toasted garlic bread with enthusiasm.

After we ate, I got dressed in black again.

"You're going to need some proper tools," Mark told me when I came out of the bedroom dressed in a black turtleneck and black jeans. "A good flashlight that you can hook on a belt, maybe your own set of lock picks, a digital camera and some sort of pry tool like a knife."

"You have all that?" I couldn't see any of it on him. His long-sleeved t-shirt molded quite well to his body. His jeans were tight enough that he couldn't have managed to hide much there.

"In the truck." He gave me a return once-over in response to my admiring up and down inspection. "With you, it seems I always have to be prepared."

"Hmm."

He laughed softly and led the way to his SUV.

The man honestly did have a tool belt with all sorts of gadgets stashed in the back. Since he was now wearing his jacket, he took what he wanted off the belt and put it in his pockets. He supplied me with a flashlight. I had already grabbed my pocketknife, but wasn't sure what good it would do.

"There shouldn't be anyone there this time of night," he said.

It was nearing eleven o'clock on New Year's Eve. We should have plenty of private time to nose around.

The streets were almost empty because normal people were already at their destination, awaiting midnight. As we drove into the parking lot at The Pavilion, I looked over at the hospital. It appeared plenty busy.

The front door to The Pavilion faced the street and the hospital, but there were two other doors located at either side of the long glass building. Large, reflective windows made the building look high tech and modern during the day, but at night, it meant our flashlights would show up a little too easily. Mark backed up behind the building in a narrow alley that housed a large garbage bin. The only streetlight was in the front of the building.

We sat quietly in the Lexus and watched for several minutes. There didn't appear to be any roaming security. My heart was a little bird fluttering in my chest.

Even by the door farthest from the streetlight, there was enough light that if anyone looked, we would be seen.

We got out of the SUV. I stayed behind Mark where I was least visible. Hopefully he would look like a lone doctor struggling to get a key in the lock.

This lock must have been a higher quality one than those at the hospital. He worked on it, cursed lightly under his breath and pulled more picks from his pocket. "Let me know if you see anyone."

I stopped watching him and started paying more attention to the surroundings. A car passed on the street, but it was impossible to know whether anyone noticed us. No one jumped out of the shadows, but they certainly had time to do so.

It took a little doing, but Mark eventually got it. "Those aren't fun. Leaves too much damage if anyone looks closely."

We ducked inside and stayed still while the door clicked closed behind us. It was hard to tell if I was breathing loudly enough to give away our position because I couldn't hear anything over the beating of my heart. I needed more practice at this breaking and entering--or less.

A long hallway stretched across to the other side of the building and the other door that led to the outside. Offices graced each side until the middle, where a lobby branched outward like a giant belly. We made our way to the belly of the beast to make sure it was empty.

The waiting area, unlike the hallway, was open to the second floor. The windows created an atrium that would be light and airy in the daytime. Live plants, some reaching the domed ceiling, decorated the lobby. The windows creaked.

There were no storage places in the open space other than a few shelves behind the reception desk that guarded the corridor. From the waiting area, looking up, I could see part of the second floor walkway exposed. Like a giant porch, it was open on the waiting room side. The doors to the offices were all on the other side of the hallway. Anyone on the second floor could look straight down and see us.

Mark frowned. "Any idea which offices you want to look in?"

I shook my head. "There's supposedly an x-ray room, and there must be some sort of storage for the files. There are at least four doctor offices with their own waiting rooms, in addition to this lobby."

We ducked back inside the first floor hallway. "Upstairs or down?" Mark asked.

"Downstairs." There was no reason to pick one over the other, but we were already down here so starting here made sense.

The first door near where we came in was a stairwell. Mark worked the lock on the next door that faced the back of the building. "Let's start with one at the back so you can use your flashlight. I'll do the front ones."

I didn't argue. I was too pleased to find that the door he had opened had an x-ray machine! "X-ray, it is," I proclaimed happily.

"What are we looking for again?" Mark asked.

"Dr. Dan said the x-rays inside the patient folders were duplicates. That means there has to be a spare set ready for false labels. If a doctor is doing all of this on his own, he could be doing it here or at the hospital after hours."

"You're assuming that one of the doctors in this office is guilty."

"Not really. We're just looking to see what we find."

"I'll check across the hall and note any x-rays."

It was a good thing he was taking the street side because it would require more stealth. He was used to this work, and I was not. The building noises made me nervous. My hands were sweating so badly, I was in danger of dropping my flashlight.

The x-ray room contained a small darkroom, a table and a digital mammogram machine. The rest of the setup was similar to that of the hospital. I poked around hoping to find x-ray cassettes. The hospital had several lying around, but I could only find one here. It was empty, rather than storing fifty duplicate x-rays just waiting to be placed in patient folders.

There were two more x-ray cassettes in the darkroom, but they were both empty as well. The drawer with unexposed films contained only small sizes, unlike the hospital, which had several shapes and sizes and cassettes for them all.

My flashlight found a doorway behind the mammogram machine. I edged over silently, peeking through. A file cabinet, desk and some shelves waited in the shadows. I scanned the books, mostly reference titles. A bright white clock ticked on the wall, keeping time with my heartbeat.

I sidled over to the desk. There were a few x-rays piled to one side in a plastic bin marked "File." Three or four more x-rays were stacked in the center of the desk. I selected an x-ray from the bin and held it up. It looked like innards of some sort. Dr. Burns' name was written on the label, possibly in Holly's handwriting. Even if it was hers, she had told me she worked over here, so that wasn't a red flag.

I picked up another x-ray and shone my flashlight through it. The picture looked very similar to the one I had just looked at. Both were fairly light, but maybe good enough to stuff a patient file.

I placed the shots on top of each other. They were close to the same picture, but not exact. One shot was more under-exposed than the other.

So how did the person expose two shots that were exactly the same? These had obviously been done twice to correct for the under-exposure of the first shot. They weren't exact duplicates although they could be used to stuff a patient file.

I didn't hear Mark approach, because I was concentrating so hard on the x-rays. It didn't help that he wasn't using his flashlight and moved without a sound.

"Did you find something?" he asked from the doorway.

I jumped and stifled a screech. Unintentionally, I threw the x-rays at him. As weapons went, they were less than dangerous.

Mark leaned over to retrieve them from the floor.

I spent the time remembering to breathe.

He held them up. "Are these important?"

"Those two are almost duplicate shots, but not exact. I am pretty sure that when Dr. Dan said the x-rays were duplicates, he meant exact ones, not shots that had been taken twice." I arranged one on top of the other and held the flashlight on them so he could see. They didn't line up perfectly. "How did the technician get two shots exactly the same? The photocopies I saw wouldn't cut it. They were much grainier and spottier. If someone takes the shot twice, they never line up perfectly."

Mark tilted his head. "Then the shots must have been taken at the same time. Can you expose two blank films at the same time?"

My mouth formed a silent "oh." I stared down at the sheets in my hand. "They take the shot with *two* pieces of film in the cassette! Take one out, label it with the correct patient name and later label the second with the fake one. Mark, you're brilliant!" I grinned. "Did you find anything?"

"Lots of models and muscles and paperwork. Dr. Fox's name on the door; looks like he does Botox work for wrinkles and some sort of collagen enhancement. The rooms on the other side of the waiting area are storage and a lab of some kind. This office complex could easily house a couple more doctors. Check upstairs?"

I agreed. We might not find anything, but hey, the night wasn't a complete waste. Mark had helped me figure out a possible way to make duplicates. I could "stuff" a cassette during work tomorrow to see if the method was reliable. Holly wouldn't notice so long as I loaded the cassette and she put it back in the pass box after taking the shot. I could develop it and check the results. Excellent.

Upstairs, Mark let me have the office away from the street again. There were only two offices on the street side before the hallway opened up to look out over the atrium area.

I lucked out and got Dr. Evans' office, while Mark took Dr. Staples' office across the hall. Evans' office had lots of birthing pictures and calcium posters. A quick glance in the few files behind one of the desks yielded mostly paper ultrasound pictures and mammograms. There were two x-rays of small bones; kids or babies. No duplicates.

I turned to leave, but before I took two steps, I heard...glass breaking? A box falling?

I froze. Belatedly, I turned off my flashlight.

The noise rippled through the dark again, a muffled crash, more than one object bouncing or sliding.

Silence.

The sound of my breathing was too loud. Should I run? Or hide? *Where was Mark?*

Had someone come up behind him and bopped him on the head? OhmyGod.

I dithered for half a second and then ran, full-tilt, grabbing my pocketknife out of my jeans pocket as I went. In the dark, I smacked into the door leading from Dr. Evans' office to the hallway.

Cursing soundlessly, I yanked open the door. The hallway was still dark and empty. Scant light came through the atrium windows down the hall, showing...nothing.

Where was Mark?

We hadn't been separated very long.

I tried the door directly across from Dr. Evans' office, but it was locked. Dammit. I hadn't thought of the fact that all the doors would be locked. Before I could make any decisions, I heard another noise, a scraping of some sort, from within.

Was someone...*moving a body*?

No way would Mark make that much noise on his own. He was too careful.

Could I possibly pry the lock open with my pocketknife without making too much noise? Then again, making noise, lots of it, might scare whoever had attacked Mark. I could hide and lie in wait...

There was nowhere to hide unless I climbed over the rail and dangled above the first floor. I hadn't propped open the door to Dr. Evans' office so I couldn't get back in there if I wanted to.

Panicked, I jiggled the doorknob and kicked it. Heart pounding, I moved to the side. I couldn't hear footsteps coming, because every noise I heard seemed to be coming from every direction.

I scrunched down, ready to spring.

The door opened. I hit it with everything I had.

Whoosh. My shoulder hurt from the contact, but that didn't stop me. The door flew backwards, accompanied by another crash. I moved into the office, spinning and weaving. "Mark?" I raised my flashlight as a weapon. I couldn't see the enemy without light, but I was afraid to turn the flashlight on.

The person who had opened the door breathed hard, bent double. I had no choice. If Mark was hurt, I had to disable this guy quickly.

I jerked forward, my flashlight high and ready to strike.

"You," the bent form gasped, "have this thing about tackling people, don't you?"

"Mark?" My arm paused. In the scant light, I could barely discern the figure at the door.

Mark's voice came from the form. "What in the hell did you do that for?"

I peered back into the office area. "Aren't you under attack?"

"Yes!"

I raised my flashlight again. "Did you get him already?" I couldn't see anyone back there, but it was pretty dark.

There was a lot of silence from behind me. I turned around.

"Sedona, the only person attacking me is *you*."

I thought about this momentarily. "But what was all the noise I heard?"

Mark rubbed his ribs. He searched the floor until he found his flashlight. He turned it on. A filter over the top kept it dim. "Come on," he sighed. "You're crazy, you know that?"

Feeling more than a little sheepish, I followed him. We went through the small waiting area into the doctor's main office. The windows started high as part of the ceiling and then curved down to form one whole wall. "Wow. Guess he doesn't do too many naked exams in here."

"They're dark glass, but yeah, I doubt it."

On the right side, long cabinets graced the wall, but the doors stood open. Mark kept his light low, but it was enough to see packets of medications in hundreds of colors and sizes spilled onto the floor. There were envelopes and packaged inserts and vials and long cards with pills waiting to be punched out the other side. "Oh wow."

"The man has more drugs than a pharmacy. I unlocked the first cabinet, but had to pull hard and next thing I knew, the whole shelf fell out."

"That must be what I heard."

He grunted. "I was trying to get it all put back when I heard someone at the door."

He might have been glaring at me, but in the dim light, I was glad to miss that part. "We better get it stuffed back in there."

"Why would he need all this?" Mark asked. "It can't all be legal."

"There are a lot of drugs here, aren't there?"

"He could sell this on the street, I bet."

"Do you think he's greedy enough to do that?" Dr. Staple certainly acted like he needed an ethics class. Or at least a "how to be human" one.

Mark swept his arm at the mess. "Looks more like he's hoarding every damn sample in the world to me."

"But he does have nice digs here doesn't he?" I surveyed the office again. "Maybe he has a lifestyle that he wants upgraded. Maybe he needs the money from a few extra procedures."

"Look for x-rays while I try to get this back in here," Mark said. He was either losing patience for this task, or he might still be peeved at me for smacking him in the ribs with the doorknob.

I dug through the desk drawers. "He could be the one to order x-rays for the type of procedure that we saw, you know." I wasn't sure how he obtained the money for the x-rays, but there had to be a way because someone was stuffing patient files with x-rays and scans.

In the bottom drawer, I did find pictures, but not x-rays. "Ugh. Don't doctors get to see enough naked women?" Okay, so these weren't naked. They were provocative swimsuit poses--a whole book of them along with a book of paintings. They were more tasteful than say, Playboy, but still. The second book looked like one of those that a guy could shop from; a catalog of pricey artwork with women barely covered by flowing scarves.

The other bottom drawer held packets from what looked like vacation pictures.

Well, well, well. At least she was clothed. Little Miss Crissa had on a very cute skiing outfit. I could see a sign behind her that said something about Vail. The next shot was of Dr. Staple and Crissa together. He looked positively wolfish. If Crissa was so happy with Dr. Staple, why had she been flirting with Mark? And going to lunch with Dr. Fox?

Then again, knowing Dr. Staple's cold personality, I could imagine why she wasn't completely thrilled with her catch.

The second packet was a bunch of Christmas pictures, more skiing antics and a happy hot chocolate picture in some lodge. "These doctors do get around, don't they?" Dr. Fox was posed with Crissa near a Christmas tree, *and* Dr. Staple showed up at the dinner table shot sitting next to her. Were they all buddies and hung out for Christmas? Or...She couldn't be dating both of them at the same time. I mean...no way, right?

The rest of the shots were of a new car, probably belonging to Dr. Staple, since we were in his office.

Pictures of innards weren't mixed in with the personal stuff, so I redirected my search.

The patient files weren't in his office, but I found them in an interior room. Dr. Staple didn't have a break area, but he probably didn't let his employees take breaks. Some of the patient files had x-rays, but there wasn't time to look through every single one for duplicates. I checked as many as possible while Mark finished straightening the mess in the office.

"Can we take a peek in Dr. Burns' office?" I asked. "He's another internist and could order the type of x-rays we left with Dr. Dan."

"We're here; we may as well."

We found Dr. Burns' office on the other side of the building in the back. I was able to use my flashlight, but other than finding a lot of food, there was nothing suspicious. Dr. Burns' wife must have stocked the place because the break room fridge contained little packets of carrots and single servings of jello, celery sticks, and fruit. The cabinets had granola bars, rice cakes, popcorn and a host of other goodies. The cleaning crew did a good job though. I only found one stray Snickers wrapper under his desk. His file cabinets, which I assumed he supplied himself, had a Halloween feast; Snickers, Butterfingers, chocolate chip cookies, you name it. It was amazing the guy wasn't a candidate for gastric bypass. If I had all this stuff around, I wouldn't fit through the door.

Instead of pictures of women, he did have x-rays, along with diagrams, patient charts, pictures of something that might have been an ultrasound, and printouts of either brainwaves or an EKG. There were no duplicates of anything except the food.

"Front office?" I suggested.

Mark led the way, but the fourth office facing the street was empty. I stared out the front windows and nearly jumped out of my shoes when firecrackers went off with a vengeance. Ambulance sirens bleeped for a few seconds too and celebratory shouts made it through the thick windows.

"Happy New Year," Mark said. "This is exactly how I pictured spending it with you."

I faced him. He smiled down at me, looking a bit resigned.

Giggles overtook me. If anyone came in the building now, it would be filled with maniacal chuckling from the empty office.

Mark laughed too, but he was quieter about it. "You are completely crazy."

"I know. But we did learn something."

"I learned that you still like to tackle."

"Not that!" I said. "I meant about the x-rays."

"Uh-huh."

We stared at each other. "I wonder what the New Year will bring?" he asked.

I would have wondered too, but it was hard to talk. He kissed me gently. "Happy New Year," he said again.

"Okay," I sighed. I hugged him tight. "Happy New Year."

He grunted and pulled back slightly.

"Oh dear. Sorry! How are your ribs?" I eased my arm back, touching his side with only my fingertips.

He stared down at me. I stopped moving. We stayed like that, watching the fireworks, but only because they were all around us. His hand pulled me in from my waist. My own fingers wanted to do some exploring, but this was neither the time nor the place.

He kissed me again, this time letting loose some of the pent up hunger. I didn't complain. I ceased caring about the fact that we were in an office building where we didn't belong.

Mark held me very close. I hugged him back, carefully. "I better get you home." His voice was husky; his breathing uneven. My heart beat as quickly as it had when we first came in, but the reasons were entirely different now. I nodded against his chest. I barely kept from reaching up to kiss his neck.

Getting out of the building was faster and easier than getting in.

Mark took me home.

The biggest disappointment was that he left right away. I had a sneaky feeling it was because he still wasn't entirely comfortable with me working on the case, and I had made it very obvious that I was involved.

He hadn't given up on me though or he wouldn't have come over in the first place. That was excellent news because I was far from ready to give up on him.

Chapter 27

Friday I was anxious to try Mark's theory on duplicating the x-rays. Unfortunately, Holly had already loaded films for the first x-ray by the time I arrived. It would be too obvious if I ran out of the dark room and jiggled the patient so that we'd have to do the x-rays over. Luckily, there were plenty of patients on the schedule. Even better, a guy who had shot a nail into his thigh with a nail gun came into the ER.

No one paid any attention to me. It was easy to slip two blank films into the cassette instead of one. Holly wouldn't discover the film because the cassettes were only opened in the dark room. Still, I nervously counted the seconds until I heard the telltale sounds of the cassette back in the pass box.

I counted to three before snatching the box out. I removed one of the films and quickly stuffed it in the back of the drawer that held the unexposed films. Later, when I had time, I would put an arbitrary name on it and process it.

I flashed the patient name onto the remaining film and developed it.

There was only one thing wrong with my plan. I hadn't paid any attention to which x-ray I developed and which one I stashed. After developing the film, it was obvious that the x-ray was too light. Was it because I had put two pieces of film in the cassette or because I should have grabbed the x-ray in front?

I dithered back and forth and finally yanked the other one out of the drawer. Crap.

I flashed it with the correct patient name and developed it, hoping she wouldn't notice the delay.

I processed it and held it up to the light. "OhmyGod." I stared at it. It was not a picture of a thigh with a nail in it. It was a chest x-ray with ribs. I looked down at the first one I had done. Yup, it was definitely a leg.

Not only was I out of time, I had just stamped and developed a chest x-ray that I knew *nothing* about. I had also put the wrong patient name on it. "Ohshitshit." Someone had put an undeveloped x-ray in the back of the drawer just as I had, and I had grabbed the wrong one!

There was an impatient knock on the door. "Ohboy." I shut the white light off, turned on the red and stuffed the chest x-ray back into the drawer. I had no idea what else to do with it. I grabbed the not-very-dark thigh x-ray and took it out to Holly.

"There's something wrong with the thigh shot," I whispered.

"Of course there is," she snapped. "The idiot fired a nail into it."

"No, I mean with the development. It came out really light."

She grabbed the x-ray and put it on the light rack. "Let's do it again. I need to adjust the exposure. I thought I checked it."

"Oh." If the reason for the x-ray being light was because I had put two pieces of film in the cassette, we would now end up with one that was too dark. I was in way too deep here.

Should I confess?

I had already processed a hidden file in the back of the drawer. Whoever had stuck it in there was going to be mighty suspicious when they saw it already developed and stamped. It was also going to be pretty obvious that I was the one who did it because of the time/date stamp. All a person had to do was look to see who was working that shift. Then again, since I was a volunteer, maybe they would suspect Holly.

I had to tell Holly. What if some diabolical criminal thought she had found the duplicate x-rays in the back of the drawer? She'd be in danger... unless she was the guilty party.

Holly looked up to find me frozen with indecision. "Go back, and I'll pass this through. We're getting backed up in here."

I scurried back inside the darkroom and waited. I tried to decide whether to shred the chest x-ray that I had mislabeled or cut the end off where the patient name, date and time stamp showed. Of course, whoever had stashed it in the back of the drawer was going to notice it was missing or tampered with.

I pulled it out and looked at it. It was evidence. I had to keep it. But I had to find a way to get it out without anyone seeing me. Uh-huh. No problem. I could just walk out of here with a fourteen by seventeen stiff plastic x-ray up my shirt. No one would notice, not at all.

The cassette rattled when Holly put the next shot in the pass box, so I got busy.

My hands shook, but I developed it. I nearly passed out because I didn't realize I was holding my breath as I studied it, expecting it to be flawed.

The leg x-ray was perfect.

Whew! I sent a prayer heavenward and made some promises about my lax church attendance.

I gave Holly the improved x-ray and hurried back inside the dark room. By now I was so tense, dying of a stroke seemed likely. With the warning light on to keep people out, I would be dead for days before anyone got permission to come in.

I pulled open the drawer with the x-ray films. There was no way to know how many exposed, but not developed x-rays, were waiting at the back of the drawer. Did the culprit wait until a feeble person was checked into the hospital, develop a likely x-ray, slap the patient's name on it and add the charges?

With the drawer open as far as it would go, I pulled film from the back. There were *eight* extra x-rays behind the last metal divider.

Which was the one I had stashed? All eight films were the same size, fourteen by seventeen.

There was no alternative. I couldn't chance taking the wrong one. I'd have to develop all of them to find the duplicate I had stashed. No way was I leaving it for someone else to find.

Like a speed-demon, I started with the last one at the end of the drawer and developed it. I didn't know what else to do.

With the lights back on, the leg shot stared back at me. It was a little on the light side, similar to the one I had taken to Holly. The only thing wrong with it was the lack of a patient name, but I wasn't about to time-stamp any more suspect x-rays on my shift. I stared at the chest x-ray that I had mistakenly developed.

What was I going to do with these two pieces of evidence? Hiding them in the drawer was out of the question. That spot was already being used by the guilty party.

More deliveries were shoved in the pass box. There was no time to waste on my petty problems. Frantic, I stuffed the evidence back in the drawer.

Grabbing the cassettes, I did my job. The pace was unrelenting. I was rattled. Was Holly guilty of helping a doctor add charges onto bills? She worked the most often.

Two more emergency patients came in, messing up the schedule. Holly shoved through the pass boxes as fast as I could develop. Between times, she knocked and provided instructions on which size films she needed. I didn't try any more duplicates. My experiments had proved the point, but I still didn't know how to get the evidence out of the place.

Just after lunchtime, we got a break in the flow of patients. Unfortunately, Holly didn't leave for lunch. She was busy entering data, trying to catch up.

There was no way to get two x-rays out of there without her seeing me. I thought again about finding a way to warn her, in case she was innocent.

"Things got pretty crazy this morning," I started.

"It's always like that when we get emergency stuff," she said, shaking her computer mouse. "Stupid computer. Slower and dumber than concrete." While she waited for the machine to catch up to her impatient clicking, she used her free hand to jerk her hair away from her face. Blond hair, hair the same color as the person in the patient record room late at night when no one was likely to be there legitimately.

"I know I wasn't very fast, but…"

She released her hair and waved me off. "No big deal. Just turn'em and churn'em. Next time, come out right away if you're not sure about something, and we can redo it. Then we don't get so far behind." She jerked open the desk drawer and pawed through the contents. "I know I had a hair clip." She tried the other drawer. "My hair is driving me nuts."

"I'm going to run and get something to eat," I said.

"Okay." She didn't look back around.

It was past lunchtime, which made it easier to find Radar. He was coming back from lunch, headed for the stairs that led to the basement. My tummy rumbled at the thought of food, but I commanded it quiet and told Radar about the films. "Can you call Mark and Huntington and tell them?"

"Why can't you?"

"Because I need to get some food, and I can't call from x-ray. The whole world would overhear."

Radar suddenly stiffened. "Can I borrow a dollar for the coke machine?"

Huh? Cover to hide our real conversation, I supposed. I dug into my jeans pocket and extracted some loose change. He was lucky I had any. Until I worked here, all my spare change was in the bottom of my backpack. Since the incident with the lunch thief, I had started pocketing cash for emergencies.

He smiled. "Thanks."

I was dying to turn around and see who was behind us, but Attila saved me the trouble. "Sedona." Her foot tapped. "I am very disappointed that you left without notice. It's unacceptable."

I closed my eyes. There was no way I could leave Radar in the lurch. No doubt the minute Attila got rid of me, she would back him into a corner. Strangely, he didn't look too concerned.

I turned around, hoping Radar would have a chance to walk away.

"Do you think I could borrow five bucks for lunch too?" he asked instead of leaving.

"Yeah, sure." Why in the world was he asking me now? Hadn't he just come from lunch? I tried to put Attila off while I searched for more money in my pockets. "Let me get my backpack--"

"I think patients take precedence over some person without lunch money *again*." Her foot tapped so hard I thought her shoe might fly off and hit me.

"I'm on my lunch break!" I defended myself. "I talked to Ellen about switching!"

"Your leaving is unacceptable. I've contacted Ellen to make sure she puts you back on a *proper* schedule." She shot equal venom at Radar and myself before spinning around and stalking off.

Whew.

"Here." I yanked bills out of my pocket.

Radar looked at the handful of money. "That's okay. I don't need it." He slapped the change I had given him in my palm. "Thanks though."

He sauntered off down the stairs leaving me standing with a handful of money. What had just happened here?

I had no idea. Not a clue.

No time to figure it out either. I needed food, and then I had to figure out how to get the evidence into the right hands.

After grabbing a sandwich across the way, I returned to x-ray. I had hoped Holly would leave for lunch or go to the bathroom so I could sneak the x-rays down to Radar or out to my car. No luck. I stayed past five o'clock, but even when Holly finally went in the bathroom, I was too afraid of getting caught to sneak them away. I finally settled for smuggling a large manila envelope into the darkroom. I put both x-rays in it and shoved the entire packet behind the cabinet. Someone could still find it there or notice the missing x-ray, but no other options seemed viable.

I went home and immediately called Huntington. Sadly, Mark didn't answer, but Huntington was impressed with my findings.

"We need to get those x-rays out and keep them safe," he instructed.

"I know, but I'll have to break in at night to do it. Holly or someone else is always around. During the day a nurse can walk in at any time with a patient."

"Break in? Is Mark over there with you?"

I followed his non sequitur since I often associated breaking into buildings with Mark. "No, why?"

He hesitated. "He's been spending a lot of time with you lately. I thought he might be over there working on the case."

As fishing went, it was lame so I didn't respond. He could ask Mark if he wanted to know what Mark was up to. Then maybe I could get Huntington to tell *me*.

I hung up, still not sure how to rescue the errant x-rays.

Chapter 28

Sleeping in was a wonderful thing, but it tended to turn me into a total slog. I could barely raise a finger to make cookies for my sugar fix late Saturday morning.

At noon, I called Amy to check on Dr. Dan and left a message so that she would know I had called. Marge was next on the list. She informed me that Rabbit was almost back to normal and Pooh was making sure that Rabbit got enough exercise.

Before I could make any further progress, the phone rang. It was Radar and from the noise, he was calling from his cell phone.

"What's up?" I asked.

"Huntington said you know where his condo is, and I should grab you on the way over."

"We're meeting with Huntington?"

"Yeah."

"Have you found something?" Could this be the end of emptying any more bedpans.

"Not really. Mostly reporting stats."

"Okay," I agreed, a tad disappointed. "When will you be here?"

"I'm in your driveway."

I rolled my eyes in exasperation. When I opened the front door, he grinned at me from inside a black Maxima. "Are you going to come in and wait while I change?" I said into the phone.

"Sure."

He hung up and came to the door.

"You couldn't just knock?"

"I was on my way when I dialed. Last time I came to pick you up without calling, you were miffed."

"It was six in the morning!" I folded my arms and glared while he stood there looking pleased with himself. I decided to enlighten him. "Next time you're going to be polite, make sure you give me enough time to change clothes *before* you arrive. *That's* the way calling works in polite society."

He didn't lose the grin.

"For example, if you decide to ask Attila out, you'll want to call well in advance before stopping over. I don't think you want to see that woman when she isn't expecting you."

To my great satisfaction, there went the smile. "I've solved that problem."

"Oh?"

"Heh-heh."

When he gave that answer, he usually had no intention of telling me any more information. "Radar!"

He relented. "I asked to borrow money every time I saw her."

"Borrow money." It took a moment for my brain to digest that information, but then I smacked my forehead with my palm. "So that was why you asked for soda money and then handed it right back. Wow. Very, very clever." What woman would want to go out with a guy who asked for handouts? Attila wanted to be wooed and petted, not support some guy who had spent all his cash. Too bad that trick wouldn't work with pushy males. They'd think a woman wanted a free lunch--and then think the woman owed them something. "Brilliant."

He looked pleased.

Before his head got any bigger, I excused myself. "I'll be right back. There's soda in the fridge if you want one and some cookies on the counter. Help yourself."

I went into the bedroom and shut the door. I exchanged my comfy sweatpants and baggy sweatshirt for jeans and a sweater. When I got back to the living room, Radar was drinking a soda and looking at my stereo. He wore a fierce frown.

"I know it's nothing special," I said.

"You got that right. Now that Huntington is paying you for all this side work, maybe you can afford a better one."

"Side work? Are you kidding me? I drew the low-end job on this one. My regular salary on this job is *zero* so I'm only making what Huntington pays."

His eyes flicked to me for a moment, and then he smiled. "Why don't you just wear sweatpants?"

"I don't go anywhere in sweatpants," I lied. If the great minds were convening, Mark was probably going to be there. Not that Mark wasn't welcome to see me in my sweatpants. But I wasn't going to go out of my way to parade around in them. At least not this early in the relationship.

"What about grocery store trips?" Radar asked.

"Don't start. You've never been to Huntington's condo?"

He shook his head and gulped some soda.

"It's very nice. Very image-worthy. The guy at the front desk might not let us in if we wear sweatpants." I looked at him critically. "He might not like your long hair. Might call the cops."

Radar didn't look perturbed in the least. "Really? That could be interesting."

"You haven't met Michael. Interesting isn't really the right word for him and his front desk job."

The Maxima was a nice car. It seemed that every person I knew had leather seats. Technically now that Huntington had given me the Mercedes I had them too, but I certainly hadn't paid for them.

Radar didn't ask me for directions.

"I thought you hadn't been to his condo?"

"Addresses are public knowledge. Doesn't even take extra trolling for gems."

I rolled my eyes. "Trolling is an interesting way to refer to illegal hacking." In order to be useful I offered, "I can tell you his parking spots unless you want the valet to park it."

He shrugged and pointed his finger in triumph. "*That* required trolling."

Trolling for no real purpose apparently. When we arrived, Radar hopped out and handed Eloy the keys. Eloy, the valet, waved at me. "Ms. O'Hala. How are you?"

"Doing okay, and you?"

Eloy smiled and saluted.

Inside the condo's plush interior, Michael didn't let me down. He stood at attention in his little dark blue and gold uniform until he saw me with Radar, who walked with his usual slouch. His lowered head and eyes that flicked quickly around any new environment tended to make him look like a skulking criminal.

Michael just about swallowed his tongue. His lips twisted as though he were auditioning for a bitter beer commercial.

He sniffed. "I'll announce you, Mizzzzz O'Hala. Perhaps I should send a warning that you are bringing in," he waved his hand, and I swear he almost said "an undesirable" but finished with, "a friend?"

"Go with a kidnapping," I replied pleasantly, hitting the call button for the elevator without waiting for his highness to come from behind the desk. "See, my friend here has me at knife point. He's going to take me upstairs and demand that Huntington come with us or else." I batted my eyelashes.

Radar slit his eyes in my direction without removing his hands from his jacket pockets. He followed me onto the elevator without a word.

Huntington's condo was on the third floor. Mark opened the door for us and maybe it was just wishful thinking, but his eyes might have lit up when he saw me.

Since there were other people around, I tried not to sound too breathless. "Hi."

"Hey." He squeezed my shoulder for a second or two as I went past him into the condo.

Immediately, I remembered the cat. Huntington was holding the beast to keep him from running amok down the hallway. How many people could a cat like that maim before he was recaptured?

Once the door was closed, Huntington put the cat down. Of course, the furry beast sauntered right over to me, black tail high in the air, and though I couldn't detect them, claws at the ready. He sniffed my shoes. He put his paws on my shoes. "No climbing," I ordered.

Radar, thankfully, leaned over and put his hand out. The enemy decided to investigate. He left my shoes to nuzzle Radar's fingertips. "Little fellow, how've you been?" He scratched the evil kitty behind the ears. The evil kitty rolled over and grabbed at his hand, no claws.

Good. Less problems for me.

"I talked to Amy this morning," Huntington said. "Dan is out of surgery and doing well."

"I tried calling a few times today, but she didn't answer," I said. "Just how well is well?"

His blue eyes traveled away from mine, and I knew he was selecting his words carefully. With men like Huntington, used to parrying with executives, it was often more important what he didn't say. "He fades in and out of consciousness. Amy said he talked once, but not only did he not know where he was, the last thing he remembered was quitting his job--the job he had *before* they moved to Denton."

"You're not saying that as part of the plan to keep him out of danger?"

He looked as though that idea had merit, but must have changed his mind because he said, "No. He's still heavily medicated, and the doctors intend to keep him that way until they are certain he'll have no more brain swelling."

"Will he...fully recover?"

Huntington shrugged. "Technically he is well on his way. Not remembering things after a severe head injury isn't unusual. Slurring words, same thing."

We all sat silently for a few minutes. Having worked in a hospital now for several weeks, I could picture Dr. Dan. Some of the patients at Crestwood were often confused, having to be told each day who they were and where they were. "How is Amy?" I asked.

"Grateful he is doing as well as he is." Huntington ran a hand through his hair. "The doctors think his memory will gradually come back. But they have acknowledged that he could go around with a pretty large gap."

"We need a new consultant, someone like Dr. Dan, who can tell us who stands to gain from fake x-rays."

"Are you crazy?" Huntington asked. "That's precisely what put Dan where he is!"

"I know, but look, all we have found so far is some patients being charged for services that didn't happen." I turned to Radar. "There were two main doctors who ordered the false x-rays we know about. Did that hold up across your stats?"

Radar shook his head. "Not really. Dr. Burns and Dr. Staple were on most of the x-rays and scans that matched the profile. Dr. Evans and Dr. Fox were on at least three others."

"When is Dr. Dan coming back?" I asked.

Huntington glared at me. "You aren't thinking of involving him again."

"If we tell him about the scans and everything else we know, it might trigger a memory. Maybe he'll recall who he talked to or who stopped by."

"If he gets lucid enough to talk to, we can think about it," Huntington said. "But right now, that's a moot point."

Radar said, "From my statistics, Crestwood does about ten percent more x-rays and scans than other hospitals of the same size. Unless I access bank accounts, I'm not going to be able to figure out who is getting a huge influx of cash." He looked hopefully at Huntington.

Huntington shook his head. "We've done several profiles already to check debt levels of some of the players, but it hasn't proved helpful. We have to narrow it down further."

Working with these guys was going to make me an all cash person. "Speaking of looking through personal records, did you find anything out about Dr. Dan's phone calls?"

Mark said, "No. Dr. Dan called the hospital's main switchboard three different times that morning. He also called Dr. Johnson, the chief of staff, but from the length of the cell phone record, it's likely he left a message."

"Maybe he did eventually talk to him," I said, thinking about the dogs again, wondering how they acted toward Dr. Johnson. "Even though Dr. Johnson isn't active with patients, he still consults and has access to patient and hospital passwords. He's been around a while so he could be accessing and changing records."

Radar said, "Whoever is duplicating scans only needs access to the electronic data, which essentially means passwords. I've tested it. Once you're in the system, the file can be copied easily and stashed in multiple electronic patient files. The x-ray scheme is probably an older one. I would bet there are fewer fake x-rays being done now that the perp has decided to add in the more expensive scans."

I had to agree with that. "The x-rays are a huge hassle. A hard copy has to be created and then manually added to the files. It's a lot riskier and requires access to an x-ray machine at least once in a while."

Huntington nodded. "The financial records indicate this has been going on for seven to ten years and that takes organization and unfettered access to the equipment."

"Why weren't these bogus charges noticed sooner?" I asked.

"The records are good enough. An audit would produce x-rays or scans and enough paperwork to make it look like the patient existed and had been in the hospital. Whoever is doing this knows the system inside and out."

"What about asking Dr. Taylor? He already knows we're…" I rolled my eyes at the looks I was getting. "Okay, okay, no more inside consulting."

Mark said, "Dr. Dan tipped someone off to the investigation. We've got to be very careful. No one asks any questions about the x-rays, Dr. Dan or money."

Well, hell. That didn't leave any questions we could ask, did it?

Chapter 29

On Sunday I managed church and karate. I was happy and almost relaxed until Attila called me at home.

"Ellen agreed it simply wasn't fair of you to give us no notice about changing departments. We can't have volunteers making these kinds of unsupervised decisions and running all over the hospital. You've been reassigned back to the third floor."

I about blew a gasket. Had I been a real volunteer I would have quit on the spot. How *dare* this madwoman go around controlling my life? "I asked about changing over--"

"Of course, this can be straightened out," the harpy interrupted me. "We can meet with Ellen later this week so that you can *request* the change, and we can do an *official* transfer. In a few weeks or so."

I hung up on her. What was she going to do, fire me? I called Ellen and tried not to rip her head off.

She sounded harassed. Apparently, Attila had been making her life miserable. "I know you want to change positions, but I do have to get along with the supervisors in order to accommodate the various programs. She could refuse volunteer help completely, and that would make it difficult for some of the others to get their hours in."

Attila would cut off her nose to spite her face. I squeezed my cheeks to keep from shouting. "I understand your position. Since you know Attila, you can probably understand mine."

"Attila?" She choked on a laugh. Then after a minute, she giggled harder. "Yes, I understand. I'll take the paperwork to her tomorrow morning and officially transfer you downstairs next week."

"How about by Thursday," I proposed. I didn't want to make it hard on Ellen, but I needed to be in x-ray. I also didn't intend to be a volunteer for very long so it was difficult for me to care about appeasing Attila.

She sighed. "I'll submit it. She might not sign it though."

Through gritted teeth I said, "Then please tell her I'm taking Thursday and Friday off." I'd report to x-ray and not clock in. I didn't care if I was given credit for the hours.

Who would have thought being a volunteer would be such a hassle???

* * *

Monday morning, I was still angry. It bugged me to no end to have to play Attila's game. It was bad enough to be a volunteer; it stunk to be a poorly treated one and not be able to do much about it. Sadly, I had to play the game long enough to work the case.

On my way to the nurses' station, I ran into Paul as he was passing out medications. "Mrs. Johanna didn't make it through the morning," he said morosely, pursing his sorry fish lips together. "Poor thing was so old. Door is closed, don't take in a breakfast tray. She needs to be taken downstairs, but I've got the med cart. You'll have to do it." He slogged away, the drug cart in front of him.

"What do you mean, downstairs?"

He stopped and looked over his shoulder. "You need to wheel her down to the morgue."

I was speechless for a full minute. "You want me to *what*?" Why, when I worked for Huntington, did I find myself doing jobs that were way beyond the call of duty?

"It's no big deal, kid. She's dead."

That was precisely the problem.

"We need to get her down there before the undertaker gets here. Her nephew called after the doctor notified the family. I told the nephew he should go to the funeral home rather than here. Trust me, it can be bad news when the family members get emotional. It's much better if the funeral home can handle things. I can't leave the med cart unattended. You can wait in the hallway for the undertaker or roll her into the morgue."

Now there was a choice or two. Gosh. Empowerment at last.

I procrastinated. My lunch was safer in my backpack, but the soup really should be refrigerated. Maybe if I tucked it way back in the vegetable bin, the thief wouldn't find it. If I were working in x-ray, as I had planned, this wouldn't have been much of a problem. Dr. Burn's wasn't down there everyday.

My jacket had to be hung just so. There were call lights blinking too; the patients still alive were more important, right? My shoe was untied, or close enough.

Fifteen minutes later, there was still no way out and no one in sight to help.

I walked slowly down the hall to three-oh-one. The door was closed. I looked up and down the hallway. No aides, no nurses, nobody. Wait, there was fish-face! Surely he was done with meds by now. "Paul--" He ducked inside a patient room without even acknowledging my call.

"Loser," I muttered. At least the door was well-oiled, and it didn't creak when I opened it.

Inside, Mrs. Johanna was covered with a sheet and thankfully someone had already put her on the wheeled bed. I checked the hallway again for help. Mornings were one of the busiest times; doctors making rounds, changing orders, meds being given, patients needing help brushing their teeth and hair.

Maybe I should go looking for someone. Crissa would help. Well, she hadn't been all that friendly since Mark left her side to come after me in the parking lot. But trying to wheel one of these beds by myself was not a good idea. What if I lost control of the bed?

Ohboy. I checked the hallway again. I definitely needed help, but how long could I stand here waiting like an idiot with…with…that…sheesh.

I swallowed hard and got moving.

It was probably impolite to wheel her quickly, but I did anyway. I tried not to look desperate or afraid, but my face felt frozen into a grimace. My eyes started burning because I didn't want to blink.

My Indian grandmother would probably have some rule against doing this. I would ask Dad. I could quote the rule next time this happened. I would decline based on religious reasons, even though both Mom and Dad were Catholic.

I refused to look at the bed. The floors might seem smooth, but that was only until you had to cart someone across them, especially a dead someone. Maybe I should drag the bed behind me so that not even my peripheral vision caught glimpses of poor Mrs. Johanna. No. Definitely not. I didn't want the body behind me either. If it sat up suddenly, I wanted to be the first to know about it.

Everything jiggled getting in the elevator, but it was worse being alone inside with…the body. What was that *smell?*

I stopped breathing. Then I wouldn't have to make a guess.

The elevator jerked, which made…the body…move.

At last, the doors slid open. The long hallway to the morgue was empty and quiet.

I gulped and forged ahead.

At the door to the ice room, I fidgeted. If the hospital were larger, there would be a pathologist to do autopsies and maybe they would come and get…bodies. As it was, anyone could go in the ice room. The security was abysmal. The room should definitely be locked, because then special personnel would be required to deliver things, right? They couldn't just send *me* down here.

What if someone was inside the ice room? Like…a bunch of séance weirdos?

"Would never happen twice," I muttered to myself.

The door opened easily. Damn. I had been hoping it would stick shut. Not that it would help really. I'd still be standing here with…her.

The inside of the morgue was completely dark. Like the other rooms in the basement there were no windows to the outside. The light from the hallway was fluorescent and not very reflective or effective in beating back the darkness.

I peered anxiously into the three-foot area and debated whether to push the bed in and run or look for a light and then drag the bed in after. Of course, Mrs. Johanna was supposed to go in the freezer, not just the room, so that meant I had to go all the way in.

I knew one thing. No way was I going in there with the lights off.

I felt along the wall for a light switch. If any substance at all, and I mean the slightest hint of goo touched my hand, that was it, I would be gone. I'd make tracks so fast, not even a supersonic ghost could catch me.

The lights took a moment to kick on even after I flipped the switch. From the doorway, I inspected the room apprehensively. No one was there. The door to the walk-in waited at the far end. There were no other carts, empty or otherwise. Whew.

A desk and a couple of cabinets were backed against the far wall. I sniffed a bit, trying not to breathe too deeply. As far as I could tell, the room didn't smell bad. Nothing was rotting that shouldn't be.

I carefully pushed Mrs. Johanna all the way in. The door clicked shut behind me. Before I could turn around, a body slammed against me, pushing my face into the nearby cabinet.

Already a nervous wreck, I let loose a scream designed to knock out walls.

Mark had been known to sneak up on me, but this was no friendly bear hug. Maybe I hadn't been as clever as I thought by working in x-ray. Maybe someone missed the chest x-ray that should have been in the back of the drawer in the development room.

My face was mashed against the cabinets. I tried to scream again. "MMMGH!" I kicked backwards and connected with something hard. My face was suddenly free. I kicked again, missed, and tried to squeeze away. If I was going to die, it was not going to be in a room for corpses.

I forced my body around and caught a glimpse of a blond head before a hand pushed my chin back into the cabinets. Metal pieces dug into my cheek, my arm and my ribs. My ear was assaulted by a screaming lunatic. "I've heard about you people! I know what you do!"

From the corner of one eye I saw the blond head lean down to grab, of all things, a bat. Blondie couldn't keep me pinned while leaning over.

"Aaaaagh!!" I twisted, squished myself against the cabinets even harder, and squirmed free. I ran around the side of the gurney.

Had this very bat been used to bash in Dr. Dan's head?

I stared in fascination at the bat, inspecting it for blood. It took me a few seconds of hard breathing and relative freedom to realize that the person holding the weapon was a he. A very short he. My assailant had probably been given the bat as a graduation present--from little league.

"Uh..." How in the hell had a kid gotten to Dr. Dan? How could a little league kid be involved in falsifying hospital records? Was he some kind of egomaniac hacker doing it for fun?

"You stop right now!" he bellowed. "I won't let you do it!"

Did crazy Mr. Silva have a relative visiting? The kid didn't look old enough to drive a car. He did look determined to score a few home runs however, and he had obviously decided my face was the ball. The only thing saving me was the bed with Mrs. Johanna. It was really, really disrespectful to keep shoving it around to keep the kid at bay.

He swung his bat wildly, walking first one way and then the other as we faced off over poor Mrs. Johanna.

"You're crazy, you're all crazy and I won't have you talking to her!" he screamed at me.

He was calling *me* crazy? "Listen kid--"

The door to the room burst open. Radar ran in, emitting a full-fledged rebel yell. It echoed weirdly across the walls. The only difference between him and the kid was that he was carrying a long pipe instead of a bat.

The kid now had a new, relatively unprotected target. He charged. "Aaarrraaaagh!"

Radar looked like he was expecting to be charged. He stepped nimbly out of the way and stuck out his foot.

Bat-man hit the wall, bounced and fell backwards on his butt with a bone-jarring crunch, dropping his bat in the process. Radar kicked it out of the way. I considered coming out from behind the gurney.

The kid grabbed Radar's leg and held on for dear life. "Leave her alone! You leave my aunt alone! She doesn't want a séance. I asked her. I came here and asked her, and she said she wasn't afraid, and we don't need a séance!"

I blinked. "Aunt?" My voice was little more than a croak.

Radar looked from me to the kid to the gurney. Maybe since he hadn't been mashed up against the cabinet and chased around by bat-man, he was quicker on the uptake. "Your aunt? She the lady on the bed?"

The kid sobbed, "Le...le..ave her alone!"

"Séance?" I rubbed my sore cheek while I tried to find words. "Listen, kid. We don't do séances."

"Ye..yes, you do!" He didn't release his death grip on Radar's leg.

"No," I repeated. "I do not. That lady was fired. I don't do séances. I don't even do bodies. I'm just a volunteer working here, and trust me, this will be the last visit I make to this room."

Something in my voice must have reached him, probably my honest disgust. He gazed up at me where I still stood on the other side of his aunt. Tears dripped down his face. Despite the fact that he had attacked me, I felt sorry for him. "I'm sorry about your aunt," I said softly.

Radar asked, "Someone actually did a *séance* down here? Are you joking?"

"It...it was in the paper," the kid hiccuped. "My aunt wants a nice little funeral. She said *no way* did she think a séance was cool. But the guys at school showed me the newspaper, and said we should sneak in and find out what she was going to say after she died."

I really wanted to scream again.

Radar said, "I gotta get a normal job."

He needed a normal job? What about me? "How did you know I needed help?"

Radar used the pipe in his hand to point at the edge of the ceiling. I followed his aim to the air vents.

"That's a pretty hefty scream you got there. Took me a while to figure out where it was coming from. I tried the janitor closet first, and there are some other locked doors down here."

I owed him one. Or two. "Well, thanks."

We both stared down at the kid. He was probably all of ten years old.

"How did you get here?" I asked the kid.

"The bus. My mom told me about my aunt this morning. I got on the downtown line. I had to walk a ways."

"Looks like things are under control," Radar said.

"Radar!"

But he didn't wait. He left me standing there with a dead body and a very unhappy kid.

"Ohboy." I didn't have a lot of experience with sympathy or kids. I pushed my feet forward, but kept an eye on the bat.

Patting him on the head didn't seem to have any positive effect at all.

I finally sat on the floor next to him. Neither of us said a word, but gradually the sobs subsided. In the end, he didn't seem to mind my awkward hug, and he let me help him up.

I used Radar's cell phone to call his mom, and then waited with him until she arrived.

By the time the ordeal was over, and I made it back upstairs, I was ready to quit. This hospital work was too much for one person to take.

Crissa cornered me. "Sedona, what happened? I heard some kid was in the room and made a big scene, and you had to call his mother. Is the kid okay?"

I glared at her. "No more bodies," I hissed. "Next time you can stack'em up in the corridor for all I care. I am *not* taking anyone else down there!" I went into the break room muttering about volunteer work. I dug money out for a soda. I needed sugar. Caffeine. Hell, food. "Want to keep volunteers happy you shouldn't be asking them to go around crating..." My lunch was gone. It wasn't even noon and my bag was gone.

"AEIII!" I yelled softly.

Crissa peered into the break room. "Sedona?"

"Who was in here? Who?" I tried to keep my shrieking down.

"Everyone," she said. "Why?"

I slammed the fridge door. "That's it. I am taking the rest of the day off. That is just it." I walked away. "Work in a hospital. Nice caring place. Nothing but a loony bin. A complete loony bin." I heard Crissa call after me, but I ignored her. "Can't eat your own lunch. Can't tell anyone you're pregnant. It's a hospital. They're supposed to like people and babies, but no, people have to go around wearing flag outfits and lying all the time."

I kept right on walking until I was outside. I needed the fresh air. I needed a life.

Chapter 30

Generally speaking, I held a grudge, even an entirely unfocused one, for quite some time. It's possible that such grudges made me a little unreasonable. The afternoon off helped marginally, but someone must have tattled about the morgue episode because Huntington called to check on me. His call would have helped except he was laughing so hard, his insincere concern only made me angrier. Mark didn't laugh, but he didn't come over to console me in person. That annoyed me too, even if we weren't far enough along in the relationship for me to feel that way.

Instead of calming down overnight, I became further enraged Tuesday morning, because I still had to report for floor work rather than to the x-ray department. Until the transfer went through, I was stuck. "Don't even get paid, and she doesn't even *like* me, but she insists I work on her precious floor." I packed my lunch very carefully. "Who put this in here?" I mimicked. "A violation to label your lunch to protect it!"

Fine. I would go with plan B even though I had to think very hard about how to get the dead snake in my lunch bag without it ruining my real meal. Originally I had planned to make a casserole with chopped up pieces of the thing and then label it snake meat. Of course the perpetrator wouldn't believe it until they tasted it.

Despite my diabolic plan, I had never gotten around to cooking said casserole, and now I was out of time.

Dealing with the stupid snake was a bit unnerving and a lot disgusting, but there was no alternative. War had been declared. I yanked the coffee can containing the snake out of the freezer. The evil snake was frozen solid, neatly coiled like a spring in the bottom of the can. I poked at it to make sure it didn't move.

Maybe, after this, Dr. Burns would think twice about grabbing food that didn't belong to him. After he got a load of this lunch he might stop eating the patients' food too.

I put my real casserole in plastic wrap, pulling the wrap tight. I set the whole thing in a container and then used tongs to put the snake on top of the food. Even Dr. Burns had to notice a snake, didn't he? After this I could just label my container, "snake meat casserole."

"Steal *my* lunch, will you?" I packed everything into the brown bag and stopped at McDonald's for breakfast. "I think I'll eat out lunch too. Forget the casserole." The bag sitting on the passenger seat watched me. Dead snake or not, I was not going to be able to unwrap the casserole and eat it. I shrugged. If the thief were caught, it would be worth it.

I put the lunch in the fridge and got started. I was barely finished with breakfast trays when Radar found me. "Got a minute?"

"Not really, but I'm in trouble most of the time anyway." I followed him back to his lab, glad for the respite.

"Check this out." He did his miracle typing and pulled up a hospital bill.

I stared at it. Tilting my head, I looked at it again. The pattern was familiar. X-rays, overnight visit, fluids. "Mrs. Johanna." The name was familiar. "Hey, she's--" I gulped, "The lady who died yesterday!"

He nodded. "That's the one. Look at the date."

I looked. The end date was this morning, not yesterday. I was pretty darn sure she hadn't gotten x-rays yesterday. Of course they could have been billed late. "Few extra charges."

"Looks that way."

"Did you call--"

"Huntington thought it was pretty interesting too. I can tell who entered the charges, but I'm positive that whoever is doing this has the passwords for all the doctors. Someone is entering the hospital tests under different doctor names. Then they must bill the insurance company. Maybe the insurance companies don't notice they are paying one particular doctor rather than the various ones who ordered the tests on the hospital records."

"I'll stop by x-ray to make sure Mrs. Johanna wasn't down there the day before or something."

"I don't think you want to be asking too many questions over there." He made his mock cutting motion across his neck, complete with gagging.

He had a point, but it was worth stopping in the x-ray department on the way back upstairs in case I thought of a clever way to ask questions. Besides, it was on the way. The long way, but in the same building, just a different floor.

Holly didn't have much time for me. Since I wasn't there to help her, I had to rush my questions. "Did you hear about Mrs. Johanna?"

Holly grinned. "I heard you chased some kid around with her in a gurney. You do get around, don't you?"

"That's not what happened," I grumbled. "Did you do her x-rays?"

"What x-rays?"

"I mean," I stumbled. "It's weird how one day you're doing x-rays on a person and then…poof."

She shrugged. "That's how it happens."

Before I could think of a better way to ask the question, a patient arrived. With Holly buzzing around, I couldn't peek at the schedule to see if Mrs. Johanna had come down at all in the past week.

With a sigh, I made my way back upstairs. No doubt there were bedpans to change and beds to make.

I was halfway to the nurses' station to check call lights when someone screamed.   At first I assumed it was some kind of medical emergency, but the screaming was ongoing and coming from the nurses' station. "What now?" People practically died around here, and no one screamed.

In fact they did die and no one made a fuss.

Screaming, on the other hand, got more attention than a "code blue." Patients who were able aimed their walkers toward the nurses' station. What would they do when they got there? Not a one of them moved faster than a "granny shuffle."

I beat them by a mile.

Attila was the focus of attention. She stood in front of the refrigerator screaming her head off. Truthfully I had already completely forgotten about the snake in my lunch bag.

My wonderful casserole was smeared across the wall and the floor. The snake was also lying in the general vicinity.

I, along with half the floor, gaped at Attila. No one had taken a step into the room after arriving. "It's not moving," I said to no one in particular.

Attila stopped screeching, but her mouth opened and closed as though she was still trying.

Since I knew the snake was dead, I took a deep breath and stepped over the threshold. I reached her and said, "It must be dead. Who could have put that in your lunch?"

I had no way to know what would happen when the thief saw the snake, but I had honestly believed the thief was Dr. Burns. I assumed he would either devour the thing without noticing or start paying more attention to what he stole in the future. He was so calm under all conditions, I hadn't worried about him panicking.

Unfortunately for Attila, I had been wrong in my assumptions. She stood there with a glassy stare, shaking from head to toe.

"It's going to be okay," I said, moving a chair between her and the snake.

She whimpered.

One thing for sure, Dr. Burns was indeed calm. He came through the mob blocking the doorway, knelt over the snake and prodded it with a pencil. "It's dead. People usually skin these before eating them."

"Unhealthy!" Attila finally gasped out. "It's bad enough that people eat junk food in my hospital, but that--"

From behind me, Crissa whispered, "My God, you eat *snakes*. I wonder what he'll think of that." I turned to find her green eyes staring at me gleefully. "I guess we'll find out, and then we'll see how easy it is for you to steal dates from other people!" She whirled around, leaving me with my mouth open and my hands hanging in midair.

How did Crissa know it was my lunch...oh yeah. She had seen me kill the "pet" and must have put two and two together.

From behind me, Attila demanded, *"Is that your lunch?"*

I turned to find her finger pointing at me. I pretended to inspect the casserole that was smeared all over the wall. "Well, it's kind of hard to say." Then, I shook my head. "No, it can't be. I planned to eat lunch out today. I think it was Crissa's lunch." Try that one on for size. Accuse me of stealing a date, and get me in trouble? Hah!

Attila didn't look convinced.

I shrugged. "I'm sure yours is probably still in the fridge, right?" I started for the fridge.

Attila blocked me. "There is no excuse for that kind of food to be in this hospital! We're professionals. We should eat healthy, low salt, low fat, high protein, low carbs! We need to set an example." She flexed her arms and clenched her fists, punctuating her words like a mantra. "I won't have unhealthy eating going on during my shifts!"

Looking at the fanatic gleam in her eye, I was pretty sure she wasn't referring to just the snake. Given her passion, I bet she regularly stole every lunch she could get her hands on, deemed it unhealthy for one reason or another, and ate it herself to "save" the rest of us.

"Snake is very low in fat, I would think," Dr. Burns commented. "Can't imagine it would cause health problems unless a person accidentally choked on a bone. It's all protein."

It took a lot of will power to keep a grin off my face and to keep myself from hugging Dr. Burns for his timely pronouncement. Before I lost my composure completely, I shrugged, blinked innocently, and scooted out of the break room to help reassure patients and visitors that all was well.

No telling what happened to the snake or the mess. Since I had cleaned up after the viper once, someone else could do it this time.

Chapter 31

The longer the evidence was left in the x-ray development room, the more danger I was in. Mark must have felt that way as well because he stopped by my place on Tuesday night, all dressed in black. "I suppose if I ask where you put the x-rays you'll insist on coming along?"

I smiled. "Of course. It will be a lot faster for us to get in and out together." I frowned as another thought occurred to me. "There were some other x-rays in that drawer that hadn't been developed. It might be a good idea to see what is on them."

"You want to develop them?"

Given the amount of hospital personnel around, it probably wasn't a good idea. "If I can get all the x-rays into a cassette, we can take them across the street and develop them at The Pavilion. There isn't likely to be anyone there if we go late enough."

"Have you eaten?"

I shook my head.

"Good. I brought steaks."

He grilled while I tossed a salad from the greens he had also brought. With the garlic bread from my freezer, we had the makings for a feast.

While we ate, we devised a plan. "The regular shifts end at eleven," I told him. "If it's busy, there might be a part-time person there."

"Is it usually busy at that time?"

"Not unless emergencies come in. None of the patients get scheduled after about five o'clock. Holly's shift ends at seven. Then it's an on-call person."

"How certain are you that those other films have something on them?"

"I'm not. I only know there were a few stuck in the very back where they weren't likely to be noticed. The one I pulled out had been exposed but not developed and stamped with a name."

"Why would someone leave them there where any of the x-ray techs could find them?"

The steak Mark had grilled was delicious. I took my time savoring a bite before answering. "The technicians know exactly where each sized x-ray is located. No one hunts through the drawer because nothing is supposed to be back there. It's always dim when the drawer is opened because only the red light is activated. Even if someone stumbled across them and developed them by mistake, they wouldn't know what to make of it."

We finished eating and did the dishes. I made coffee for Mark and tea for myself. My nerves were always strung tight with Mark around. I didn't really need the caffeine.

It was barely ten o'clock, but I changed into dark clothing in preparation. We had two hours to kill. Every time I caught Mark's eyes I had this great idea of how to spend the time. Of course, there would have been no need to put my midnight outfit on if that were the case.

Mark may have been thinking the same thing. His eyes raked over me as I stood there in my tight silk sweater and black jeans. "I should have rented a movie," he said.

"We could go out to see one." My voice squeaked at the end. He looked...dangerous, staring at me as if I were dessert.

"That's a good idea." He jerked up from the chair and grabbed his jacket. "We probably look like hoodlums both dressed in black."

I didn't point out that he always looked like a hoodlum and that was part of the attraction. I got my leather jacket and followed him out to the SUV. He tucked me in, but we were both thinking too hard.

Instead of closing the door after holding it open for me, he reached in and grabbed my chin. I think he meant for it to be a quick kiss, but as soon as he touched me, I melted. My lips were as soft as the rest of me, and it was too much of an invitation. He kissed me hungrily. I wanted to taste him too, and I wanted to be closer. I put my arms around his neck, lost my balance and slid down from the seat across his hard body while our tongues tangled. He growled something unintelligible before picking me up unceremoniously and depositing me back in the SUV. "I *really* wish we did not have to do this tonight."

It was the last thing he said until we pulled up to the theater, but I finally understood what he meant about the job interfering with the romance.

Mark muttered something about "comedy" and got tickets.

We took seats in the back. He put his hand on my thigh.

I jumped.

He chuckled low. From the flickering illumination coming from the picture screen, I could see he was pleased. I put my hand on his, and he twined his fingers through mine. He glanced over at me, but I wasn't prepared to meet his eyes.

By the time we left, I had impressions of people moving across the screen, some shooting and a couple of explosions, but if there was a plot, I missed it.

With a real purpose at last, I was calmer and focused. The hospital was familiar territory, and I had done this before, at least most of it. We left our jackets by the escape door in the basement so we wouldn't look like what we were--thieves roaming the hallways about to grab something and run.

Dark shadows, we crept up the stairwell and through the corridor to the x-ray room. The outer door was locked, but once inside, the door to the dark room wasn't. We ducked inside and locked the door.

There were eight films in the back drawer. I transferred them to a cassette with only the red light to illuminate my movements.

Mark touched my arm. "If someone notices these are gone, it could be dangerous for you."

I hesitated. "Can we afford to leave them here? Right now only one is missing; the one I accidentally developed. Maybe it won't be noticed."

He thought about it and then shook his head. "Someone knows we're looking or Dr. Dan wouldn't have been hit. We need the evidence."

"Okay, then." I sealed the cassette and reached behind the cabinet to get the one I had already developed. The envelope was right where I left it. "Let's go."

He nodded, checked the outer room and waved me after him out into the hallway.

We were back in the SUV before I knew it.

"Warm and cozy?" he asked with a lazy grin.

"I'm getting good at this, aren't I?"

He grazed my chin with his fist. "Don't get cocky or I'll make you pick the lock on the next door."

I grinned. Unbelievably, I was having fun. I was safe with Mark, and he was right. He was doing most of the work, although I suppose I was just as culpable. All I had to do was follow.

Oh, if only it were always so easy.

Chapter 32

Instead of going through the difficult side door, Mark had obtained a key for the front entrance at The Pavilion. It took a mere second for him to unlock the door. We looked like we belonged there.

I felt quite clever about it until we got inside. The front of the building was more of a greenhouse than a building; the sloping cascade of glass partitions went above the first floor where it met the building. The second story rose above us. The glass was tinted, but we were still very exposed.

Enough light came from outside that flashlights weren't necessary; not that we would have risked it in the open anyway. The long reception desk was elevated a bit, directly centered so that the hallway and offices branched to both the left and right. It would be more difficult for someone to see us once we were behind the desk and under the cover of the overlook from the second floor. Having been on the second floor, I knew the railing area above allowed people to look down over our current position.

We hadn't taken two steps forward when a clicking noise, much like a door closing softly, broke the quiet. Both of us froze.

Listening hard, we heard it again; a door opened and closed. I tried to figure out where it came from, but only had a vague impression that it was to our left. The lovely atrium caused echoes.

Mark reached for my hand. Silently, we moved behind a group of tall potted plants. "Stay here," he murmured against my ear. He took the x-ray cassette from me and set it down in the potted plant. Our backs were against the window, making me feel as though we could easily be spotted from the outside.

Mark closed my fingers around the butt of cold steel. I moved my other hand up to help hold the gun. "Okay?" he whispered.

I nodded without looking directly at him. My eyes were too busy hunting the darkness. Someone was out there.

It was too easy to hear things; the wind, the creaking building, my own breathing. The sound of hissing air from the heat vents was relentless. The more I tried to filter it out, the less I could hear.

Mark disappeared down the hallway without making a sound. The obvious place to check was the x-ray room. There were no lights on upstairs. There were offices on the other side of the hallway and offices downstairs, but I couldn't tell whether any of those lights might be on. Whoever was in the building was too quiet to be a legitimate presence.

I stayed behind the potted plant, watched the entrance hall and listened myself into a symphony of false alarms.

Thankfully, no one appeared. And even if someone had, I couldn't shoot into the hallway. It could be Mark coming back.

But what if someone crept up on Mark?

He had another gun. He'd be okay. And I knew to stay put so that Mark didn't accidentally shoot me.

I braced myself, pushing down into that place where the hissing of air and the errant creaking of the building didn't exist. I was Mark's best protection. If anyone came through the front door or chased after him, I had to stop them.

The seconds were interminable. The scattered moonlight broke into a dark shape on the second floor. It was soundless, but human.

Was it Mark?

The ghostly presence drifted across the second level atrium, hovering at the railing. He stopped, but reached over the railing to the area below. In the milky light I saw the gun. It was aimed down, but not at me.

My focus shifted back to the hallway. Mark, his stride already familiar and dear to me, appeared behind the desk from the left side of the hallway. Before I could open my mouth to warn him, he moved confidently into the open, approaching my hiding place.

My arms moved up. The guy must have known Mark was going to walk out. He already had his gun aimed.

My scream of, "*down,*" merged with the shot fired from upstairs and that of my own gun. The partition shattered.

I fired again and kept right on firing without any regard to whether or not I hit him. I stayed down and punched holes through the railing partition.

After four shots, maybe five, I paused. The survivor in me knew I might need more bullets.

Chapter 33

Mark was furious. I never heard the side door to the building slam, although later, Mark said he had heard the gunman run down the stairs and slam the door on the way out.

Though my eyes were glued to the second floor, I never saw the gunman move. I was dimly aware of Mark reaching my side. I heard nothing except the ringing in my ears. There was no movement on the second floor.

We must have retreated quickly, but I didn't remember going back to Mark's SUV. There were no other vehicles in the parking lot, but there hadn't been any there when we arrived either.

By the time we got home, Mark was almost capable of yelling, but he didn't get out of the truck. His jaw clenched so tight it hurt mine to look at him. He finally broke the silence. "I should have made you go back in the truck."

"I am not sure if I hit the guy because I aimed for the part of his body behind the gun in hopes I'd hit his gun and mess up his shot." My ears hadn't stopped ringing. "It wasn't Holly. Or Dr. Evans. It was definitely a man. He had on dark clothes. I couldn't see anything else." It wasn't likely Dr. Burns, because he was bald and round from all the food that he tended to nab, but whoever it was had been wearing a jacket. That added enough bulk that it could have been anyone.

Mark got out and was at the passenger door before I did more than open it. He slammed it shut behind me and took my arm. I knew he wasn't trying to propel me forward, but he wanted me inside, behind a locked door with the illusion of safety.

When the front door was behind us, he didn't let go of my arm. He grabbed the other one and just held on. He started to say something, changed his mind and tried again. "You--"

He pulled me to him at the same time that I burrowed my head in his shoulder. He held me for a long time before he kissed me.

I slid backwards toward the couch while he unzipped my jacket. His hands didn't wander; they were on a more systematic mission to check every inch to make certain I was intact.

I don't know how we ended up in the bedroom because the walls, the floor, and the entire house disappeared.

If Mark's intent was to tell me that I belonged to him, to brand me with memories instead of gunshots, he succeeded. I had a few messages of my own, and I'm pretty sure he got the point. Both of us had a lot to say, and we said it more than a few times without ever uttering a word.

Chapter 34

Going into work the next morning was pretty much the last thing I wanted to do, but since Mark left very, very early, there was no good excuse to sleep in. Maybe it was the ringing in my ears and the adrenaline left over from the midnight excursion that made me feel like I was plugged into a light socket, but honestly, I think it was Mark.

On top of the crazy emotions running through me, I was afraid of the hospital. There would be no avoiding the doctors, suspect or no. Whoever had been in The Pavilion may have seen more of me than I saw of him. Both Dr. Staple and Dr. Burns' offices were on the second floor of The Pavilion. They had legitimate reasons to be there. Of course, the x-ray equipment was on the first floor, so that didn't really implicate either one of them, and whoever had been in the building had been sneaking around, not doing paperwork upstairs in an office.

I was afraid of Holly, Attila, cats, dogs and definitely snakes. At least I was off the official schedule. That allowed me to show up after ten when Holly's shift started.

X-ray was already busy. It was easy to slide into the dark room and stay there, safe and sound. I steadily developed x-rays without interruption, until someone knocked at the door. I closed the drawers, made sure the films were all properly covered and opened it.

"Do you know where the storage room is?" Holly asked breathlessly. "Attila called down and said Crissa isn't answering her page. She needs some older x-rays for Dr. Staple. I'm too backed up to go." She tilted her head toward Dr. Burns and Dr. Fox. Burns was lost in an x-ray, staring at it like a bowl of candy.

Dr. Fox said, "Let's do an MRI first."

It had to be bad news when more than one doctor was consulted.

"Yes," I said, "I know where the storage files are kept."

"Great. Finish this last set I'm about to put in and then run down and look for them, okay? I'll leave the key to the storage room on my desk along with the patient name and info."

"Sure, no problem." I ducked back in, did the development and after letting Holly check them to make sure they were okay, I grabbed the key and piece of paper with the patient info off of her desk. The doctors were either gone or in the other room with the patient.

Normally I would have stopped in to give Radar an update, but Holly wouldn't have sent me unless there was a rush, so I skipped the visit.

The storage room light was on, but since I hated walking into dark rooms I was glad--at least until the door clanged shut behind me.

As soon as it did, the adrenaline from the previous night returned. Long rows of files towered over me. All I could think of was how easy it would be for Dr. Staple to wait behind any one of them.

I fidgeted first on one foot, then the other. The fluorescent lights hummed. They weren't ticking though. I think that meant they had been on a while. Or maybe it meant they had just been turned on.

I had no idea how common it was to retrieve x-rays. Did Dr. Staple really need them?

I looked down at the patient name and year. The first thing I noticed was that it was the same year of the other patient records Mark and I had pulled.

Coincidence. Had to be. I took a deep breath and looked back at the aisles going off in either direction. How much trouble would I get in if I didn't return with the file? Maybe I should get Radar to help me look.

I took a step forward, but then backed right up, keeping my eyes on the rows. There was no sound of breathing so there was no way anyone was down here with me.

My hand was on the doorknob when I heard it; the sound of something brushing against the files.

I turned the knob, not making any noise at all.

Dr. Fox stepped out of the aisle. If he hadn't had a scalpel in his hand, that shiny surface that cuts into a person's flesh, I might have said hello and walked away. Even with the knife, I momentarily tried to convince myself that he was just down here on his own innocent file-finding mission.

Nope. That scalpel was definitely bad news. He held it like a prized diamond, letting the light glint off the very sharp surface.

"Looking for these?" He waved a folder full of x-rays. "I heard you were coming down this way. I pulled them for you."

I looked down at the patient name, but it was pointless. A lot of things crashed into my head at the same time, but the biggest questions of all were still unanswered. "Why did you order extra x-rays to pad your earnings? And how did you get the money from them?" Dr. Fox was a surgeon. He only made money if he performed surgery.

"You're not as smart as you think, are you? Neither was Dan." He laughed. "All I needed was a few tests to show surgery was necessary to back up my billing records. I can't believe Hernandez didn't think of that until I was standing in front of him. I thought he'd already guessed."

My mouth formed a little round oh. "You billed for surgeries based on *faked* x-rays showing a fake problem?"

He smirked, his chest swelled with pride. "I only needed to show a surgery was necessary in order to bill for it. But this next surgery," he purred,

"This one is entirely necessary Don't worry. I won't be billing you for it.
It's on me." His green eyes looked pleased, but not generous.

"You can't cut me up! You can't leave body parts strewn about down
here like…" I didn't want to think what it was like. "Everyone will know it
was you!'

"What's one more body in the morgue? They'll pick you up from the
back room, like any other body. The hospital won't have the right paperwork,
and you'll lie there like a homeless derelict. It will be days before they even
figure out who you are."

He swung the scalpel with hypnotic appeal. When he moved left, I
went right. We danced back and forth, but he was getting closer.

I swallowed. "That looks sharp." My attention was focused on the
scalpel with an intensity that would have greatly disappointed my karate
teacher. We had been told to watch the eyes. When the knife was a rubber
toy in a practice session that hadn't been a problem.

"It's going to be hard for you in this profession if you don't get used to
a little blood and gore," he said soothingly.

I managed to tear my eyes away from the knife long enough to notice
that his grin wasn't nearly so handsome now. His green eyes were like
stones, cold and dead. What was it like to be on the operating table and go
under while those emotionless eyes looked down? Did they shout out at the
last minute that they didn't trust this guy?

"Can't save every patient. It's really too late."

"But," I yanked on the door. It was entirely too heavy, which was why
it slammed shut so easily. In karate, that lovely class I so often skipped, we
were told not to turn our backs on the enemy. The lesson seemed irrelevant,
and since I couldn't get the door opened without turning and pulling harder, I
turned my back.

Dr. Fox rushed at me with the knife raised over his head.

That wasn't the way we were taught to attack with a knife in karate
either, but I wasn't about to correct him.

I screamed. The silver blade flashed down.

I ducked under it and stuck my arm out in a blind panic. Dr. Fox
plunged at me, but I only felt pressure, no pain, at least not right away.
Leaned over, I moved forward, forgetting to twist and diving into Dr. Fox's
stomach instead of turning neatly and pushing away.

Dr. Fox stumbled backwards.

I sucked in oxygen and dove for the door again, this time keeping my
head turned so I could see him.

Blood dripped down my arm. I couldn't get the door open. My hand
was slippery, and he was coming at me again.

When he slashed, I slid away along the wall, one hand still on the
doorknob.

I kicked.

It didn't work. Given the man's flirtatious habits, his divorce and now his criminal tendencies, he had probably been hit below the belt before. He kept coming, crouched, livid and not really breathing.

I blocked the scalpel, but he pressed forward. Like two giant timbers, we swayed against the wall. I slid sideways, but his weight bore down on me. He tried to hold onto me with one hand and stab me with the other.

Gravity won. I crashed to the ground, almost hitting my head against the nearest wheeled ladder. I pushed with my legs, gaining perhaps a foot. My head was now between the shelves and the ladder. That didn't stop me from trying to get away.

Dr. Fox must have dropped the scalpel because he used both arms to grab me. He scrabbled forward, sitting on my legs and stretching up to pin my arms.

I threw files at him, yanking them out of the shelf above me and stuffing them in his face while I tried to free my legs by kicking and wiggling. Panting, I screamed again. "Help!"

Too late, I realized I should have leaned forward and screamed in his ear. He was the only one likely to hear me. The air ducts that had brought Radar to my rescue the last time were on the other side of the hallway.

Dr. Fox let out a giant sneeze and lunged further forward.

He saw the scalpel at the same time I did. Still heavy on my knees, he reached for the knife, exposing his head.

I rammed the ladder towards him with every ounce of strength I had. The wheels screamed in protest, but connected with his head, making a satisfying crack.

I pushed against the ladder as leverage to free my legs. Undaunted, Dr. Fox never stopped reaching for the knife. Talk about concentration.

I slammed the ladder into him again, catching his shoulder. Without bothering to stand, I made my legs run. I kept my attention on the door, and this time, I made it out before he could catch me.

My respite didn't last long. He followed, an angry animal, his head down, snarling and growling.

I stumbled away, a desperate fool, screaming my head off. "*Help! Police! Ambulance!*" Reaching the elevator in time was out of the question. The stairwell was as poor a place to die as the x-ray storage room.

Radar was my only hope. He was the only one down here. Whimpering, I yanked the door opened.

It immediately yielded a mop, a bucket and Crissa locked in an embrace with Dr. Staple. Dr. Staple must have been leaning against the door because he fell backward into me.

I crashed hard, smearing a line of blood across the linoleum squares.

Dr. Fox, clutching his scalpel like a mad scientist, stopped in his tracks. Dr. Staple pulled at his pants because it was probably embarrassing to have everything unzipped and unfastened in public. Crissa stood frozen, her blouse off one shoulder.

"Geez, Dad, no one ever comes down here and...Don't even start in on me about what people will think. You cheated on Mom how many times?"

"*Dad?*" I gasped. For half a second I thought maybe she was talking to Dr. Staple, which made no sense at all given the closet embrace, but then I looked up and stared right into her green eyes.

The same green eyes were looking at me from Dr. Fox's face.

"Dad?" I repeated stupidly.

"It's none of your business anyway!" She seemed to notice the scalpel in "Dad's" hand. In confusion, she looked back at me. "What are you doing down here?"

The four of us stared at each other, none of us moving. All of us breathed as though it could be our last.

"I guess this is why you didn't answer the page when Attila was looking for you," I said.

Crissa tugged her shirt back into place. "Stupid bitch," she muttered and stalked off. "Now you're spying on me."

I couldn't believe it.

I heard the distinct sound of a door clicking closed. I prayed it was Radar going for help. At least I hoped he remembered to call for help before he started hacking the records of these people.

Dr. Fox's eyes flicked backwards when the door clicked. He stood up straight, extracted some sort of cover for the scalpel, put it in his pocket and calmly walked off down the hall towards the morgue and back entrance.

I looked up to find Dr. Staple staring intently at my arm. I scrambled to my feet and instinctively covered the cut with my hand. Almost as fast as before, I hightailed it to the stairwell. Somehow I couldn't see letting a guy who had been in the middle of what he had been in the middle of touching my arm. Ye-ick.

I ran all the way to the ER.

Dr. Taylor looked resigned when he saw me.

Chapter 35

Dr. Taylor cleaned my wound without asking anything but medical questions. I thought about Crissa and her blond hair. It could have easily been her in the storage room the night Mark and I broke in. Later, I had seen her and Dr. Fox together, but only at a distance. It never occurred to me that she was his daughter. She didn't have the same last name, but apparently she was married or had been.

I remembered the photographs in Dr. Staple's office. Crissa had been in the pictures with both Staple and Fox, but I had "dating" on the brain. I had only been half right. Fox with Crissa was a family picture. Staple was likely a friend of the family--and was apparently sometimes a very close friend to Crissa. Ugh.

Through the curtain, I watched Mark barrel into the back section of the ER, ignoring the triage nurse voicing her objections.

There went my plan to sneak back to the x-ray department, get my coat and leave. Radar must have called him. Radar talked to Mark briefly before Mark came through the curtain where I sat, forlorn. Radar, as was his usual mode of operation, never said boo to me; he just faded away down the corridor.

Mark's face was glowing. Well, it was actually a deep red underneath his tan. He looked tense.

"Hi," I mumbled. I wasn't certain, but getting picked up at the hospital by a boyfriend might be worse than asking my brother to take me home.

Nah. Sean didn't know I was working here. If he found out for certain, he'd have carted me off and locked me away from Brenda until after she had her baby.

I held out my arm. The stitches were covered with a nice bandage, and it hadn't leaked yet. "It's fine." The statement would have been more impressive had my voice not cracked in the middle.

He gathered me up and wrapped me in his arms. That sort of thing always made me a bit teary even without painful stitches. Dr. Taylor had used Novocain before he sewed me up, but he must not like me much because it felt as if he hadn't used enough.

Mark just held me, staring over my head without saying anything. Asking if he was mad would be too stupid. "I can drive," I said.

He laughed then, softly. "I'm sure you can. Superwoman can do anything." He stroked my hair before squeezing me hard. He finally backed off, scrutinized me head to toe, and then sat on the doctor's stool. "What happened?"

Having dealt with angry brothers before I knew elaborating now wasn't a good idea. Men didn't react well to accidents, problems and... attacks. In fact, there was never going to be a good time to tell Mark what happened. "I suppose Radar told you that Doctor," I choked on the name, "Dr. Fox had some issues with my part in the investigation?"

The muscle in his jaw clenched. "*Issues*? Sedona, the man was trying to kill you!"

I picked at the edge of the bandage on my arm. "Well, yeah, he mentioned that was his intent."

"And he already tried to kill Dr. Hernandez." Mark stopped and took a deep breath. Dr. Taylor drew back the curtain and glared in.

"Will you take her home and chew her out? This is a hospital where we try to present some dignity and calm. People are sick. They are in pain." At the mention of pain, he glanced at my arm. "I'll give you a prescription for a pain killer. You'll need to have those stitches out in ten days."

Maybe Mark hadn't known for sure there were stitches underneath the bandage, because his jaw twitched. "Thanks Doc," he said.

Dr. Taylor unbent a little. "It's my job."

"It would probably help," Mark sighed, "if some of us got different jobs, wouldn't it?"

Dr. Taylor looked at me and opened his mouth to snap out a reply. Maybe because I was so pathetic, he relented. "I guess if you weren't doing your job, I would end up with more accidents like this one and the head trauma Dr. Hernandez suffered. Eventually people who don't have any consideration for human life take more than one."

He pulled out a pad and wrote a prescription. "You might not want to volunteer for a few days." He ripped the sheet off and gave it to me. "Or do whatever else it is that you do." He smiled at his own cleverness and departed.

I hopped gingerly off the table. Mark put his arm around my waist. It felt good.

Chapter 36

It didn't take long for me to recover. After a good night's rest I was almost feeling normal, and barely in time, too. There were a lot of people with questions. My brother was one of them. Whenever he had questions, he came over, made himself at home and started making demands. Of course, not only did he want answers, he wanted food.

Brenda had kindly brought some food, and even nicer than usual, she hadn't made it herself. She was dressed as a pregnant woman; wearing one of the coverall outfits without the benefit of extra padding, cuffs or capes. She looked great.

Mark had not left my side since the hospital so when Radar showed up, followed by Huntington and the Hernandez's it looked like we were going to have more people than food.

"How are you?" I enclosed Dr. Dan in a huge hug. Amy smiled at me from behind him and held up a cake.

"Payback!" she said cheerfully, squeezing around everyone and taking it to the kitchen table.

Sean wasn't one to stand on ceremony. He helped himself to the plates and silverware so that she could serve.

"He's been arrested?" I asked when I saw the triumphant look in Huntington's blue eyes.

He nodded. "Got him a couple hours ago boarding a plane to Bermuda."

I smiled and a large knot inside unwound.

"For the record," he added with a smirk, "he had a bullet wound in one leg and another grazed spot along his ribs."

I sucked in a breath and tried not to remember the shooting. Mark looked over my head the way he did when he was annoyed with me.

"Has he confessed?" Brenda asked. "I still can't believe it. He was always so nice."

Sean gave her a disparaging look. "Criminals don't wear signs, which is why you should be more careful. Sedona never should have involved you in this at all."

Before Sean could throttle me, Huntington provided a distraction. "He didn't confess, but it doesn't matter. We have enough of a paper trail."

"Don't we have *too* much of a paper trail?" The number of hospital bills and x-rays had stumped us from the beginning.

Huntington shook his head. "Most of the fake x-rays and scans weren't done to line his pockets, they were done to cover his tracks."

Dr. Dan agreed. "I thought by talking to Alex--Dr. Fox, I was safe. He couldn't have anything to do with the x-rays, because there was no way he would gain from the phony x-rays. It didn't occur to me that the x-rays were a cover-up for surgery billing that I couldn't see because he billed from his office and it wasn't in the files."

Radar's eureka finger went in the air. "And insurance didn't flag it because the other tests on record backed up the procedure he was charging for."

Dr. Dan added, "I didn't want to involve Henry--Dr. Johnson--until I had figured out what was going on. But after I woke up in the hospital, I couldn't remember who I talked to. I may have talked to Dr. Fox because he was the head surgeon and knew all the players. Either way, he must have realized that I was getting too close and attacked me."

"So when he showed up while you were walking the dogs what happened?" I prompted.

Dr. Dan shook his head. "That part still eludes me."

Amy couldn't help herself. She leaned over and gave him a hug. "It's for the best."

Huntington didn't look like he fully agreed and neither did Sean. Neither had enough manners to keep their mouths shut, but my brother beat Huntington out. "It would be better if you remembered. Then you could testify against Dr. Fox. What did he hit you with?"

Dan put his hands out, palms up. "No idea. I don't remember a thing about it, not even going out for a walk."

I turned to Radar. "What else did you figure out?"

"Remember Mrs. Johanna?"

Hard to forget the one dead body I had to take to the morgue. "What about her?"

"I followed her billing after those late charges showed up. I asked the nephew to check the bills for his aunt. Kid was more than happy to help."

My mouth dropped. "You asked the kid? The one who attacked me in the morgue?"

"Donald," Radar helpfully supplied his name. "He found a bill from Dr. Fox for a tumor extraction."

I frowned. "I thought we agreed we weren't going to go asking questions and raising suspicions. What if the kid was a diabolical hacker that some doctor had hired to break into the system?"

Radar smiled. "That *could* have been the case." He helped himself to another piece of cake. "All along I presumed a hacker was entering charges. Turns out that Dr. Fox spied on his peers until he knew all the passwords. I found they had been used from his office machine at the Pavilion. He could enter all kinds of charges for preliminary tests that would lead to surgery."

Mark added, "And Crissa worked in x-ray at least once a month. Like you, she learned to run the machines. She could collect batches of x-rays that would work for Dr. Fox and stamp them over at The Pavilion. When that was done, she took them down and added them to the patient's files."

"Why is her last name Sheldon, not Fox?" Brenda wondered.

Huntington answered. "Sheldon was her mother's maiden name. Dr. Fox divorced his first wife a long time ago when he was still a medical student. The mother got full custody and made sure Crissa had her name."

"But she followed in Dad's footsteps anyway." In more ways than one, if her closet episodes were common.

Radar stood up and glanced at his watch. "Thanks for the cake. I've got a few more things to track down." He grinned at Huntington.

"We need to get going as well," Amy announced. "I don't want Dan to overdo it. He's still recovering and needs his rest."

Her husband started to protest, but he was going to look perpetually tired until his hair had a chance to grow back over his wound.

I accompanied them to the door. When I returned to the dining area, Sean and Brenda were arguing in a loud whisper about whether it was appropriate to stay for dinner, even though there wasn't any dinner to be had. I gave Sean my best warning look, which he took to heart with a loud sigh.

The door was barely shut behind them when the doorbell rang. I assumed one of them had forgotten something, but it was a courier.

The courier barely waited for my signature. I finished signing and ripped the tab off. There was only a single sheet of paper within, which I read quickly. Mark and Huntington stared at me, waiting.

"Wow," I exclaimed. "I've been fired from my volunteer job. I wonder how often that happens?"

I shouldn't have asked.

Mark couldn't quite conceal his grin. Huntington didn't even try.

"It all works out," Huntington announced happily. "You'll be available when I need your skills again."

"Huntington," I warned, "don't you think it would be a better idea if I got a real job?"

Mark solemnly nodded his agreement with my assessment.

Huntington shrugged. "How can you possibly go back to a single income?"

I bristled. "Have you noticed that this last job only had one income? And I never know how long the jobs will last. I have to save as much money as possible, because I never know what is going to happen next."

"Plus you get fired a lot," he added quite unnecessarily. "It's probably a good thing you save your money."

"Acetel will still take me back." I said it with more self-confidence than I really felt. "It wasn't the best pay, but it would suffice until I found something else."

Mark winced.

Huntington grinned like a cat.

"What?" I demanded.

"They filed for bankruptcy last week," Huntington explained. "Investors pulled out of the stock after the scandal came out. When customers heard about it, several decided to stop using Acetel's services. Don't you read the papers?"

I glared at Huntington, but he was unperturbed. "You might not have noticed, but I was a little preoccupied." We all knew that I could still work at Strandfrost, but only until they found out I wasn't pregnant. I sighed. Huntington's grin did not fade.

"This time, it's a perfectly safe case," he said. "I don't even need Mark's help. It'll be easy."

Ohboy. With Huntington, it was never that safe--or easy.

Mark closed his eyes and reached for my hand. I held on tight. Huntington might not need Mark, but new case or not, I did.

More Books by Maria E. Schneider

Executive Dirt, the fourth Sedona O'Hala mystery has been published!

Most of my other works are also mysteries. **One Good Eclair** is the start of my latest cozy mystery series.

Under Witch Moon is the first in an urban fantasy series: When dead bodies start turning up Adriel has no choice but to talk to White Feather, an undercover cop. Unfortunately, Adriel is a witch, and White Feather isn't convinced she's innocent of wrongdoing. She's going to have to talk fast-- and set spells even faster to get herself out of trouble.

Dragons of Wendal is a fantasy romance adventure: Learning new magic isn't as easy as Zoe expected, especially when the mages at Gorgon University seem dead set against teaching. Add in some necessary late-night sneaking about, and Zoe is almost certain to be kicked out. As for exploring the intriguing mysteries across the border in Wendal, well, it has more teeth than she ever imagined.

To find out what I'm currently up to, visit me at my blog: www.BearMountainBooks.com.

www.ingramcontent.com/pod-product-compliance
Lightning Source LLC
Chambersburg PA
CBHW021038130626
46552CB00005B/1903